RULES OF THE GAME

It was clear to both the new Lady April Glenville and her bridegroom, Lord Adam, what the rules of their marriage would be.

He would mold this unkempt young lady into a fashionable beauty and dazzling hostess fit to occupy a public position as his wife.

She would refuse him entrance to her bedchamber despite all the seductive skill and overwhelming attractiveness of this man who until recently had been the most sought-after catch in London.

Thus the game was begun — with both of them knowing very well that the first one to fall in love would lose. . . .

THE
BLACKMAILED
BRIDEGROOM

SIGNET Regency Romances You'll Enjoy

The Blackmailed Bridegroom

by

Dorothy Mack

A SIGNET BOOK

NEW AMERICAN LIBRARY

NAL BOOKS ARE AVAILABLE AT QUANTITY DISCOUNTS WHEN USED TO PROMOTE PRODUCTS OR SERVICES. FOR INFORMATION PLEASE WRITE THE PREMIUM MARKETING DIVISION, THE NEW AMERICAN LIBRARY, INC., 1633 BROADWAY, NEW YORK, NEW YORK 10019.

SIGNET, SIGNET CLASSIC, MENTOR, PLUME, MERIDIAN and NAL BOOKS are published by The New American Library, Inc., 1633 Broadway, New York, New York 10019

First Printing, February, 1984

1 2 3 4 5 6 7 8 9

PRINTED IN THE UNITED STATES OF AMERICA

Prologue

It was a glorious day proclaiming the annual renewal of the earth. Early-morning showers had washed the London streets and then given way to clearing skies and a warm spring sun. Most of the puddles were gone now, but the freshness clung to the shrubs and branches in the gardens in the square, whence voices of children drifted, calling excitedly to each other. A young housemaid tripped down the steps on one great stone house on the south side of the square and called to another leaving a doorway a hundred feet farther on. The one hailed waited for her friend, and the two proceeded on their errands in company. A stiffly starched nanny crossed the street toward the gardens holding the hand of a little boy who toted a huge red ball under his free arm. Halfway across, the ball squirted from its insecure position and bounced away. Boy and attendant gave laughing chase and succeeded in retrieving it near the gates to the gardens. They disappeared inside.

The only person in evidence who seemed not to share in the air of general bonhomie was a man who approached from the western boundary of the square with a purposeful but oddly reluctant stride. He was still a young man, probably two or three years under thirty, a tall, well-set-up figure with the easy grace of the born athlete. His countenance too would have been described as well favored by most, though its appeal was marred at the moment by a vivid half-healed slash across one cheekbone. He was neatly dressed in the blue coat, light colored smalls, and impeccable Hessians that constituted correct morning dress for a gentleman paying calls, and a curly-brimmed beaver reposed at an exact angle atop dark-brown locks brushed to repress a tendency to curl.

The eyes of the two young maids swiveled involuntarily to survey his person with shy approbation as he stood politely aside for them to pass him. Their conversation ceased abruptly, then resumed amid self-conscious giggling before they were quite out of earshot.

The gentleman remained impervious to their interest as he continued along the flagway absorbed in his own thoughts. That these thoughts were of a serious nature was attested to by a certain somberness of expression that was evident when he glanced up occasionally as if checking the numbers of the houses he was passing. At last he paused at a red brick edifice whose entrance was hung with black crape. For a few seconds his gaze was transfixed by this symbol of mourning, then he squared his shoulders and climbed the steps.

The door was opened by an expressionless individual whose bearing and sober costume proclaimed his importance in the household. The caller inquired for Lady Wendover and was told by the butler that her ladyship was indisposed.

"*Please!*" exclaimed the young man. "It is extremely important that I see Lady Wendover. Would you take my card up to her at least?"

A coin changed hands; the butler bowed and stepped back to admit the gentleman into the hall to wait while he carried the calling card up to his mistress. In the next few minutes the young man stood motionless near the door, staring with an unhappy intensity at the hat he was twisting in his gloved hands. He glanced up eagerly as descending footsteps announced the butler's return.

"I regret, Mr. Harding, that her ladyship cannot receive you. She is seeing no one today."

At that moment a door toward the back of the hall opened to admit a girl dressed from head to toe in unrelieved black. As she came toward the entrance the man thought he had never seen hair so fair; there was almost a look of silver to it, but perhaps that was due to the contrast with her black raiment. Becoming aware of people in her vicinity, the girl raised a pale face.

"What is it, Condon?"

"Nothing, Miss April," that worthy replied soothingly. "This gentleman was wishful to see her ladyship, but she is unable to receive him." He opened the door as he spoke.

The girl would have proceeded to the stairway without comment, but the caller demanded:

"Are you Miss Wendover? Perhaps you would convey to your mother my earnest desire to speak with her whenever she feels able to receive me?"

She turned an inquiring glance in his direction but made no reply.

"My name is Adam Harding. I—"

"Adam Harding!"

The girl's lifeless countenance was transformed with bitterness; her red-rimmed eyes flashed hatred as they dwelled on the wound on the man's cheek. *"Adam Harding!"* she repeated in tones that blended astonishment and loathing. "I wonder, sir, that you have the temerity to call at this house! Is there some further harm you have yet to deal us? Was it not enough that you drove my father to suicide? Did you have to kill my brother too?" She was shaking with emotion, her fists clenched at her sides, as she glared up at the man, whose face had lost all its color at the spate of invective.

He stepped back a pace and bowed slightly as he returned her look for a pregnant instant, his countenance rigid, his mouth a tight line of repression.

"I apologize for my presumption in coming here, Miss Wendover, and will bid you good day." The caller spun on his heel and walked quickly through the door being held open by the butler without even noting the reluctant sympathy in the latter's eyes. At the bottom of the steps he directed a final bleak look at the black-draped door before replacing his hat and striding away.

Chapter One

A loud crack stopped Mr. Jeremy Choate in his tracks, and the jerky movement caused the tankards on the tin tray he carried to spill a considerable portion of their liquid contents onto the tray and one grimy hand. This occurrence evoked no more than an absentminded oath from Mr. Choate, whose frowning attention was directed at the window whence the noise issued. He resumed his progress toward the only occupied table in the public room after locating a sleepy-eyed lad who was endeavoring to make himself inconspicuous by tending to the fire. The proprietor of the Cap and Bells, one of the lesser-used coaching inns on the Great North Road, indicated the window with a movement of his head.

"You there, Todd, get outside and fasten that shutter, and this time make sure it's tight."

As the boy thus addressed got to his feet with discernible reluctance, another spatter of wind-delivered rain hammered the window and the loose shutter set up a continuous banging.

"Look smart, you devil's whelp, before that there wind rips the shutter clear off." The lash in his tones changed to an ingratiating purr as he set the tray down on the table where three men sat in lounging attitudes.

"Here you be, gen'lemen, three pints o' the best ale within thirty miles o' London." He removed his wet hand from the tray and wiped it casually down the side of his catskin waistcoat, which, judging by the various stains thereon, already bore witness to similar treatment with regard to numerous items on the menu. While responding wholeheartedly to the jocularity of his guests, the landlord managed to keep one eye on the boy, who had donned a dirty cap unearthed from the vicinity of the hearth and was struggling to afford himself some increased protection from the elements by forcing as many of the remaining buttons on his ragged coat as possible into their holes, a procedure complicated by the undersized nature of the garment, which had never been meant to cover a gangly adolescent. Quailing under an impatient scowl directed at him by his employer, the lad abandoned the effort and departed hastily.

In the brief interval before the taproom door closed behind the boy a spate of rain and the noise of the storm entered the snug room along with another familiar sound, that of an approaching carriage. This last caused the innkeeper to leave his post by the occupied table to investigate.

"Sounds like more company," declared one of the members of the merry drinking party.

To this statement of the obvious Mr. Choate made no reply. He arrived at the door just in time to be forced to step smartly back to avoid a collision with a figure erupting into the room, a collision that would have had no very beneficial effect on Mr. Choate's person, for he was a small thin individual, roughly half the size of the man who entered.

The newcomer, intent on slapping the excess water from the once elegant beaver he had removed from his dripping locks, remained unaware of the near accident. "Filthy night," he said by way of a general greeting before beginning to struggle out of a sodden driving coat whose numerous shoulder capes must have marked it as all the crack when in its pristine condition.

"Lor, gov'nor, you ain't been driving in an open carriage in this weather?" expostulated the innkeeper, automatically coming to the assistance of this new arrival.

"Tried to beat the storm, the more fool I," explained the stranger with an economy of words that matched his manner as he handed over the coat and hat into his host's extended arms. He gave a cursory glance around the dimly lighted room, nodding slightly to the interested spectators at the far table before heading straight for the warmth of the fireplace. "This is a welcome sight," he added, holding out his hands to the blaze.

"You . . . you wouldn't be wanting a room for the night, would you?" asked the landlord, whose sharp-featured face had taken on a worried aspect.

The stranger stopped chafing his hands and favored the speaker with a direct stare. "Naturally, I want a room and a meal too—why else should I be here?"

The impatient query seemed to increase Mr. Choate's discomfort. "Well, you're welcome to the meal, though you'll have to take what's left in the kitchen at this hour, and you're welcome to stay here by the fire, but I'm afeared I can't oblige your honor with a room, because the fact is, there ain't an empty room in the place tonight." He recoiled visibly from the thunderous scowl that descended on the stranger's black-browed visage and quavered, "I'm right sorry, your honor."

"Look, I'm not overparticular about the style of room— any place I can lay my head will do. I've been driving for fourteen hours, and I'll be damned if I go out in that again," with a hunch of his shoulders in the direction of the rain-beaten window.

"I'm that sorry not to be able to oblige your honor, but all my rooms are taken."

"Do some rearranging," ordered his unwelcome guest. "I'll pay you double, triple the rate for your best chamber for any room with a bed and a door that locks." Having expressed his wishes in the tone of one accustomed to being obeyed, he turned away from the innkeeper and resumed drying his person by the fire.

His host stood irresolute for a second or two, but his shrewd little eyes had already assessed the value of his guest's raiment, and he was not totally unaccustomed to the ways of the quality. His inn, while perfectly respectable, did not cater to the nobility in a general way, but there was no denying it would be a feather in his cap to accommodate one whose lofty manner clearly marked him as a member of this class. His quick greedy brain had been turning over possibilities, and he spoke now to the unconcerned back of the traveler in the manner of a man working out a problem.

"There are a couple of abigails in single rooms who appeared to strike up an acquaintance at dinner tonight. O' course it's late, after ten o'clock, but if the ladies was agreeable to sharing a room, I could make it worth their while, refund the price o' one room with no one the wiser, and your honor could have t' other."

"Fine," said the newcomer with patent indifference. "I'll want a meal for my groom when he gets in from the stables. He can bed down here for the night, if you've no objection."

"O' course, your honor, always happy to oblige a gentleman." His host's obsequious smile lasted until the door opened, admitting the now soaked adolescent, who had evidently succeeded in fastening the shutters. "I'll want you in the kitchen," he said, directing the boy toward the hall with a well-placed push and following in his wet footsteps after another ingratiating smile for the man who watched him with a sardonic expression on his stern-featured face.

It was almost eleven o'clock when the traveler was finally established in his room, seated in a chair that offered more comfort than its shabby appearance promised. He had changed his damp coat for a warm velvet dressing gown, and though the small room didn't boast a fireplace, the inn was solidly built and relatively free from drafts. There was a hot brick between the sheets of the single bed, promising additional comfort when it became too cold to read any longer. For the present, he was content to repose his limbs in the high wingback chair with its once garishly printed upholstery faded to a murky monochrome and lose himself in the company of his favorite poet. A branch of candles stood on the table at his elbow. From time to time he refreshed himself with sips of a surprisingly smooth brandy from his host's cellar. The storm still raged outside, but the only sounds in the cozy room were the faint rustling of pages and the occasional quiet click of a glass being returned to the table.

The soft tapping had barely penetrated his abstraction when it was succeeded by a somewhat breathless speech from the vicinity of the door behind him.

"Thank goodness you are still up, Mattie! I was reading and didn't realize how late it had grown. Diana's sound asleep and I cannot undo these pestilential buttons. Be a dear and help me, please!"

The man had replaced his glass and risen swiftly from the depths of the chair to confront the girl who followed her voice into the room, leaving the door open behind her. His initial impression was a regretful confirmation of the thought that had surged to his mind on hearing her first words — that no face could possibly match the beauty of that voice, low-pitched and melodious. It didn't.

The female who stared at him in openmouthed astonishment was past her first youth certainly, but he suspected it was a lack of interest in her appearance, not advancing years, that heightened the discrepancy between the vibrant voice and the rather drab impression created by the owner of the voice.

He bowed punctiliously. "I regret that I am not Mattie, but will respectfully offer my poor services in her stead if I may be of assistance?"

The presumption in this remark caused the woman's cheeks to flame and drove up her chin, but she ignored the suggestion and replied with creditable composure.

"I beg your pardon for the intrusion, sir, but I was under the impression that this room was occupied by my maid; in fact, I know it was! What have you done with her?" Voice and eyes conveyed accusation.

"I trust you don't suspect there is blood on my hands," he drawled, noting her tightened mouth with perverse satisfaction. "Your maid — er, Mattie, was it? — very kindly volunteered to move in with another abigail so the landlord might accommodate a weary traveler on this very wet night. I would deem it an honor to ascertain her exact whereabouts if you require her services tonight, but before we embark on what could be a time-consuming errand at this hour, may I, without the least intention of offending, reiterate my offer to deputize for her?"

Large eyes of a rare light gray surveyed him coolly. She permitted herself a slight supercilious curve to her mouth but declined his offer with well-bred civility. During the whole of their brief interview she had faced him with one hand behind her clutching the partially unbuttoned dress together at the waistline. Now she retreated a step with the evident intention of accomplishing the short trek to her own chamber by walking backward. The thought of this feat produced a widening of his lips, but at that moment an unctuous voice from the doorway wiped the smile from his face and caused the woman to spin around, her eyes dilating in alarm.

"I trust I don't intrude?"

A man already dressed for sleeping, wearing a black brocade dressing gown over his nightclothes, lounged against the doorjamb regarding the couple within the room with an expression of malicious enjoyment on his attractive but curiously lined face.

"Considering that you've perfected a natural talent for intruding down through the years, I presume you ask that question in a strictly rhetorical spirit," countered the owner of the room in accents that blended indifference and disdain.

The woman remained mute, but she edged back a pace in reaction to the malevolence that this offensive remark brought to the features of the man in the doorway. He was nearly as large as the occupant of the room, and for an instant gave the appearance of tensing for an attack on the latter, but he evidently thought better of this idea. The ugly look faded, he straightened his posture, and his voice retained its smoothness.

"How unfortunate for you that I just happened to be across the hall and opened my door in time to hear your familiar tones," he remarked to the room's occupant.

"Unfortunate? Unpleasant, I'll grant you, but in what way unfortunate?"

The cold blue eyes of the man in the doorway narrowed, and his too full lips bunched unattractively as his insulting glance swept from the unknown woman to the man he seemed to know all too well. *"Unfortunate* if the minister proves to be, shall we say, less broad-minded than you might hope about condoning intrigues among his subordinates, especially when these intrigues involve cits."

The woman opened her lips to protest angrily, but the man cut in first.

"Don't be a damned fool, Allerton. There is a perfectly innocent explanation for this scene, and—"

"Then you must hope the minister believes it!" sneered the other. "You will have your chance to lay your explanation before him as soon as you get to town. I'll bid you good night, Glenville . . . madam." He made the outraged woman a mocking bow and retreated across the corridor.

"Do your worst," invited his antagonist with perfect unconcern. This changed abruptly to alarm as his glance lighted on the woman for the first time since they had been interrupted. She was staring at him in outright horror, and her complexion was drained of any life or color. "Here, don't collapse on me!" he begged, reaching out instinctively to support her wilting frame. His concern gave way to a puzzled frown as she recoiled sharply from his outstretched hand, but he forbore to touch her, going instead to the big chair, which he seized by its wings and wrestled forward. "Sit down," he ordered, but when she had obeyed the brusque command, he subdued his irritation and infused a more gentle note into his voice.

"Don't allow that cretin's idle threats to distress you, ma'am. He doesn't know your identity; you'll never see him again. No one will ever learn of this incident." Something speculative yet disdainful in the quality of the stare she was directing at him caused him to break off his assurances in midstream.

The woman spoke for the first time since the recent

unpleasantness. Her voice was cold and very clear. "I'm afraid that is not quite true. He *will* discover my identity because I have discovered yours, Lord Glenville. I should have recognized you from the scar!"

"So, we have met before? It does not signify. Allerton doesn't know what room you are occupying. Just keep out of sight tomorrow until after he leaves. He'll have no way of identifying you."

"I am constrained to differ with you. He *will* know who I am."

The man's frown deepened. "How will he know?"

"If necessary, I shall tell him."

This bald statement uttered in perfectly composed tones brought a dangerous look to the man's already stern-featured countenance. There was a short, tension-packed silence during which dark-gray eyes warred with light.

"I begin to comprehend. Underneath that respectable exterior lurks the soul of an adventuress, after all," he sneered. "What is your game, blackmail? I should advise you not to try it, my girl. I'm an ill bird for plucking. You will suffer more than I by any recounting of tonight's activities."

"I think not, Lord Glenville."

He had turned abruptly away from her to stalk across the room, feeling it was safer to put a distance between them, but at this he whirled around and snapped, "Why not?"

She rose from the chair and met his challenging regard squarely. "You haven't asked my name, Lord Glenville."

"I suppose that provocative statement is meant to convey something to me. You are too young to be one of the royal princesses," he said with an insulting little laugh. "Very well, I'll bite; who are you?"

"My name is April Wendover."

There was a definite quality of menace to the stillness that followed this disclosure. The man's hands were clenched at his sides, and a spasm of some strong emotion contorted his features momentarily. He inhaled deeply.

"I see."

She continued with cold calm. "You have managed to climb steadily in the ranks of government despite what happened nine years ago, but I seriously doubt whether your career would withstand the notoriety attendant on charges of seducing the daughter and sister of the men you killed. You'd be an embarrassment to your party."

"You know that isn't true, any part of it!"

"Not the seduction part, no, but you cannot deny you are responsible for my father's and brother's deaths."

"I could deny it and do, but it is a waste of breath. You refused to believe me nine years ago, and you obviously have not softened your position in the interim. What is it you want of me, money or revenge?"

For a moment the woman squirmed under his hard stare and her eyes refused to meet his. Before he could press the momentary advantage, however, she had herself in hand again. Her slightly pointed chin tilted upward, and she spoke without any feeling at all.

"I don't know whether you ever bothered to discover what became of the family of the men you killed. My father was ruined, of course. He had gambled away all his private fortune. The estate was entailed, and when my brother died it went to a distant cousin who had long been estranged from our branch of the family. My mother's constitution was always delicate. She never recovered from the double shock, although she clung to life until I came of age to be legally responsible for my young sister. Then she just . . . faded away. I was seventeen and betrothed when my father and brother died, but I soon discovered my fiancé was quite willing to release me from the engagement when he learned my marriage portion had gone with all the rest. Mother had a tiny income and we lived frugally in a rented cottage in the country, but with her long illness we were forced to use some of the capital. It is nearly gone now. I could manage if I had only myself to consider, but my sister is now seventeen and very lovely. She *must* have her chance to marry, but how can I give it to her? We are here tonight because I decided to swallow my pride and approach my cousin to plead with him to do something for Diana. We were on our way to London to see him."

During this recitation Glenville's stare never wavered from the woman's wooden countenance. Now he said with a sardonic inflection, "But, having met me in, shall we say, unusual circumstances, you now feel that I might take your cousin's place as benefactor to your sister. Do I take your meaning correctly, Miss Wendover?"

Icy clear gray eyes bored into his darker ones. "Having met you in *sordid* circumstances, I now feel that as my *husband* you can give Diana all the advantages of a court presentation and sponsorship into the polite world to which she belongs by right of birth and which you took away from her when you killed her brother."

He had been prepared for a demand for money. It took a few seconds for the meaning of her words to strike home, then he reacted with leashed violence.

"*Marry* you? I'm more likely to *murder* you! What's to stop me from strangling you this very minute?" He flexed long fingers as he flung the angry words at her and noted the signs of fear she could not control. Her answer, however, came straightly back.

"The assurance that the crime would be brought home to you. That man across the hall would see to that!"

Reluctant admiration for the courage that enabled her to stand her ground warred with fury over the weakness of his own position. She had him in a cleft stick, damn her! The patronage of the minister disarmed his enemies at present, but he was well aware that there were those who would make discrediting him their first priority if they could see their way to accomplishing the feat. He eyed her consideringly for a long moment, but it never occurred to him to call her bluff. He paid Miss Wendover the tacit compliment of believing she meant exactly what she had threatened. There was determination and more than a little desperation beneath that carefully preserved calm of hers. Like her father before her, she was staking all on a desperate gamble. He was almost light-headed from rancor and frustration. She continued to stand a pace or two away from him, a quiet, expressionless, almost characterless female who held his future career in her hands.

He wrenched out of the paralyzing tension holding the two of them in place and walked stiffly over to the table near where the chair had stood such a short time before, though it seemed an eon had passed since he had been happily absorbed in the book reposing on its scratched surface. The brandy glass still held half an inch of liquid, and he reached for it, downing the contents under the girl's eye. He did not apologize for the rudeness, nor did she acknowledge the slight by so much as the flicker of an eyelid. With great deliberation he replaced the empty glass and remarked softly, almost casually:

"A matter of coercion, in fact. Allow me to congratulate you on your original methods of husband hunting, Miss Wendover. Are they the ones you employed in extracting your first proposal?"

He thought she winced slightly, but her reply was couched in the terms of sweet reason. "There is nothing to be gained by prolonging this discussion, my lord. We will both be more rational after a night's repose. I'll leave you now." She turned away from him, but her steps were arrested by his voice before she reached the door.

"You've forgotten something, have you not, Miss Wendover?"

"Forgotten something?" Her voice was carefully unaccented, but a certain wariness leaped into the smoky eyes.

"Your gown is still partially fastened," he pointed out without emphasis. "Unless you propose to sleep in it you had best let me undo those buttons."

She presented her back to him without comment, and he accomplished the task in a like silence. He did not offer to see her to her door.

"Thank you, Lord Glenville. Goodnight."

The door closed quietly behind his affianced bride.

Chapter Two

Adam Harding, eighth Earl of Glenville, watched the door to an inn bedchamber swing slowly into place with a wild sense of disbelief mixed with fury. The soft snick of the catch released him from the paralysis that seemed to grip his limbs and brain alike. He surged forward. This farce could not be allowed to continue a minute longer! He must have been mad to agree to a marriage with that female icicle. Not that it would be a marriage, of course, but the very fact of her existence — and there was a sister too, he recalled — would irretrievably alter his comfortable way of life for the worse. His hand was on the latch, the door was open, permitting an unobstructed view of the closed door across the corridor, the door behind which his long-despised opponent, Allerton, lay, most probably dreaming of the damage he would do to Glenville's political career with the scandal he felt he had unearthed.

A long moment of frustration and indecision elapsed with nothing to break the silence but a creaking shutter outside and the sound of his own harsh breathing in the room. At the end of it he shut the door quietly and walked over to the winged chair and dropped into its comfortable depths. He made no move to return it to its original place by the table where the candles still burned steadily. There would be no more reading tonight, and he did not require light to pursue his dark thoughts.

They were always present at some level of his awareness, ready to prey on him in moments of weakness or depression.

These had grown fewer with the passage of time as he had reconstructed his life, but he had never quite succeeded in putting the events of that bleak period permanently aside.

He had been a young care-for-naught in those days after the death of his father, leading the aimless existence of young men of his class, his interests bounded by sporting pursuits in the daytime and gambling and dalliance in the evening. His father had been the second son of the fifth earl, and since his uncle had secured the succession with the production of two strapping sons, Adam had been allowed to pursue his own interests, which had in the main been frivolous. His father's property was small but well run, and on his death when Adam was four and twenty, his heir found himself able to afford most of his expensive habits if he didn't draw the bustle too outrageously. His mother was living in London at the time, having returned after her husband's death from an extended sojourn on the Continent. She had very little influence in his life, having deserted husband and child before Adam was old enough for Eton. Now married to the wealthy peer with whom she had eloped, she had resumed her social career with as much success as money could buy. The *ton* had a long memory, though, and there remained houses whose thresholds she could not hope to cross. He kept his own contacts with her to a minimum, never failing in the public courtesy owed to a parent and never allowing her one scrap of the affection she had forfeited by her desertion. In this pleasant, purposeless style he had reached the age of eight and twenty without making any commitments to the future when the affair with the Wendovers, *père et fils,* had blown up in his face.

Sir Charles Wendover was a chronic gambler. For months there had been rumors circulating among the clubs that he was all to bits and would soon be forced to sell out of the Funds. Being much younger than Wendover, Adam had no more than a nodding acquaintance with him, though he knew his young cub of a son, Basil, for whom he cherished a mild dislike that was reciprocated tenfold on the part of one always bested at every turn by Harding's superior strength and skill at various sports.

Looking back, he could see it was no more than a quirk of malicious Fate that he should have come to the attention of Sir Charles at the lowest point in the latter's fortunes. On the night in question he had just arisen from a most successful session of piquet with a man noted for his play and had found it impossible to refuse to give Sir Charles a game. The man was in his cups before play got under way and continued to make indentures on the burgundy throughout the contest. He had overriden Adam's tentative attempts to keep the stakes low, forcing up the price of each game and recklessly signing chits as he lost heavily. Perhaps a contemporary of Sir Charles's could have extricated himself from such a mismatch, but Adam had not known how to accomplish it without mortally offending a man old enough to be his father. He had pleaded fatigue and finally illness before the grimly obsessed baronet released him in the small hours of the morning, and he had departed for his rooms with no desire and little expectation of collecting his winnings. However, the payment had arrived the next day and with it the unwelcome news that Wendover had blown his brains out.

There had been witnesses enough at White's to absolve him of any suspicion of lying in wait for a victim incapacitated by drink, but he had experienced all the natural regret of a man involved in the senseless tragedy of another. Sir Charles was scarcely in his grave when the situation took an unexpected turn. Basil Wendover, in the presence of witnesses, had accused Adam of cheating his father, and Basil was *not* foxed at the time. He had convinced himself that this was the true situation and was not to be persuaded otherwise. Adam, at the mercy of a man determined to force a quarrel, had been unable to refuse the challenge. He had chosen swords, confident that his superior skill would enable him to give the young hothead satisfaction without having to hurt him seriously. And so it had turned out. He had himself sustained a deep cut on his face and had pricked Basil in the shoulder. Who could have foreseen the tragic series of misadventures that culminated in young Wendover's eventual death from blood poisoning? The wound had been minor, but he had not received adequate medical care and within a week he was dead. Adam had been wracked by remorse at the double tragedy, though he could not accept guilt where it did not exist.

In the rapidly chilling inn chamber, Glenville raised his head from his hand and rested it against the high back of the chair. His eyes, staring at nothing, were full of grim memories. He recalled his only previous meeting with Miss Wendover and experienced again the weight of her vilification and bitterness. That had been the worst moment of all, staring into the suffering face of a young girl who was uttering manifestly unfair accusations, and being powerless to change the situation. Suddenly he lunged out of the chair and started an aimless quartering of the room's limited floor space as he pictured the cold features of the woman who had just left him. He had thought he would never forget her face, but tonight he had failed to recognize her. Frowning, he went over her appearance in detail. The hair, that was it! He recalled the incredible blondness of the young April Wendover and realized that her hair had been almost entirely hidden by a cap tonight. The image in his mind, though fixed, was actually fuzzy about details after nine years. Then she had been pasty-faced and her eyes had been swollen from weeping. Now that he dwelled on it he did recall that they had been of an unusual light gray, which tallied with his observation tonight. This older version had been coldly controlled in contrast to the unbridled passion of the young girl, but it was the same person. He no longer felt surprise that a comparatively young woman should look so *quenched*. Nor did he find himself unmoved by the bald tale she had recounted of her life for the past nine years. Enough rain had fallen in Miss Wendover's life to quench anyone's fire. He merely resented having everything laid to *his* account.

But nine years had made no difference to her hatred. Evidently she had not been able to take a more reasonable view of events even after grief had long abated. Tonight she had been living in the past with an ever fresh desire to revenge herself on the man she held responsible for her relatives' deaths and all the unhappiness that had followed. The thought was appalling enough to send a chill feathering along his nerves. And this was the woman he was to wed? A woman whose loyalty would always be to the past? To invite an enemy into one's house would be to carry self-destructiveness to extremes! Surely they could come to some other arrangement which would enable her to accomplish both her purposes. If he paid her expenses she would be extracting her revenge and, with her cousin's sponsorship, should be able to launch her sister into society.

Mentally he passed the present baronet under review and was forced to the conclusion that Sir Neville Granby, saddled with a hatchet-faced wife and an antidote for a daughter, was hardly the man to lend his patronage to cousins he barely knew, especially if one of them was likely to cast his unwed daughter into the shade. He paused in his pacing as another, more primary objection presented itself. Allerton would be bound to recognize Miss Wendover if he met her in society, and then the fat would be in the fire. A reluctant smile drove the sternness from his expression as he imagined the effect on the *ton* of his alleged partner-in-sin's attempt to insinuate her sister into its ranks in the light of disclosures of this nature. The smile faded as quickly as it had appeared. It would have to be marriage. Still, if he *must* nourish a viper in his bosom, then, by God, he'd see to it that the viper's fangs were pulled! Miss Wendover would find this marriage a two-way street!

On this thought he surrendered to the creeping chill in the room and, after undressing in record time and extinguishing the remains of the candles, crawled into bed and pushed the now cold brick aside, wrapping the comforter tightly around him.

Lord Glenville would have been surprised to learn that

the scene in the next room was not so very different from his own experience during the past hour. Miss Wendover had beaten a strategic retreat from his room, her recent triumph slightly dimmed by the humiliating necessity of submitting to his ministrations with regard to her gown. She closed her door behind her with great care so as not to awaken her sister and sagged back against its reassuring firmness. Her fingers crept up to massage her temples. How had she *dared* try to coerce that terrible man into marrying her? He had accused her of blackmail, and she stood convicted of that heinous crime in her own eyes! From the moment she had become aware of his identity some other self she did not know had taken over her mind and body and led her to act in a manner she would never have considered in her saner moments. She pressed her fingers across her eyes. Yes, that was it, she must have been *mad* for those few moments, but the madness must cease!

She whirled about and seized the latch. The door was already open when a cold draft on her back brought her own state of disarray sharply before her mind's eye. What would he think if she should reappear at his door half undressed? A deep flush rose from her throat and suffused her cheeks, but she berated herself soundly for a fool. What did it signify what he thought if she released him from all obligation to wed her? He'd be too relieved to notice her appearance. As she lingered in the doorway a sound reached her from the big bed across the room. Diana had moaned softly and turned in her sleep.

Diana! Her eyes flew to the darkened corner even as her hand pushed the door gently shut. Diana's future was the impetus for what she had just done. It was on Diana's behalf that she had undertaken this quixotic journey to London in the first place. She had come to terms with their reduction in circumstances for her own sake, but Diana was too lovely and too ill equipped to endure poverty. Her sister was urging her to marry Mr. Lynley, a retired merchant who had been exceedingly kind to the small family during Lady Wendover's last years.

It was through Mr. Lynley's influence that she had been able to start a school for village children, which brought in a pittance, but there was no denying their existence would be precarious indeed when their remaining capital ran out. Unless Diana made a good marriage or she herself consented to become Mr. Lynley's wife, it was inevitable that the money would run out eventually. And if she did manage to subdue her own instinctive revulsion of the senses and marry a man who, though good-natured and kind, was twice her age and physically unappealing, then Diana would be permanently barred from forming an advantageous connection. Mr. Lynley's money would keep her in comfort, but Mr. Lynley's lack of breeding would close forever those doors which her own birth entitled her to enter. This circumstance her sister seemed unable to grasp in her urgent desire to have the wherewithal to buy pretty clothes and go to parties. The older Diana became, the more pressing Mr. Lynley's suit and the more acute the problem.

It was in reaction to the seemingly inevitable surrender of her freedom that she had evolved this plan to appeal to her cousin for assistance. It had been her devout hope that he could be persuaded to underwrite the expense of Diana's debut if Diana's sister made herself available to his wife as an unpaid governess to their numerous offspring. Failing this full support, Miss Wendover had one more option in reserve. If Sir Neville could at least be induced to sponsor Diana's comeout to the extent of allowing his wife to chaperon her for the season, she would ask Mr. Lynley for the necessary funds to provide her sister with a suitable wardrobe, pledging herself to marry him when Diana contracted an eligible alliance. She resolutely refused to dwell on the necessity of fading out of her sister's life in such an eventuality. This last-ditch plan she had divulged to no one as yet. Nor had she been able to bring herself to depress Diana's optimism by confiding her own fears that one look at her beautiful sister on the part of Lady Granby would set up the latter's back and cause her to refuse to allow her own plain daughter to be brought out in the company of one who was bound to eclipse her. Instead she had permitted Mr. Lynley to persuade her to accept the use of his coach and horses for the journey, and look where the move had landed them!

Miss Wendover, standing wearily near the door, shivered in the cold air and forced herself to begin preparation for sleep. Anything she might have to say to Lord Glenville would be better said in the morning. And what she was to say to him she couldn't hope to know, the state her confused intellect was in at present. Making herself consider all possibilities as she folded her clothing with automatic precision, she acknowledged that the best they could hope for would be complete support from their cousin, and the least attractive option would be marriage with the man responsible for the deaths of her father and brother. Or would that necessarily be worse than marriage with a man she liked but shrank from? Her busy hands ceased their efforts as she summoned up an image of Mr. Lynley before her eyes. His short stature and tendency toward corpulence didn't repel her, but his noisy and greedy enjoyment of food and drink and the uncared-for nature of his pudgy hands with their dirty nails did. And she always found herself looking away from his too wet mouth with its thick lips covering yellowed teeth.

The hated Lord Glenville, on the other hand, though of a rather harsh aspect, seemed to be of a fastidious nature, and she had noted the well-shaped hand and immaculate nails. He might be a Bluebeard for all she knew to the contrary, but one thing she had learned was that he had no interest in her as a female. His look had been an insult, but it was a relief too.

Miss Wendover had no very good opinion of the stronger sex. She had loved her father and brother, but love and loyalty had not blinded her to the defects in their characters. At seventeen she had been flattered by the attentions of her fiancé, who had caused her youthful heart to flutter with what she had assumed to be love, but his protestations of devotion had meant so little that he had jumped at her offer to release him from the engagement when it became obvious that she would be a penniless bride. On the two occasions on which she had observed her cousin Neville, he had struck her as being a conceited popinjay without the intellect or resolution to stand up to his harridan of a wife.

At this point in her summing up, Miss Wendover realized that she was too exhausted and too mistrustful of the future to make any rational decision. Her last thought on edging into bed beside her sleeping sister was that if it really came to a choice between a marriage in name only to a man of her own class whom she hated or a union in which she would be expected to undertake a wife's obligations with a man of lesser breeding whose touch caused her to shrivel inside, she would elect the former. And so, protesting to herself that she could not make a decision, Miss Wendover drifted into an uneasy sleep, having already made her decision.

Chapter Three

Miss Wendover, not surprisingly, was loath to rise the next morning. Her rest in a strange bed was never guaranteed under the best of circumstances, and after the shattering events of the previous evening she had endured a disturbed night, finally sinking into a deep sleep just before dawn. Miss Diana Wendover, eager to embark upon the last leg of the journey that she, with the unbounded optimism of the very young, confidently expected would result in setting the mechanics of her presentation in train, rose betimes and was nearly dressed when Miss Matilda Denby arrived to wait upon the surviving members of the family she had served for nearly forty years.

This redoubtable lady had joined the Wendover household as a kitchen maid at the age of thirteen and had advanced to second housemaid by the time the late Sir Charles brought his bride home to the Grange. The new Lady Wendover had taken a great fancy to the discreetly efficient young woman and, when anticipating her first Happy Event, had declared she would have no other to act as nurse to her children. In the guise of a benevolent despot who stood no nonsense from her charges, Mattie had ruled the nursery until the tragic events that led to the dissolution of the estate. There was never any question that she would go wherever her lady and her daughters established themselves. Being of an intensely practical nature, she had taken the reins of the reduced household into her capable hands and had seen to it that Lady Wendover was not troubled with domestic matters during her final unhappy years. It was she who trained Miss Wendover in the mundane details of domestic management, which had not formed part of the education imparted by a very expensive French governess. Miss Wendover, impelled by the promptings of necessity, had proved an apt pupil, learning among diverse skills how to dress a joint, plan the stocking of a still room, and choose the most efficacious mixture for cleaning and polishing every surface in a home that could ever be thought to need maintenance. Later, she herself had taught her sister those accomplishments such as ease with the French tongue, watercolor painting, and needlework which were indispensable to a lady's education, but neither Miss Wendover nor Mattie had so far succeeded in implanting much practical or domestic knowledge in Diana's lovely head.

This morning Diana opened the door to the maid, who entered with her customary brisk stride, glancing in some surprise from the still-occupied bed to the girl engaged in buttoning the sleeves of a most becoming carriage dress of dark-green wool.

"Well, Miss Diana, you are up bright and early." She accepted the slim wrist thrust at her for assistance, but once her capable fingers had fastened the buttons her eyes returned to the bed.

"What's wrong with Miss April?"

"Nothing—that is, I do not imagine there is anything wrong. She was reading when I fell asleep. I don't know what time she came to bed. You know her way when she gets absorbed in a book. Wake her, will you, Mattie? I am persuaded she meant to get an early start, and, Mattie, you'll have to finish packing for me. Look what a muddle I have made of my nightclothes. I don't have your knack of folding things neatly."

"If you took more time, Miss Diana, you wouldn't need help."

"Dear Mattie," wheedled the girl, "you know I am a hopeless case past praying for. Please do it for me and I shall rouse April. I vow I am famished for my breakfast."

"Don't play off your tricks on me, missy. You know I take no notice of such nonsense." Though the words were minatory, Miss Denby's austere features softened at sight of the pretty, mischievous face confronting her, and she proceeded to repack the cloak bag, clucking her tongue in disapproval at the state of its contents. Her head with its uncompromising knot of salt-and-pepper hair was bent to her task, but her alert black eyes strayed frequently to the scene taking place in the corner.

"April, wake up, it's nearly eight o'clock. Don't pretend you're asleep, I saw your eyelids twitch. Oh no, you don't!" Diana pulled the blanket down from her sister's ears and continued alternately abusing and cajoling her until her victim rolled over with a groan and opened her eyes.

"Diana, you wretch, what is the big rush? Good morning, Mattie. Am I really so very late?" Miss Wendover gave a huge yawn and swung her legs out of bed, accepting the wrapper her sister handed her. She glanced briefly at the maid, then avoided the searching look the other bent on her, concentrating her attention on the vital task of tying the girdle of her wrapper. Now that the moment had come to disclose the fundamental change that was about to occur in their lives, she found herself woefully inadequate to the task. Anything less than an absolutely truthful rendition of the events leading up to the decision taken last night would sound fantastic, but every instinct of discretion forbade such a revelation. Besides, it was not beyond the bounds of imagination that Lord Glenville might have had second thoughts about capitulating to what was no better than blackmail. He might have made his escape at dawn, gambling that a woman in her position would not have the resources to follow up her threat to expose him. And she did not even know whether to regard such a possibility as a calamity or a blessing. She began to wash and dress for the day, thankful for Diana's excited chatter that covered her own lack of conversation. Her mind was still totally blank by the time she had donned the same brown dress she had removed the night before and brushed her hair into some kind of order before confining it under the cap she had taken to wearing since beginning her career as a teacher.

"Miss April!"

"Yes, Mattie?"

"Is something wrong? Do you feel unwell this morning?"

"No, no, I am fine, thank you, Mattie, but I haven't much appetite at the moment. Why do not you and Diana go down to the coffee room. All I wish is coffee, if you'll send some up to me. I'll finish packing in the meantime."

She summoned up the nerve to return the maid's concerned regard, but knew herself for a craven coward. The thought of coming face-to-face with Lord Glenville or his enemy, the man he called Allerton, in the public dining room robbed her of any desire for food, and she was inclined to think they would be well out of a bad situation if she never met either again. Diana and Mattie were staring at her in bewilderment when a knock sounded at the door. Miss Wendover jumped and put out a hand in an instinctive gesture of repudiation, then dropped the hand to her side as Mattie crossed to the door.

The landlord wished the ladies a cheerful good day and presented Miss Denby with a screw of paper for Miss Wendover. He prevented Miss Denby from closing the door by the simple expedient of a foot in the opening. "I'm to wait for a reply," he declared, noting with interest that one of the ladies had turned pale as a ghost on seeing the missive. When this was put into her reluctant hands, the trembling of those hands was obvious to all three observers. There was complete silence in the sunny room while she smoothed the sheet of paper and read the message thereon. It might have been a long message or the handwriting might have been difficult, because the lady's eyes remained fixed on the paper for an appreciable length of time. Finally she raised her head, ignoring the younger lady's importunities to be told what was happening, and spoke directly to the innkeeper.

"Tell Lord Glenville we shall be pleased to accept his kind invitation in fifteen minutes."

"Who is Lord Glenville?" asked Diana before the door had even shut behind Mr. Choate. "Invitation for what?"

Miss Wendover looked from her sister's puzzled face to the knowledgeable one of Miss Denby and spoke to the latter. "Yes, it is he, and . . . and I am, in all likelihood, going to marry him," she finished in a rush of words, the tone of which was slightly defiant, like that of a child confessing to an act of disobedience.

Her audience was stunned for an instant, then found its collective tongue.

"*Marry* him? Marry *whom*, for the Lord's sake? Are you funning, April?"

"*No*, Miss April, you *can't!*" Miss Denby's harsh whisper drowned out Diana's query.

"Yes, I can, Mattie. Don't you see, it would be the answer to all our problems!"

"It would be a disaster, mark my words! Nothing but misery could come from such a move," Miss Denby stated in a prophetic tone.

The eyes of the older women had been locked in a battle of wills since Miss Wendover had made her annoucement. Hers were pleading but determined, and her former nurse projected fear and rejection as her lips clamped in a thin line. Diana, who had been ignored during the interchange, looked from face to face, unable to make any sense out of what was happening. She stamped her foot impatiently.

"Will someone please tell me what this is all about? Who is this Lord Glenville?"

"He is a man I knew a long time ago before Mother died." Miss Wendover spoke slowly, addressing her sister, but she continued to look at Miss Denby. Some unspoken agreement had been forged between them, for Miss Denby remained mute, her expression grave but resigned.

"And he wishes to marry you? How did he know we were here? Have you seen him?" Diana was determined to get to the bottom of the mystery she scented in the atmosphere of the room.

"It is a long story, and there is no time now for explanations. He has invited us to have breakfast with him in a private dining room. We must not keep him waiting." As she spoke, Miss Wendover had collected her reticule, and now she tucked a clean handkerchief into it. "Are you ready?" she inquired of Diana, who gave a last pat to the curls Mattie had arranged for her while her sister finished dressing.

"I suppose so. I do not understand any of this, but there's no denying it's exciting," Diana replied sunnily. "What kind of a lord is he?"

Miss Denby emitted what sounded suspiciously like a sniff of disdain.

"He is the eighth Earl of Glenville," said Miss Wendover, avoiding her handmaiden's eye. "He inherited the title about seven years ago from a cousin who drowned in a boating accident together with the brother who was his heir."

"Goodness, you'll be a *countess,* April!" cried Diana, much impressed. "But why did he not ask you to marry him when he came into the title?"

Diana's reasonable question was greeted by a brief silence as Miss Wendover paused at the open door to await the others' exit. "There were reasons," she said at last in a manner calculated to discourage further questioning. That this end was achieved was due more to the brisk pace she set and the presence of the landlord at the bottom of the stairway than to any inhibiting effect her firmness had on her curious sister.

Mr. Choate bowed and conducted the ladies to the private dining room Lord Glenville had hired, where he stood aside for them to enter. The tall man with his back to the fireplace approached after a swift look at Miss Wendover and bowed formally. Miss Wendover made the introductions with a cool grace that would have concealed her nervousness from a casual eye, but Lord Glenville's was no casual eye. His first quick appraisal had assured him of both her determination and her uneasiness. She had more color this morning, but any claim to more than average looks was totally nullified by the sparkling young girl beside her. So this was the jewel that must not be left to shine unnoticed in the country even if it meant her sister must sacrifice her own interest and act in a manner contrary to her upbringing to achieve the opportunity to display her before the *ton*. He concentrated a hard stare upon the girl, who met his look with the natural assurance of one confident of her appeal. The absence of any signs of shyness on the part of a seventeen-year-old girl who had spent most of her life away from society struck him as rather significant.

There was a faint family resemblance, he thought, bending politely over the small hand, but the younger Miss Wendover was a more vivid edition, her hair a mass of bright-gold curls, her eyes thickly lashed and deeply blue, her complexion of rose-leaf perfection. Like her sister she was of moderate height and graceful carriage, but in her case a slim nicely curved figure was displayed to advantage by a beautifully cut dress that flattered her coloring and, to his discerning eye, had cost at least three times as much as the nondescript brown thing Miss Wendover was once again attired in. Pretty? Yes, decidedly so, but in a style often seen among the buds at Almack's each year, and owing more to the eager glow of youthful spirits than to any bone-deep loveliness that would escape the ravages of time.

"I am delighted to make your acquaintance, Lord Glenville," Miss Diana Wendover declared with apparent sincerity, "but I must tell you that Mattie and I are still reeling with surprise. April has never mentioned you to me until just now when your invitation was delivered, but she says you have known each other since before our mother died."

"That is correct, Miss Diana," he concurred smoothly at the same time one level eyebrow elevated slightly as he flicked a glance at her sister's rigid countenance and tightly clasped hands.

"Lord Glenville, this is our good friend Miss Matilda Denby, who has been with our family since before Diana and I were born," Miss Wendover said before her sister could pursue the topic of their past acquaintance.

Miss Denby dropped him the merest suggestion of a curtsy

and treated him to a stare every bit as measuring as his own and much less approving from a pair of snapping black eyes that enlivened a gaunt-featured face. He responded with a genuine smile that narrowed those eyes as he murmured his pleasure at the introduction. The younger Miss Wendover, not about to see the conversation taken out of her hands, intervened in a voice that lacked the musical quality of her sister's but was not deficient in carrying power.

"April says that you are probably going to marry. Pray, what does that mean precisely, sir?"

His smile, tinged with amusement now, turned toward the curious face of his prospective sister-in-law. "Why, it means that your sister has done me the honor to accept my offer." He could sense the momentary relaxation in the woman on his right at this reply and the subsequent stiffening as he continued, "And that we shall be married later today in London when I have procured a special license."

"*Today!* But I . . . you—"

"Yes, why wait, my dear?" he said to the stricken female beside him. "Wasn't it Shakespeare who said, 'If it were done when 'tis done, then 'twere well it were done quickly'? This way we shall avoid any awkwardness about your arrival in town."

Whatever the well-read Miss Wendover's indignation at having her marriage likened to an assassination might have prompted her to reply in retaliation was aborted by the appearance just then of a waiter bearing a huge tray. She had to be content with shooting her intended husband a glance of undistilled loathing as he seated her at the table with an ostentatious courtesy that was an affront under the circumstances.

The meal that followed was destined to remain in her memory as one of the most unpleasant of her life. Her appetite had deserted her long before the actual confrontation with the man she had coerced into marrying her, but now as it became apparent that the balance of power had swung sharply in his direction, she found it a test of her endurance just to remain seated at the well-appointed table while her intended husband calmly played host and announced plans that would radically alter all their lives with the same degree of emotion he might expend on a decision as to which slice of meat to take onto his plate. The very smell of the food induced a sensation of nausea within her, which wasn't aided by a rising panic as she felt the trap she had designed closing relentlessly around her. Nor did the suspicion that she had bitten off more than she could chew contribute to her peace of mind. Her instinctive attempts to assert herself and prevent Lord Glenville from having everything his own way were enfeebled at the start by her urgent desire to keep Diana ignorant of the true circumstances behind this sudden decision to marry. Thus as the breakfast ordeal progressed she found herself agreeing between clenched teeth to a private wedding that very day wearing the clothes she stood up in, to the dismissal of Mr. Lynley's coach in favor of a post chaise hired by Lord Glenville, and most alarming of all, to the installation of the three of them in his lordship's town house immediately following the marriage. He apologized suavely for the lack of preparation for their reception at his home, sliding over the precipitate nature of the marriage when Diana would have explored the topic more thoroughly. In his future bride's somewhat biased view he exerted a shameless charm of manner (undoubtedly assumed for the occasion) accompanied by liberal doses of flattery to achieve his ends with an inexperienced girl.

His maneuvers were highly successful. Diana was quite won over by the calm good sense of his arguments and showed herself sparklingly responsive to the masculine magnetism he projected seemingly effortlessly. Even Miss Denby unbent a trifle under the benign influence of good food and hot coffee presented to her by a courteous host who contrived to appear attentive to her needs, a rare experience in her work-filled life. She and Diana made a very good meal, but April could not physically swallow anything but coffee even to supplement an earnest desire to conceal her mental agitation from the others. It was a slight degree of consolation to realize as the meal dragged on that her future husband was not making very deep inroads on the platters of eggs and cold meats despite the impression he gave to the contrary. Though common sense insisted he simply might not be a big-breakfast eater, she chose to believe he was finding the meeting as nerve-racking as she was. The thought revived her flagging courage enough to allow her to maintain a fragile composure imposed over a panicky desire to rise from the table and literally flee anywhere that offered an escape from the situation she had created.

It was a profound relief when Lord Glenville took out his watch and announced that it was time they took their departure in view of the busy day that lay ahead of them once they arrived in London.

Miss Wendover was on her feet before he had finished speaking. "Yes, of course. I must just pay our reckoning at the desk. We will not keep you waiting above a minute or two."

"Don't be foolish." His impatient words caught her before she reached the door. "The bill is already taken care of. There is nothing to be done except board the chaise at your convenience. I will see to the loading of your baggage if it is ready."

Suddenly it was imperative that she get away from him—from everyone—for a moment of privacy before embarking on a journey that was to turn her life upside down. "I . . . I must just write a note to Mr. Lynley to explain the return of his coach," she said in desperation. "My writing things are upstairs. I beg you will excuse me, please." She fled on the words but found him beside her as she reached the staircase.

"Is anything wrong?" he inquired with polite formality while his eyes remained watchful.

"No, of course not. I—"

"Quickly, put on your gloves!"

April stared at the enigmatic dark face that had leaned toward her. "I beg your pardon?"

"I said put your gloves on. *Do it!*"

The urgency in his low tones caused her to obey him without further delay. As she struggled into the worn kid gloves she noted that his attention was no longer on her, and her glance followed his up the staircase. Her cheeks reddened as she recognized the tall man slowly descending, and her hands shook slightly as she buttoned her gloves. It seemed there was to be no avoiding another embarrassing confrontation with their tormentor of the night before. She would have to pass Allerton to get upstairs, and Lord Glenville was standing like a monument at her side blocking any return to the dining room. As the victim of a bad dream she watched the approach of the man who hoped to ruin her future husband. Her fingers itched to slap the leering expression from his face, and her teeth went tight. She could feel the man next to her grow rigid. Later, the recollection of her own uncivilized reaction enabled her to better understand what happened next.

"You must be reluctant indeed to leave the delights of this very mediocre inn, Glenville, to forgo your usual crack-of-dawn departure." Allerton's insolent gaze lingered on Miss Wendover, who felt besmirched.

"My wife was tired from her journey, so we delayed our departure," the man at her side replied in an offhand manner.

The words had an electric effect on his listeners. Miss Wendover gave an uncontrolled start, but a warning grip on her arm kept her silent. She stared, fascinated, as the leer on Allerton's face gave way to mingled fury and incredulity.

"*Married!* Since when?"

"Since yesterday, but I'd rather the world at large remain unenlightened until I have told my mother."

"Rather a sudden decision then?"

"Just so."

"Strange you did not think to present your *wife* to me last night." Allerton had recovered his self-possession, though his whole manner bespoke disbelief.

"My marital status is none of your business, but as I said, I would prefer that my mother hear the news from me." He turned to Miss Wendover, who was giving an excellent imitation of a statue, and said with gentle solicitude, "Do you still wish to retrieve your writing materials, darling?"

"Yes," she whispered, unable to contribute more positively to this talented performance but eager to seize the opportunity to efface herself.

"Wait!" Allerton's command halted her foot on the first step and sent a shiver of apprehension down her spine. Had he guessed the truth? She turned with reluctance.

"You must allow me to offer my felicitations on your marriage, Lady Glenville. You have *captured* . . . the heart of one of England's most eligible and resistant bachelors."

She allowed him to take her hand for an instant then, though every instinct bade her ignore his outstretched hand. Her upbringing demanded that she respond, but she could not bring herself to utter more than a brief thank-you before resuming her ascent up the stairs, which only the severest self-discipline kept from resembling the rout it was.

Chapter Four

Some six hours later, April was seated in a chair in the bed-chamber that was henceforth to be hers in the large town house in Hanover Square that had been inherited by the earl along with the title and estates. She had been sitting in the same limp attitude since dismissing Mattie a half hour ago to assist Diana in settling into her new quarters. For the past two hours she had been a married woman, April Harding, Countess of Glenville. She repeated the title now aloud, but that didn't seem to give any additional substance to the fantasy world she had been inhabiting for less than twenty-four hours. Incredible that one's existence could be changed forever in less than a single revolution of the earth on its axis! And not just her own existence either. That was the truly frightening part, that by her harsh, perhaps even criminal action, she had radically altered the course of at least three other lives. She shivered and rubbed her upper arms fiercely to shake off the sudden chill. The one sure thing was that sitting here nursing regrets would not mend matters. She had to go on from here.

For the first time her eyes roved around the room, whose furnishings had not yet impinged on her consciousness. The results of this survey were not particularly encouraging. This morning Lord Glenville had dispatched his groom to Hanover Square on horseback with instructions that rooms be made ready for his wife and sister-in-law. Certainly there was evidence of a hasty dusting and airing in here, but April's fastidious soul was affronted by the atmosphere of neglect that clung to the room. The satinwood furniture was good, if a trifle old-fashioned, but would have been improved by a thorough application of beeswax. The brass fireplace appointments wanted polishing, and only heaven and the housekeeper knew when the draperies and bed curtains had last been taken down and cleaned. Not that cleaning would improve the look of them, she thought sourly, eyeing the faded wine-red draperies with disfavor. Then she brought herself up sharply. Pretty well for a woman who had been living in a cottage and teaching in a village school for the last several years to be criticizing such luxurious surroundings! She ought to be on her knees thanking the Providence that had led her to this place.

Only it hadn't been Providence at all but her own unchristian and, yes, *immoral* act that had achieved this new status. All it took was a few solitary moments when she was off guard to bring the whole sordid episode before her again. How could she, April Wendover, who had always considered her principles to be of the highest and her conduct above criticism, sink to such depths of degradation? Every moment spent in the company of Lord Glenville was a stinging reproach. She recalled his stern features as he had stood by her side for the brief marriage ceremony in St. Clement Dane's earlier. She had not yet learned to discern his emotions behind that unreadable face he presented to the world, but something in the set of his finely molded lips at that moment smote her heart. Even though she had done it for Diana's sake, she must be held deeply accountable. Did Diana's need give her the right to coerce another's actions? Last night she had answered one way, but today when it was too late to undo the wrong, her heart gave her a different answer.

Too restless now to sit, she prowled about the large square apartment, opening drawers and staring blankly at their equally blank interiors. Lord Glenville had already made plans to send for those of their belongings they wished to bring to London. Mattie was to go tomorrow to supervise the packing and removal. Could anything be more final? She sighed deeply, then straightened slim shoulders. What was done was done—irrevocably.

A knock brought her attention sharply back to the present. It didn't seem to come from the door through which a maid had led her, nor the open door to the sitting room beyond. Her eyes lighted on another door she hadn't noticed until now in the fireplace wall. After a momentary hesitation she crossed to it and pulled it open to stare in surprise at Lord Glenville—her husband, she reminded herself.

"I hope I am not disturbing you?" he inquired politely. "Were you in the sitting room?" He waited for her to step aside so he might enter, and with reluctance she did so.

"No, I was in this room. You did not interrupt anything of importance, my lord." Her voice sounded strange in her own ears, and he must have thought so too, for a small frown appeared between his eyes.

"My name is Adam. You really cannot go about addressing me as 'my lord,' you know, my dear April, or we shall undo all our careful work."

She essayed a tentative smile. "You are quite right, of course, Adam. It is a name I have always liked. Things . . . seem a bit strange to me at present, but I shall try to . . . to fit into your life with the least possible disruption." The eyes she raised to his were eloquent of unspoken apology.

He stared deeply into them for a moment before acknowledging this overture with an unsmiling bow. He glanced around the room, his expression gradually darkening. "You don't fit into this room, I fear. I had not realized how gloomy and old-fashioned it is. You must effect any changes you wish to make it more comfortable. Throw everything away and start from the beginning if you like."

"Thank you, my lord—I mean, Adam. You are most generous."

"Not at all. I am planning a few changes also. I thought to approach the subject tactfully, but that was rather presumptuous; it cannot be done other than directly."

"Wh . . . what changes?"

There was an evanescent gleam that might have been

amusement in the dark eyes staring down at her, but it was quickly submerged by determination.

"Changes in your appearance. As my wife you'll be greatly talked about, and I intend that the talk be flattering. The first step is to discard this." They had been standing in the middle of April's bedchamber, but now he took a step forward and snatched the muslin-and-lace cap from her head. "Permanently," he added, tossing the rejected cap onto the bed and watching unmoved as she inched backward from his vicinity, her eyes wide with shock. Fetching up against the dressing-table bench, she dropped onto it, putting up a protesting hand to her tousled head, whose smooth coil had been disarranged by his rough action. She entered an unsteady demur.

"At my age it is necessary to wear a cap."

"Why? To prove you are an ape leader? Well, you are no longer April Wendover, spinster, of this or any other parish. You are the Countess of Glenville and one of society's fashion setters. At least," he amended, "you will be when I have finished refurbishing you."

April's heart had started an irregular hammering action that forced part of her attention away from the disturbing man looking her over so coolly. It took her a moment to assure herself that this vital organ, though noisy, was still functioning properly. She must remain calm. Lord Glenville, this *stranger*, had no power over her. Even as the thought took shape, she recognized the futility of it. Her *husband* had a great deal of power over her life, validated by law and tradition stretching back in time, but, as anger began to rise, her *appearance* was not his province. Just let him try to dictate to her! Her chin acquired a belligerent tilt as she brought her eyes back to the man, who seemed to be making a thoughtful inventory of her attributes. Oddly enough, she wasn't suffering any pangs of embarrassment at all. Indignation had its uses, evidently.

Lord Glenville spoke then, confirming her impressions. "You are no classic beauty, but with those strange eyes and that hair you could be eye-catching at the very least. It's simply a matter of emphasizing your assets." He continued to survey her person with a cool impartiality that caused her to show hackle despite a short-lived resolve to remain impervious. It was neither embarrassment nor offended modesty that brought about a faint becoming rise of color in her pale cheeks but a fierce resentment at this judgmental air, and it cost her something to maintain her stolid calm as she replied with entirely spurious mildness:

"I have no slightest wish to be eye-catching and am quite reconciled to my physical limitations."

"Well, I am not, and now is as good a time as any to inform you that your wishes on this and other matters ceased to be of paramount importance the moment you coerced my acceptance of marriage between us." He ignored the sudden indrawn breath of the figure seated rigidly on the dressing-table bench as he leaned over her shoulder and tapped the gold band on the slim finger of one clenched hand. "To you that ring may represent the security of social position you require to ensure your sister's success, but it grants me a whole set of rights too that you'd do well to keep in mind."

Up to this point she had maintained a steely composure, but now the clear gray eyes widened, then dropped before the threat in his. Recognizing the flicker of fear, he nodded, satisfied that his message had been received, before he resumed his original assessment. "Your figure is good even in that outmoded gown and will appear to advantage in the styles I intend to select for you."

This brought her startled glance back to his face. "*You* intend to select my gowns?"

An abrupt turn to finger the mother-of-pearl-backed brushes on the dressing table behind her concealed his amusement at the expression of disbelief and outrage that momentarily animated her previously impassive features. The drawl became more pronounced. "Why not? Surely my taste could not help but be an improvement over that which selected the gown you are wearing. It's several years out of date and all the wrong color for you." In the mirror he watched her straight back grow even straighter, but there was no heat in the quiet reply.

"This gown was not considered dowdy when I purchased it five years ago. It has not been within my means to replace it."

He abandoned the mirror and faced her once more, a pace or two from where she sat on the bench. "Yet your sister is wearing a most attractive dress and pelisse, not expensive, I grant you, but certainly in the current mode."

"My sister is very young and very lovely. Clothes mean a lot to girls at this stage in their lives. She has missed out on so much because of the life we have been compelled to lead since the deaths of our father and brother."

He could almost hear the struggle within her to keep all defensiveness out of her explanation but chose to ignore it as he summed up the situation dispassionately. "By trapping me into marriage you have achieved your main objective." A pause produced no reaction save a slight firming of the soft mouth. Those unusual eyes looked unwaveringly back. "Your sister will make her bow to society rigged out in all the trappings girls set such store by. She will undoubtedly create something of a sensation, initially at least, and quite possibly might make an advantageous marriage if I settle enough money on her. I hope it will afford you great satisfaction to witness this triumph, because *you* will be paying for it with the loss of your freedom. I shall leave the dressing of your sister in your hands. I take no interest in members of the infantry, but you are my wife and your appearance and your deportment will reflect on me. *No one* is to guess that this marriage is anything other than an impetuous love match. I don't choose to set up as a laughingstock among any acquaintance!" Again he paused, but there was not the least reaction in the woman watching him with grave attention.

"I intend to orchestrate every detail of your debut as Lady Glenville. I may not have wished for a wife, but, by God, now that I have one she'll do me credit or I'll know the reason why!"

Again the implied threat, but this time curiosity was stronger than intimidation. "What precisely do you have in mind, my lord?"

"As I said before, it is my intention that you be decidedly eye-catching. I shan't stint you on what you expend on your sister's raiment, but I do not intend that you shall ever be cast into the shade by a brainless chit with yellow curls and a provocative smile!"

Her eyes flashed as she assimilated the insult to her sister, but the temper was concealed immediately by lowered lids. Her voice was merely curious. "And how will you prevent this, my lord, in the light of the fact that Diana is younger, prettier, and livelier than I and, if I may accept your words at face value, will herself be dressed in the height of fashion?"

His smile was neither warming nor reassuring, because it was not directed toward the woman seated a few feet away but at some inner vision he did not propose to share with her. "You may safely entrust that task to my, shall we say, more experienced judgment. I may not have any great liking for your sex, but I am generally accorded something of a connoisseur when it is a question of beauty."

"But as you have already pointed out, I am not a beauty."

"You haven't a classically beautiful face," he corrected. "Often the unconventional has a more potent appeal. Your sister is like a hundred other pretty girls and will appeal to ordinary men. When I am finished with you, you will attract those who reject the commonplace." He rather enjoyed her expression of doubt mingled with reluctant expectation as he proceeded to the heart of the matter.

"We'll start with your hair. Does it curl naturally?"

"No."

The hint of satisfaction in her denial was not lost upon him. She had no intention of cooperating wholeheartedly, and, perversely, this attitude lent an additional measure of enjoyment to the exercise.

"Good. Everyone must notice the unusual color at once, and I intend that their eyes return to it frequently. You will never under any circumstances wear any ornament, jewel, feather, or ribbon in your hair. We are going to draw attention by the silken smoothness of the style I shall devise so that every movement of your head will cause the light to catch and accentuate the silvery tone. The first step is a good cut."

Her hand went up to the prim coil in an instinctive gesture of protection. "You . . . you do not propose to do the cutting yourself?"

"No, but it will be done under my direction. I think we shall turn you into a feminine version of a medieval page. Your forehead is too broad, but with a long fringe almost to your eyebrows we can disguise that and at the same time call attention to your pointed chin. With those eyes the effect will be slightly feline, but I have no objection to cats."

"But I don't wish to look like a cat!" she protested, aghast at the picture of herself forming in her confused mind. "And no one appears with straight hair. Do you desire to turn me into a figure of ridicule? Is this your revenge for having married me against your will?"

"Must I remind you again that your wishes are of absolutely no interest to me?" he replied in bored accents. "You may rid your mind of any fear that I would ever allow my wife to make a figure of herself among my friends and enemies. You will be occupying a more elevated position than you ever dreamed of, and I intend that you make a decided impression. If people talk about the unconventional aspect, well and good; that is infinitely preferable to fading into the background. There is no denying your quality, and I presume you have sufficient understanding to converse on a social level with those of my colleagues whom I shall be entertaining. You will not find it all that taxing," he added somewhat dryly.

When she made no reply, he returned to his inventory of her features. "Fortunately your lashes are thick and sufficiently dark to enhance those eyes, but your brows must be darkened." He paid no attention to her gasp of indignation. "They are beautifully arched, but too fair to be effective. Don't worry about censure from the high sticklers. It can be done with subtlety. It would not be to my advantage to have people speculating whether I'd picked my wife from the corps de ballet at the Opera. You haven't much natural color; however, I'm not sure that cannot be regarded as an asset. Your skin is as fine-grained as alabaster, and a slight hint of fragility won't come amiss." He was ticking things off on his fingers like a shopping list. "Hairstyles, eyebrows, coloring, I think that's the lot, except to inform you that when we have attended to these alterations, this afternoon if possible, I shall make myself available to accompany you to a modiste that I can trust not to load you up with ruffles and furbelows. I shan't be able to spare more than one day, so it's best to instruct you about my wishes in the matter of dress now. It will save the annoyance of having to return unsatisfactory purchases at a later date." The light-gray eyes had widened with a reluctant fascination. He sensed her resentment and was amused by it.

"You are a trifle too slender, but I won't quibble about that. Statuesque females tend to run to fat in middle age, and that I cannot abide. The image I shall create demands simplicity in style at all times, *costly* simplicity, emphasizing perfect fit and made up in the choicest fabrics. Never succumb to an impulse to adorn yourself in strong colors. They're not for you, the crimsons and deep blues that your sister will undoubtedly choose. They will overpower your delicate coloring and render you insignificant, as does that brown thing you are wearing. Confine your choices to pearly grays, pale rose, muted shades of blue and green and the various mauve tints. Avoid deep yellow and never try to wear dead white, though an oyster or champagne shade might be flattering. You'll see what I mean when we call at Mélisande's tomorrow."

Lord Glenville had come to the end of his assessment of his wife's potentialities, for he fell silent and raised one dark eyebrow, apparently inviting comment on one or all aspects of his discourse. After an expectant pause when nothing ensued from the expressionless figure on the bench, he bowed mockingly and strolled to the door that led to his own rooms, pausing only to mention in passing that he had sent for a coiffeur and had left word that he was to be notified on the arrival of this personage.

She was on her feet before the door quite closed, racing across the room to lock it behind him in a childish gesture of defiance that was foiled by the absence of any key for the purpose. How dare he treat her like some little lightskirt he had picked up on Bond Street! He was going to turn her into a lady of fashion, was he? She'd see about that! She turned from the door with an angry flounce and marched back to the dressing table to stare into its mirror. *A cat!* He thought she looked like a cat and he actually wished to emphasize the likeness! The man was mad, *utterly mad!*

It had been a very long time since April had taken the least interest in her looks. She had had no reason to bother about how she looked for longer than she cared to remember. Now she peered with impartial concentration at her own features. There was no denying her chin was a trifle pointed, and her eyes, now that she really studied them, were set at a slightly oblique angle, but they certainly weren't yellow like a cat's eyes. In fact, they didn't seem to possess any distinct color at all. She had always dismissed them as an uninteresting gray, but they did tend to acquire a blue or violet or green tinge if she wore those colors. Perhaps they weren't so uninteresting after all. She leaned closer to the glass to examine her lashes with new appreciation. She had never paid them any particular attention in the long-ago days of her comeout, but Lord Glenville's casual observation of their length and thickness was strangely comforting many years later. Recalling the outspoken strictures of her governess and Mattie against the sin of vanity when, prior to her presentation, she had demanded their opinion of her chances of being one of the successes of her season, and their insistence on concentrating her efforts on appearing modest and well mannered, she laughed aloud at the picture she would present to the long-departed Mademoiselle Fautier and the ever present Mattie if they could see her now, staring (at her advanced age) into

a mirror, assessing her looks with all the anxiety of a
seventeen-year-old. Feeling herself back in Diana's stage, although it must be admitted her sister never suffered from
any qualms of insecurity with regard to her appearance, she
abandoned the search for hidden beauty after a brief
frowning inspection of her forehead. He was right, this
annoyingly perceptive husband of hers, it was much too
broad. Her hand went to her hair in a tentative gesture. She
was unaware of the wistful expression in her eyes as they
lingered on the shining silvery mass. At least he thought her
hair an asset, she reminded herself with a touch of shamefaced defiance before eschewing the ridiculous, unprofitable
exercise in which she had been engaging for a wasted half
hour.

Several hours later, April allowed a surprisingly approving Mattie to slip her least-dated dinner dress over her
shining head in preparation for the first meal in her new
home in the company of her husband and sister, the two
people whose interests she must advance and protect. She
offered a silent prayer that these interests should never
collide and turned her back obligingly at Mattie's command.

"Stand still, Miss April, do. How am I to do up these
pesky buttons with you wriggling about like a fish on a
hook?" The maid's eyes followed those of her mistress to the
dressing-table mirror, and the lines of her face softened.
"Though mind you, I don't blame you for wanting to look in
the glass tonight. That's a right becoming haircut that
Monsoor Maurice gave you. I disremember when I've seen
you look so pretty with your hair all silky and shinin' in the
candlelight."

"Thank you, Mattie. You . . . you don't think perhaps it's
a bit young for me?"

The abigail's firm disclaimer was aimed at the suggestion
of anxiety underlying this hesitant question.

"Young is it? And why shouldn't you look young, that's
what I say. You *are* young, though small chance you've had
to act it these last years." She cast an appraising eye over the

sleek, below-chin-length hair that curved gently into April's graceful neck. "It's a mite unusual, of course. That straight fringe in front comin' down almost to your eyebrows and curving past the top of your ears is not what I've ever seen even in old pictures, but there's no gainsaying it suits you down to the ground. Makes you look entirely different from anyone else."

"Lord Glenville says he wishes me to be a leader of fashion," April offered doubtfully.

"And why not? He won't be the first man to want to show off a good-looking young wife."

This was almost heresy! April gazed in astonishment at her old nurse, unable to credit the transformation that her marriage to a peer of the realm had apparently wrought in one whose stern moral precepts had included vanity and worldliness among the seven deadly sins. "Handsome is as handsome does" had pretty well summed up Miss Denby's attitude in raising her charges. She was about to question the source of this turnabout when a knock sounded at the hall door and her sister entered.

The excitement of the journey and their sudden change in circumstances had caught up with Diana, and, once settled in her new apartment, she had fallen victim to the lure of a comfortable bed to indulge in a restorative nap. Now she bounced into the room eager to impart the odd snippets of information concerning the inhabitants of the household dropped by Alice, the maid detailed to wait upon her. She had just launched into a secondhand account of the head housemaid's lumbago when her sister's changed appearance registered. Her pretty mouth fell open, then snapped shut while she drew breath.

"April! What have you done to yourself? Where is your hair?"

"Most of it is in the fireplace," confessed her sister with a smile. "Do you like this style?"

Diana looked rather taken aback. "I'm not sure. Your hair seems very pale and smooth, but it makes you look different, much younger," she finished almost accusingly.

"You don't look like yourself, and you've darkened your eyebrows!"

"Well, yes, a little. Adam insisted, but he said no one would notice."

"Well, I noticed!" stated Diana primly, then added a trifle grudgingly, "I don't suppose anyone who didn't know you well would guess. You won't be in the current fashion with that hairstyle, though," she pointed out, "and how can you ever wear ornaments or feathers if there isn't length enough to put up?"

"Adam doesn't wish me to wear any ornaments in my hair at all."

"*Adam* doesn't wish it? Poor April! All I can say is that *I* shall never allow a man to dictate to *me* in matters of fashion!" She tossed her bright-gold curls to emphasize her independence from masculine domination.

At which point, April, feeling thoroughly dominated, thanked Mattie for her assistance, complimented her sister on her appearance, and proceeded to lead the way to the main saloon, where they found Lord Glenville awaiting them. The soft gray cotton gown with its low-cut neckline edged with lace and long tight-fitting sleeves was quite her most becoming, April thought, and in combination with the distinctive new hairstyle produced an almost forgotten sensation of mild satisfaction with her appearance. Having been subjected earlier to a gratuitous and unflattering assessment of the picture she presented in her dowager's cap and brown traveling dress, her tattered self-esteem would have benefited greatly by any comment from her husband on the dramatic improvement. This satisfaction was denied her, however, as Lord Glenville merely wished her a good evening in a bored voice before turning his attention to his young sister-in-law. For Diana there was no lack of smoothly expressed compliments, and April was astounded and disturbed at the depth of her own disappointment. She brought herself roundly to task. Surely the insincere and practiced compliments of a man of the town had no value for her, and besides, did she not already know his opinion of herself? An adventuress, he had called her, and had all but spelled out his doubts that her youthful betrothal had been in any way a tribute to her person. He had weighed her few assets as if she were a horse he was contemplating buying.

There had been a moment this afternoon, however, when Monsieur Maurice had nearly finished cutting her hair, when she had surprised an expression in her husband's eyes very unlike the impersonal appraisal she had resented earlier. It had been a dark, brooding look full of a significance that eluded her, and in any case it had been almost instantly supplanted by a measured judgment as he had indicated to the coiffeur that he wished the tips of her ears to remain exposed to show off earrings. At that moment, recalling her Ovid, the image of Pygmalion came into her mind. With just the same intentness must the legendary sculptor have fashioned his ideal woman. In the next instant she dismissed the comparison as inapt. Pygmalion had fallen in love with his Galatea, and one had to be human to fall in love. She had already noted and been repelled by an odd inhuman detachment about the man she had married. To the Frenchman's enthusiastic praises of the results of his handiwork, Lord Glenville had merely allowed that the artist had achieved the look he sought for his wife before taking an abrupt leave of them in the manner of a man who had already wasted too much time on trivialities.

He was talking charming trivialities with Diana now as April's considering gaze assessed him with some of his own detachment. Not precisely handsome, she concluded. His features were a bit too strong and his aspect too stern for that epithet, though each individual item of his physiognomy was good taken by itself. His brow was wide and not overly high, with fine lines crossing it when he looked thoughtful. Nose and mouth were perfectly carved, but she found his jaw too square and attributed the impression of harshness largely to this and to the deep vertical lines that creased his lean cheeks from nose to mouth. She liked his eyes least. Though full of intelligence and well opened with clear dark irises and long curving lashes wasted on a man, the hardness of his habitual expression negated nature's softer design. In the few seconds that had elapsed between seeing him for the first time nine years ago and discovering his identity, she had formed a swift impression of virile good looks, but that impression had been swamped by her emotional response to his name. Studying him now, she conceded the virility, but the quality that had made it a pleasure to look at him in his youth had not endured. Except for his mouth when it wasn't clamped in a straight line, nothing of youth remained in his face. There were even a few gray hairs among the brown over his temples.

She was roused from her covert study of her husband by his voice asking a question; in fact, repeating a question, one eyebrow slightly elevated as he waited for her reply. Fortunately Diana came to her rescue with a laughing rejoinder which gave April time to recover her poise and take an interest in the conversation.

It was an uncomfortable meal for the new bride despite her sister's animated chatter. Diana kept the wheel of conversation in her determined hands, steering her course through all the prospective delights of the season that would soon be upon them, plying her new brother-in-law with eager questions about Almack's, the Opera, and the possibilities of full-dress balls and rout parties. Lord Glenville was kept busy responding to this barrage, and April found she had nothing to do but supply an occasional word of agreement. The better part of her mind was free to contemplate the ramifications of the decision she had made less than twenty-four hours before, but there was no comfort to be derived from this line of thought. She was throbbingly aware of the brooding presence of the man sitting opposite her, an enigmatic personality beneath the surface charm. As dinner progressed she pushed most of the food around on her plate, making only a pretense of eating. This was only the second meal with the man who was now her husband, but if she continued to feel his presence like a blight on her appetite she would soon expire from malnutrition.

At some point she became aware that there were

empirical grounds for avoiding the food at Glenville House. The quality of the offerings from her husband's kitchen was, to set it at the most charitable, uneven. Granted there had been only a few hours' warning that the household was to receive a new mistress, that news should not have thrown a competent chef into a flat spin. She could only guess at the kitchen disasters that could have produced at one meal rubbery chicken in an overthickened, cold Madeira sauce, burned peas, fish that had definitely gone off, and inedible pastry covering an unidentifiable filling masquerading as a tart. The earl placed a modest amount of various foods in his mouth with no discernible reaction of pleasure or disgust, mechanically chewing and swallowing indiscriminately. Once April saw Diana's quick frown at her plate as she tasted some of the chicken, but in essence her sister was too intent on her conversation to notice what she ate. April's thoughtful glance dwelled with increasing frequency on Morton, the dour butler who served the meal with the aid of a young footman.

Nearer fifty than forty, the ascetic-looking gray-haired butler was above the average in height, but he walked with a round-shouldered stoop that, combined with shadow thinness, reduced his stature a bit. Except for this characteristic, which may have been the result of some illness, his appearance in his neat livery was impeccable. There was nothing to object to in his pale, smooth-skinned face with its thinly chiseled nose and mouth and light-blue eyes except perhaps an expression in those eyes that April had discovered once or twice in their brief encounters. For the most part they were almost expressionless, but when Morton had greeted his master on their arrival this afternoon, she had noted a glitter of something that came and went so quickly that she hesitated to put a name to it. Being all but excluded from the lively interrogation of her husband that Diana had conducted throughout the meal, April had been at leisure to observe the movements of the servants. Jacob, the pleasant-faced footman, was young and a bit awkward. He looked to the quiet-footed butler for guidance in the carrying out of his duties. Morton directed him unobtrusively, his eyes never losing the chilling ice-blue impersonality that she found a bit daunting when leveled on her. Once when she looked up swiftly at hearing her husband's rare laugh, she caught a repetition of the disturbing glitter as Morton stood motionless regarding Lord Glenville for a moment before heavy lids descended and he deftly retrieved a dish of vegetables from the table. The next instant the impersonal mask of the well-trained servant was back in place, but it was April's uncomfortable impression that the butler never fully removed his attention (his *hostile* attention?) from the earl. All in all she found her nerves at the stretch when the final serving platter was at last cleared and a bottle of port was set before Lord Glenville. As she prepared to rise, Morton's colorless voice inquired:

"Do you wish the tea tray brought to the main saloon or some other location, my lady?"

Since no help was forthcoming from her husband, April indicated that the saloon would be fine, and turned as the butler pulled out her chair to confront her sister wearing a look of almost comical dismay.

"Oh, Lord, until Morton called you 'my lady' I had forgotten this was your wedding dinner!" Diana burst out in consternation. "You two must be wishing me at Jericho! I won't come to the saloon tonight."

"Don't be nonsensical!" April returned sharply, her cheeks aflame. At a warning look from the earl, she achieved a light laugh and softened her response. "I doubt you would find Jericho at all to your liking, my dear, and you cannot retire at such an early hour after napping all afternoon. Besides, I am persuaded Adam would like to hear you play and sing."

"I should indeed," her husband replied cordially. "I'll join you both presently." He escorted the ladies to the door the footman had opened and bowed them out with a charming smile for each.

Diana made another feeble protest as April headed for the main saloon but allowed herself to be persuaded by her determined sister. Once she had glimpsed the beautiful black-and-gold-lacquered pianoforte she was eager to try it and complied good-naturedly with her brother-in-law's requests. Although her voice was not particularly strong, it was true and had been well trained by her sister. Neither was there any necessity to apologize for her performance on the pianoforte. She knew herself to be a competent musician and suffered no qualms of shyness when invited to perform. Her audience tonight, at least the feminine half, seemed loath to release her, but after one quick cup of tea she bade her sister and the earl a determined goodnight at ten o'clock.

April, who had formed the intention of retiring with Diana, was thwarted in this resolve by the earl, who had informed her in an aside during the performance that he desired to have private speech with her before she went upstairs. As the door closed behind Diana he broke the strained silence that had existed between husband and wife the whole evening.

"I won't keep you from your bed above a moment or two." He observed the yawn she was attempting to conceal, or pretending to conceal, and smiled a trifle sardonically. "Please try to relax. You remind me of a bird ready for immediate flight. It has occurred to me that I might reduce this wariness in my presence if I were to assure you that I have no designs on your virtue."

Her eyes flew to his as to a magnet, but she appeared incapable of speech, and he went on, "You may have noticed that there is no key to the door between our rooms. I am sorry not to give it into your keeping, but I do not wish the servants to speculate about our relationship. Will you accept my word that I will not enter without an invitation?"

Smoky eyes full of relief tinged with curiosity searched his. "Yes, of course. Are you, that is . . . do you—*no*, never mind—" She broke off, flushing hotly, and jumped to her feet to wish him an abrupt goodnight, but he raised a hand to detain her. His expression was wry.

"If all that stammering means that you are wondering

whether I prefer young boys, the answer is no; nor am I a monk, but I have never found it necessary to force myself upon unwilling females, and it is especially unlikely in your case. Do I make myself clear?"

"Very clear. Goodnight, my lord." Her voice was almost strangled by embarrassment and she sought release, but he arrested her flight once more.

"Whoa! There is one more item on the agenda before we adjourn this delightful meeting. I wish to present you to my mother tomorrow morning, but we must call at Mélisande's first. This afternoon I sent your measurements to her work-room so they might begin making up a dress and pelisse for you immediately. Please be ready to leave by nine so Mélisande can fit you and they can finish the outfit while you set about choosing fabrics and designs for the most pressing items of your new wardrobe. We shall not send out any 'at home' cards until these initial requirements have been met."

April was staring at him in disbelief. "My measurements!" she echoed, going right to the heart of the matter. "How could you know my measurements?"

"I asked Mattie, of course," he replied coolly. "What is there in that to upset you?"

Her voice outdid his in coolness. "You must pardon my missishness, my lord—I mean, *Adam*—but I am as yet unused to the intimacies of marriage. I shall study to do better in future."

"Thank you," he said gravely, and this time she did flee before he could subject her to any additional shocking revelations.

The earl remained where he was seated, staring at the closed door, his face unreadable, until Morton came in to remove the tea tray.

"Will there by anything else, my lord?"

"No, thank you, Morton. Send the servants to bed, and go yourself after you lock up the house."

"Very good, my lord. I'll bid you goodnight."

The earl continued to sit unmoving for some little while

longer, his gaze fixed in space, a slight frown furrowing his brow. Eventually he emerged from his reverie and, after checking the condition of the fire and extinguishing the candles, left the room. He took up the lamp in the hall and entered his bedchamber, only to reappear five minutes later wearing a greatcoat and carrying a black beaver. In the entrance hall he took a large key from the drawer in a console table and proceeded to unlock the front door.

Once out on the street, he pocketed the key and hauled on his gloves before setting off at a brisk pace for Oxford Street, where he hailed a passing hackney cab. A few minutes drive brought him to Tavistock Street. After paying off the jarvey, he mounted the steps to the entrance door of a slim house and let himself in, using another key he produced from a pocket in his coat.

Chapter Five

Upstairs in a surprisingly luxurious boudoir for what was from its exterior a modest house, sat a woman, comfortably established on a pink satin daybed, a mass of rose-colored wool in her lap. Evidently she had been reading earlier, for a book resposed on a table beside her that also held a good working lamp. From time to time her attention wandered from the slipper she was knitting and her eyes would roam aimlessly about the good-sized apartment, coming to rest with a wistful expression on a door in the wall opposite. They did so now, and her hands stilled in her lap for a moment before she sighed deeply, soundlessly, and resumed her task.

To a disinterested observer the woman thus occupied matched the elegant, slightly overdone furnishings of the room, which featured quantities of the same bright-pink fabric at the windows, as a skirt for the dressing table, and for elaborate bed draperies and covering. She was not by any means in the first blush of youth but was an exceedingly handsome creature in the full flower of her beauty. Thick black hair crowned her head, caught in a knot on top and allowed to frame her face in carefully careless ringlets. Her eyes, which she again focused on the door, were large and a deep velvety brown, enchanced by the thick black curling lashes and set in a complexion of pink-and-white smoothness. If a skillfull use of cosmetics had heightened the perfection of her complexion, this fact did nothing to negate nature's own benevolence in endowing the lady with abundant gifts. Her features were regular and, despite the high coloring, contrived to arrange themselves in a serene order, giving her face something of the look of a calm madonna. Her figure, on the other hand, was most voluptuously rounded and would never go unnoticed whatever the lady wore. In the rich red velvet dressing gown cascading over the pink upholstery of the day bed, she had achieved a spectacular background for her brunette beauty. Her hands and feet were small and plump, the former adorned with several sparkling rings that flashed as her fingers moved among the wool, the latter encased in red velvet slippers trimmed in brilliants and boasting absurdly high heels.

She teetered on those heels now as she rose with an abrupt movement that was alien to the image she presented of indolent sensuality. The unfinished slipper and rosy wool slid unnoticed to the floor. Her alert ears had caught a sound on the stairs, and she strained now to confirm her hopes, her hands clasped together in front of her ample bosom, her dark eyes fixed on a miniature of the Earl of Glenville which held pride of place on the bedside table. It had been almost a fortnight since he had last visited her, and, as always when he was away, the time had passed with a dreadful crawling slowness. An eager smile illuminated her lovely face as she recognized the tread, and she ran to the door (awkwardly on those heels) and flung it open.

"I did not think to see you back for another day or two, my lord. What a delightful surprise!" Her voice was something of a surprise, its quality slightly nasal and revealing remnants of a country accent which was out of character with its owner's elegant and costly appearance. Her face was alight with happy welcome as she raised it unself-consciously to the man, who halted near her to struggle out of one glove.

"Hallo, Molly." He smiled and took her chin in his ungloved fingers before kissing the upturned lips briefly. "How are you?"

As she responded to this greeting, he strolled over to the daybed and picked up the fallen evidence of her previous activity, tossing the yarn back onto the pink cushions. He glanced from the book on the table to the woman watching him and a look of amusement crept into his eyes. "Have you been reading Donne's poetry? How do you find it?"

"I'm afraid I find much of it beyond my comprehension, my lord," she confessed, then added with a desire to please, "But it does sound lovely read aloud, and I finished that last novel you brought me, *Sense and Sensibility.* I enjoyed that. Of course it wasn't very exciting, but it was a very good picture of the way respectable people live." Her earnest words, carefully enunciated to suppress a Suffolk accent, deepened the look of amusement on the earl's face.

"Respectability is a fetish with you, Molly, my sweet," he said with careless good humor. "At heart you are the most respectable creature I know. You should be married with a brood of children to keep you too busy to read, and much too busy to eat chocolates at all hours." He grinned, glancing at the open box on the table.

Molly looked a little guilty for an instant at the mention of chocolates, then returned his smile as she came forward to help him off with his coat. "It wasn't respectability I was headed for when you came into my life seven years ago, my lord," she replied quietly. "You saved my life and Charlotte's too, and I've no complaint to make about my lot. I'd lost my chance for a respectable marriage before she was born, but, thanks to you, Charlotte will have hers." She moved behind him to take his coat as he shrugged out of it.

"I've something to tell you, Molly. I was married myself this morning."

No sound escaped the lips of the woman behind him at this news, but she closed her eyes tightly and willed herself not to faint. Her hands clutched the collar of his coat with a deathgrip, but she was momentarily incapable of further movement. When the silence had continued for another second or two, the earl turned with one arm still in his coat and looked at her questioningly.

"Did you hear what I said, Molly?"

She tried twice before she could produce a voice. "I . . . yes, my lord."

"Well?"

She looked at him fleetingly, then dropped her eyes and remained silent as she accepted the coat and folded it carefully over her arm, all of her attention concentrated on the performance of this simple task.

"Have you nothing to say, no comment to offer?" he persisted.

"I . . . this is a great . . . surprise. I was not aware that you thought of marriage." Her voice was curiously lifeless, but he replied to the words only.

"I hadn't until yesterday."

Molly in turn seemed unaware of the emotion behind the words as she asked hesitantly, "Are you . . . very much in love?"

"*Lord, no!*" He read the puzzlement in her eyes and softened his response. "I'd scarcely be here tonight if I were in love with my wife, would I? There were sufficient reasons for the marriage, but love wasn't among them."

"Is she very young and beautiful?" The question was put with some timidity.

"No, she's not much younger than you. How old are you, Molly?"

"Almost one and thirty."

"April is twenty-six or seven, I believe."

"That is her name, April?"

"Yes."

"It's unusual but pretty." She avoided his glance as she aimlessly smoothed the collar of the greatcoat enfolded in her arms. "Is she as pretty as her name?" The question seemed forced out of her against her will, but silence was something to be avoided at all costs while she wondered if she dared voice her real concern.

He considered the question. "Pretty? Not really, but she has a certain appeal that is more intriguing than mere prettiness."

Molly had turned away from him during this explanation while she laid the coat on the chaise with elaborate care. Now, with her back to him, she took a deep breath and plunged, "Does this mean that you won't be coming here anymore?"

"Of course not, Molly!" He seized her shoulders and turned her gently to face him. "Is that what's bothering you? You know that I shall always take care of you and Charlotte, don't you? Don't you?" he repeated as her head remained bent. "Look at me, Molly!"

She obeyed, searching his face for something but unsure of whether she had found it.

"You need never fear that I'll fail to provide for you and Charlotte, Molly, no matter what happens," he promised in a gentle tone. "Do you believe me?"

She nodded, her eyes clinging to his.

"That's better." He released her shoulders after giving them a mock shake and stepped back to sit on the bed. "How is Charlotte? Have you heard from her lately?"

"I received a letter last week," she said with the first sign of animation on her lovely face since Lord Glenville had made his announcement. "She has a new dearest friend— this is the fourth since the term began—and she has taken the new dancing master in dislike, although she doesn't make it clear why this should be so."

The earl grinned. "That's to be preferred to having her take an unaccountable liking to him. Perhaps at twelve she's too young for that, though!" His coat was off and he was trying to remove the studs from his shirt as he spoke. After a short unavailing struggle he directed a plaintive plea to the woman watching him silently. "Molly, I need help."

Swiftly, wordlessly, she went to his assistance.

Hours later she heard him making preparations to leave as he dressed by the light of a single candle. Very rarely would he stay the night, and this time she experienced to an intolerably heightened degree the desolation that his leaving always brought sweeping over her in a tidal wave. She moved quietly in the bed, her hungry eyes following his every move, but she did not speak, having learned long since that he disliked conversation at this point. In a few minutes the door closed softly behind him and she fell back on the pillows, the scent of the candle he had just blown out filling her nostrils in the deepened darkness. Despair penetrated more deeply into her soul, spreading as the odor from the candle but not destined to be equally short-lived. There had been no joy in their lovemaking tonight, at least not for her. Despite the earl's reassurances that he would always take care of her, the existence of his wife meant the death knell to all her hopes, unadmitted even to herself until now. Thank heavens she had had the strength not to betray the agony that his announcement had dealt her! The earl had attributed her reaction to the fear, which would have been reasonable had she not known him so thoroughly, that his marriage would mean the withdrawal of his monetary support. Knowing full well what manner of man it was that she loved, this worry had not so much as crossed her mind.

She moved restlessly on the large, now cold bed, trying to force final acceptance of what she had always known. Members of the gentry didn't marry farmers' daughters, even farmers' daughters without illegitimate children. She had never expected, never really hoped for marriage, she insisted to herself. In the beginning when the earl offered her a *carte blanche* she had accepted out of a desire to see the end of the perilous existence she had led since the man who had seduced her and eloped with her had finally deserted her and their baby daughter. At three and twenty she had still been able to trade on her striking beauty to support herself and Charlotte, but the next step would have been the streets, and fear of this end enabled her to bear the shame of several short-lived liaisons with young men of good family who had provided generously while their passion for her charms endured. The earl had never pretended to love her —indeed, they had met just after his serious courtship of a well-known society beauty had ended with the clear-sighted lady marrying for a title and fortune just weeks before the earl had come into a title and fortune of his own. He proposed to keep Molly in comfort in return for exclusive rights to use her for his pleasure, and she had been relieved and happy to accept an arrangement that allowed her to provide an outwardly normal life for her daughter. When Charlotte became old enough for boarding school he made all the arrangements, achieving an acceptance at a prestigious institution whose directors would have shunned Charlotte had they known the truth about her background.

Looking back through the years, Molly could not discover when gratitude had become love. Most probably it had been a gradual evolution, but at this distance it seemed she had loved him with single-minded intensity ever since first clapping eyes on him. Her initial experience with a man had cured her of the error of self-deception, however, and she had never permitted herself the false comfort of believing the earl returned her feelings. True, she hoped continually, fool that she was, for signs of a deepening attachment on his part, searching for some new meaning behind each gift he made her and the ever present concern he displayed for her welfare. There was affection, certainly, and an ease born of familiarity, but never anything that could nourish her starving soul. In fact, on isolated occasions in the recent past she had wondered with a sinking heart if he actually found the weight of her undeclared but obvious emotion becoming something of a burden to him. She moved her head in torment on the pillow. It was not beyond her comprehension that love unsought and unreturned might tend to irritate a man of decent sensibilities, who would then feel guilty and resentful. She tried never to overstep the boundaries he had set for their relationship, instinctively responding to what she perceived as his attitude upon any specific occasion. Even tonight she had set aside her shock and misery to accommodate his mood, which had turned playful once he had reassured her of her future security.

Reassurance! What a bitter taste the word had on her lips! He might not love his wife—indeed, she believed him when he said this; he might never grow to love this April, but it was imperative that she accept the fact that he had had ample time and opportunity to fall in love with herself without doing so. The most she could hope for was a continuation of their liaison for some while longer. Truth was a bitter medicine and her reluctance to swallow it extreme. However, she had the rest of the long lonely night to begin the process. Certainly sleep was an unattainable goal this unhappy night.

After a most convincing reassurance of his lack of interest from her husband's own lips, April enjoyed an excellent night's sleep on the most comfortable bed she had encountered in many years. The next morning she was ready for their outing before the time set by the earl but was delayed by her sister, whose vocal disappointment at not being included in this first shopping expedition had to be tactfully dealt with. By the time Diana had been cajoled into a better humor by a promise to take her out shopping that very afternoon if the earl had no objection, so that she reconsidered her avowed intention of sending her breakfast tray back to the kitchen untouched, it was ten minutes past the hour. As April ran down the main stairs still tying the ribbons on her hat, the earl appeared at the foot of the staircase wearing an unmistakable air of impatience. The sight of his forbidding expression banished what little anticipation of pleasure in this rare treat had remained after the scene just enacted with Diana.

She greeted him soberly, offering an unadorned apology for her tardiness, which he accepted with a courtesy she knew was due solely to the presence in the hall at that moment of Jacob, the footman, who opened the door for them. He assisted his wife into the carriage in an unamiable silence that remained unbroken until they arrived at their destination. By this time April had overcome her lowness of spirits by allowing full rein to a silent but grim determination to show the man at her side just how little importance she attached to his boorish manners. Consequently it was a composed young woman whose proud carriage belied her *démodé* attire who entered the premises of the renowned modiste on the arm of her husband.

Fortunately for the picture of newly wedded bliss the earl

intended to present to this world, the events of the next two
hours were productive of enough satisfaction to improve the
tempers of both parties to this audacious deception. They
were received with an eagerness bordering on servility by
Mélisande herself, a buxom, florid blonde of uncertain age
and dubious French accent who soon won April's confidence
by her businesslike efficiency and undoubted good taste. It
was a decidedly modish young woman who finally emerged
wearing an elegant carriage dress of softest mauve wool,
covered by a matching pelisse sumptuously trimmed in
ermine. The dashing high-crowned hat of ermine now
setting off her silvery hair to perfection had been delivered
along with two others for her consideration from a well-
known shop whose canny proprietress had been only too
happy to accommodate the new Countess of Glenville as a
beginning of what she confidently expected to be a mutually
beneficial relationship. Clothilde herself had stripped the
sage-green satin ribbons and feathered trim from the most
becoming hat, substituting a single curled ostrich plume
dyed a deeper shade of mauve which caressed one cheek
from a position on the underside of the curving brim. This
innovation came about at the suggestion of the earl, who
had watched critically as each hat had been tried on by his
wife. The result had been greeted with instant rapture by
Clothilde, who envisioned the style becoming all the rage
once Lady Glenville had been seen abroad in it, and with
more moderately expressed approval by Mélisande, who
agreed the hat became her client and complemented the
pelisse, which was one of her own designs. The milliner then
returned to her own shop full of creative ideas guaranteed to
elicit the continued patronage of Lady Glenville.

The earl, with no more explanation than a promise to be
back shortly, had himself left the modiste's establishment for
almost three quarters of an hour while the final sewing of
the mauve costume was being accomplished in record time
by four of Mélisande's stitchers in her workroom at the back
of the premises. He had left his wife to look over styles and

fabrics being presented for her approval by the designer. Considering Adam's insistence only yesterday that he would guide her choice, April was surprised to see him absent himself at this point but delighted in exercising her own judgment without fear of contradiction. She spent an enjoyable half hour browsing through Mélisande's sketches and admiring fabric samples, only to find upon the earl's return that he had every intention of reviewing her decisions. To her chagrin he did reject several of her choices of fabrics, and she was not best pleased to witness the dressmaker's immediate about-face when the rejected samples had been largely accepted by April at her instigation in the first place. However, she swallowed her spleen and permitted herself to be overruled with a good grace, secretly rather gratified at the extent of the earl's involvement with the dressing of his wife. When he finally handed her up into the carriage after a cordial leave-taking from the designer, she tried to thank him for his generosity and assistance. Her shy expression of gratitude was brushed aside with a wounding brusqueness that deprived her of further speech.

She had entered the carriage more confident of her attractiveness than ever before in her life, but thanks to the earl's manifest disinterest now that there was no audience, her satisfaction was destined to be ephemeral. Her expanding spirit retreated to its former humility. How foolish she had been to allow herself to be taken in by Adam's performance as a devoted husband before the modiste and hatmaker. It had simply been an effective piece of acting. The knowledge of her new attractiveness in the stylish outfit had led her to credit him with an opinion he had already made it clear he did not hold of her desirability. Well, now she knew and would not again make the mistake of reading anything personal into his public performance of doting husband. Actually, life was much less complicated this way; the last thing she wanted was devotion from the man she had hated for nine years! It was a bit lowering to discover in herself a childish craving for admiration, a weakness she'd root out from this moment on. Lest he should think she was sulking over his lack of interest she roused herself to inquire pleasantly:

"What time is your mother expecting us to call, Adam? I trust we shall not keep her waiting."

The earl lifted one eyebrow. "She is not expecting us at all. What gave you to think that she might be?"

April gazed at him blankly. "Why I . . . naturally I assumed you had sent a message to her yesterday acquainting her with the fact of your marriage." Her voice tailed off as she continued to study her husband's unrevealing countenance.

"Why should you assume anything of this nature?"

"You would not wish your mother to learn of your marriage from another source, surely? You said as much to that awful man at the inn."

"Allerton is scarcely likely to call upon my mother to acquaint her with the news," he replied carelessly. "The latest crim. cons. are more in his style."

April assimilated this. "Then . . . then your mother will have no inkling of the truth when we arrive?"

"No. Why should she?"

"You . . . you plan to simply produce a daughter-in-law out of thin air, as it were?" Her voice held a rising note of panic and some of her color had faded.

"My mother's reaction need not concern you. You will not be much in her society. We meet but seldom. By the way, she is married again; she is Lady Ellsmere now, not Mrs. Harding."

April did not know what to make of the curious note in her husband's voice. She was shaken by the knowledge that he had not bothered to inform his parent of his marriage before confronting her with a daughter-in-law. She could sense his unwillingness to discuss his relationship with his mother, so she subsided, stifling her curiosity but unable to suppress her agitation at the thought of the awkward meeting to come.

After a moment's uneasy silence Adam said casually, "I

visited Rundell and Bridge while you were choosing gowns this morning. I'd like you to wear this."

April raised her eyes to his extended hand thrust in front of her nose. Held between thumb and index finger was a ring that featured a large diamond surrounded by a circle of smaller ones. Her breath caught in a gasp of admiration, but she made no move to take the glittering object as she stared into his impassive countenance. He tapped her mauve kid glove with the fingers holding the ring, and she began to pull it off slowly with a reluctance she barely understood. When her glove was removed he slipped the ring on her finger, noting with satisfaction that the jeweler had guessed correctly as to size. She kept her eyes fixed on the sparkling stones, but he didn't seem to expect any thanks from her; in fact, as she opened her lips he forestalled her by slipping a hand into an inner pocket of his coat.

"I also selected these to be worn with this outfit."

"These" turned out to be a pair of amethyst earrings in a delicate gold filigree setting. A half hour ago April would have been thrilled with something so exquisite to complement her lovely new costume, but her husband's coldness on entering the carriage had completely erased her pleasure in her appearance. "Thank you," she said politely. "They are lovely."

"Put them on," he ordered curtly.

She toyed with the idea of refusing so peremptory a request, but one covert glance at his firm jaw decided her against a course of action guaranteed further to increase the tension in the air. Wordlessly she untied the satin ribbons of the ermine hat, took it off, and placed it carefully on the matching muff reposing on her lap. She removed the gloves and accepted first one and then the other earring, which she inserted into the lobes of her ears under his steady gaze. She took the bonnet in both hands, but before she could complete the motion, Adam took her chin in his fingers. He tilted it upward, then from side to side to study the effect of the jewels. April kept her eyes lowered, unconsciously affording her husband an excellent view of the luxuriant thickness of her lashes. After a second she found herself released, and she proceeded to replace the hat and pull on her gloves. No words had been exchanged during this operation, and neither ventured any further remarks during the rest of the short ride.

Adam, sitting relaxed in his corner, was congratulating himself on his accurate analysis of his bride's potentialities. She had no power to attract him, but it was quite intellectually satisfying to see how really lovely she was when her assets were emphasized. At this moment she appeared scarcely older than her sister in his eyes. He found he was looking forward to presenting this glowing girl to his mother. He was going to enjoy the coming interview.

In her corner, April was a far cry from sharing her husband's complaisance. She had been horrified by the discovery that her existence was not yet known to Lady Ellsmere, and, though unconfirmed in words, there persisted a niggling little suspicion that Adam was seriously estranged from his remaining parent. Instinctively she knew that her sartorial transformation was meant for Lady Ellsmere's benefit and could only hope that Adam felt she did him credit. Nothing in his manner or words told her whether the results were satisfactory, however, so her anxiety over the imminent meeting increased as they drew nearer the Ellsmere residence. When the carriage halted she barely glanced at the impressive facade as her husband hustled her up the shallow steps to evade the drizzle that had begun to permeate the atmosphere.

The somewhat intimidating aspect of the silver-haired individual who appeared at the entrance altered substantially when he recognized the man on the doorstep, and he hastened to assure Lord Glenville that although Lady Ellsmere was not receiving this morning this prohibition did not of course include her son. The earl acknowledged this favor with a tiny smile. "Thank you, Foulting."

He did not attempt to gratify the butler's curiosity as to the identity of his companion, a curiosity that could only be guessed at, since Foulting permitted himself merely one lambent flick at April from under heavy-lidded dark eyes before leading the way up a singularly beautiful carpeted, curved, and carved staircase of some rich dark wood, polished and gleaming. At any other time she would have been eager to inspect the paintings in massive gold frames that lined the wall along their ascent, but in her present state of anxious anticipation she did no more than dimly record their existence in passing.

They were ushered into an unoccupied saloon and left with a promise that her ladyship would join them presently. The earl waited until his wife had tentatively seated herself on the edge of the nearest chair before taking a chair a few feet away. Slanting a glance at him from under her lashes, April was vaguely annoyed at his seeming lack of any emotion or tension when she was uncomfortably aware of an increased heart rate and a clamminess in her palms beneath their thin covering of kid. She could not recall ever before anticipating an introduction with such dread, but then, never before had she been called upon to sustain an introduction to the mother of a man she had forced to marry her! Adam was determined to conceal the truth from everyone, but how could a mother fail to guess after one look at her son's face?

In an effort to distract her mind from this unprofitable line of thought, she forced herself to take stock of their surroundings. They had been shown into a large well-proportioned apartment expensively furnished by someone with lavish tastes, judging by the sumptuous fabrics at the windows and on the upholstered pieces and the quantity of valuable ornaments disposed about the room. Even to April's inexpert eye the candelabra illuminating the glorious Venetian mirror over the fireplace were of gold and beautifully scrolled. On either side of the double entrance doors stood matching glass-fronted cabinets of rosewood containing a collection of china and porcelain figurines that might have come from Germany. She found most of them excessively convoluted and ornate, but though not to her personal taste, there was no denying their value. The outsize

carpet beneath her feet was reminiscent of a small one from
China that had been her mother's pride. Pale blue, pink,
green, and gold formed an intriguing design against a
cream-colored background. It was difficult to tear her eyes
away from its serene beauty, but everywhere in the room
beautiful items called out for attention, from the French
ornamental clock on the mantel to a choice gold filigree
pomander ball on the table beside her which her fingers
itched to examine more closely. Strangely enough, despite
the lovely decor and the number of choice objects, the atmosphere of the room was a trifle oppressive. It screamed of
wealth carefully spent and cried out for admiration of its
creator's artistic taste, but April would have exchanged a
bit of the artistic perfection for some sensation of warmth.
If anything could be considered too perfect, this room
achieved the distinction. She glanced again at her husband,
but any comments she might have ventured were frozen on
her tongue by the frigidity of his aspect.

Just then the doors opened, though for an instant April
was so confounded by the animation that leaped into
Adam's face that she almost missed the entrance of her
mother-in-law. Dragging fascinated eyes from her husband's
countenance, she focused somewhat reluctantly on the
woman poised between the two doors, a hand on each, while
she smiled at them, fully aware, April was instantly persuaded, of the graceful picture she presented in her blue silk
morning dress.

Two thoughts made immediate impact on April's mind
while she rose to her feet—that here was the embodiment
and creator of the beautiful room and, more prosaically,
that Lady Ellsmere did not appear nearly old enough to be
Adam's mother. She didn't know his age, but he looked to
be deep in his thirties. Perforce, this slim woman of erect
and graceful carriage with no trace of gray in her rich brown
hair was well over fifty. It was scarcely to be credited
visually, but her laughing voice somewhat distorted the
illusion of youth. It was deep and assured and contained a
hint of sly malice.

"My dear Adam, how do you do? Foulting informed me my son awaited *with a female companion.* I nearly accused him of imbibing the burgundy behind my back, but I see that he spoke no less than the truth." A gleaming white-toothed smile was produced to indicate her words were mere funning.

April's bemused attention was fixed on the woman who addressed herself to her son at the same time she assessed his companion with a lightning-quick female inventory that missed nothing from the curling ostrich plume on her hat to the tips of her mauve kid half boots. She realized with sudden unaccountable relief that her hand was being held in a comforting clasp as Adam drew her closer to his side. He met his mother's smile with one of his own and said gently:

"Mother, I'd like to present my companion to you. This is my wife, April."

Lady Ellsmere's smile solidified for an instant before disappearing completely. *"Wife!* You've married and I not there? When? How?" The assured tones threatened to escalate into stridency.

It seemed to April's hectic imagination that the others were unaware of her presence for the moment, that a duel was being waged between two pairs of dark-gray eyes, and then her husband spoke even more gently than before.

"Don't upset yourself, ma'am. We were married very quietly, but except for one other, you are the first to wish us happy."

Lady Ellsmere strove with herself to regain control of the situation, though she still could not bring herself to look at her daughter-in-law. She gestured toward the settee and chairs grouped behind them. "Shall we sit?"

When April and Adam were seated on the blue settee facing their hostess across a mahogany tea table, she disposed herself gracefully in a giltwood chair covered in straw-colored satin. After a deliberate survey of her son's wife, she conceded coolly, "At least she is exquisitely dressed and looks a lady, though not quite in your style, I would have judged."

"And just what, in your informed opinion, is my style?" inquired Adam with interest, not at all put out at the tone of his wife's reception by his mother.

"Ripe and luscious, I'd have said," his parent countered quickly, and turned to find a pair of light eyes, slightly violet-tinged, fixed on her face with unwavering intensity. "Perhaps after all she is not so young and unfledged as she appears at first sight," Lady Ellsmere remarked after sustaining that regard for a further few seconds. "Who is she?"

Deciding she had sat mumchance long enough while these two antagonists waged war over her corpse, April spoke up clearly. "Both my parents have been dead for some years, Lady Ellsmere. My father was Sir Charles Wendover, and my mother's family—"

"*Wendover!*" Lady Ellsmere interrupted her daughter-in-law and rounded on her son. "Adam, have you taken leave of your senses? Haven't you suffered enough at the hands of that feckless family? And not a penny to bless herself with, I'll wager! When I recollect some of the lovely and eligible girls I have introduced to your notice in the last half-dozen years I vow and declare you must be the most perverse creature in nature!" Her angry words trailed off as she caught her son's sardonic regard, and red coins stained her cheeks. She avoided the younger woman's eyes.

"May I suggest, ma'am, that you essay to take comfort in the knowledge that no other girl in the kingdom, no matter how eligible or beautiful, could have prompted me to marriage save April."

April caught her breath and lowered her glance to hide the anger that surged up in her heart. Oddly enough, she was less upset by the insulting comments bordering on the vulgar made by Lady Ellsmere than by the truthful words so softly spoken and so misleading from the lips of her husband. Feeling her hand seized, she raised her eyes to her mother-in-law's now smiling face.

"Please believe, my dear April, that there was nothing personal in my earlier remarks. They were entirely prompted by concern for my son's future. Naturally I am prepared to welcome Adam's wife into the family." The sound of the opening door spared April from the necessity of formulating any civil lies as her hostess's attention was drawn to the stolid figure of the butler approaching with a silver tray upon which rested a bottle and several glasses. "Ah, here is Foulting with some Madeira. Shall I ask him to bring champagne instead? Yes, of course we must drink to your happiness in champagne."

Adam demurred that Madeira was as acceptable as champagne for pledging their happiness, but Lady Ellsmere, evidently determined to atone for her previous lack of enthusiasm, insisted that nothing but champagne would do, and they had perforce to await the arrival of this token. In the hiatus she subjected her daughter-in-law to a barrage of questions concerning her background and her plans for the upcoming season. For the most part Adam answered before his bride could speak, but April upheld her end of the conversation with grave courtesy when she could edge in a word. When the champagne arrived she accepted her glass and went through the motions of sipping it but put the glass on the mahogany tea table immediately afterward, and there it remained for the duration of their call. She owed it to her breeding to be polite, but nowhere was it written that one must drink with enemies, and however harsh the term, she felt it was the *mot juste* to describe her companions at that moment. As for Lady Ellsmere's earlier complaint, she did not take it as meant for her personally, although it had been made painfully obvious that his mother had wished and actively worked for a more brilliant match for Adam. April had no way of learning the root and reason for the antagonism that simmered between mother and son, but she was shocked, chilled, and oppressed by its existence.

It was a palpable relief to be able to quit the beautiful soulless room when Adam at last stood up to make their adieux. It did not escape April's notice that her husband had been strangely ambiguous about any future social plans in conjunction with Lady Ellsmere, politely brushing aside a

tentative suggestion on his mother's part that she host a
dinner party to welcome April to London. Since her own
reaction to her slightly overpowering mother-in-law had not
been without a reciprocal touch of the hostility that seemed
to simmer just below the surface cordiality, she was glad to
follow Adam's lead, and they took their leave without
committing themselves to any definite engagement.

The earl was just handing his thoughtful-looking wife up
into the carriage when a jovial masculine voice hailed him.

"I say, Adam, I did not look to see you in town again so
soon. Seems to me I recall Freddy's saying you weren't due
back for another day or two yet, but he was more than half
foxed at the time. How are you?"

"Good morning, Damien."

A tug at her elbow caused April to pause in her ascent,
and she turned to inspect the man smiling up at Adam.

He was well worth inspecting. A few years younger than
the earl, he was almost as tall but less broadly built, and
appeared slim and straight in a drab overcoat featuring
nearly as many shoulder capes as a coachman's. Waved and
pomaded golden locks gleamed beneath his hat, and when
he turned to include April in his regard she was almost
stunned by the perfection of his chiseled features. In the
instant before her husband's voice interrupted her assessment it flashed through her mind that he could be a Greek
statue come to life.

"April, this Jack O'Dandy is my cousin, Damien Harding.
Damien, may I present my wife?"

"Your *wife!*" Mr. Harding was facing April with his hat
raised. For a split second he froze in incredulity and a look
flashed into his eyes that nearly caused her to step backward
instinctively, but before she could withdraw the hand she
had extended, Mr. Harding was smiling again as he saluted
her fingers with consummate charm.

"This is indeed a great pleasure, Lady Glenville, but how
like Adam to spring a wife on the *ton* with no warning! You
will have to suffer all the indignity of being a nine days'
wonder before you will be allowed to take your rightful place

as one of society's loveliest ornaments. Heartiest congratulation, coz," he added, turning to shake Adam's hand for the second time, his grin wide and knowing. "You have proved once again that you still have the best eye for beauty of any of 'em. Your April is the loveliest creature to appear on the London scene in years."

April accorded this extravagant compliment a cool little smile that matched the coolness of her rainwater eyes. She had no illusions about her nonexistent pretensions to beauty despite the recent transformation Adam had wrought in her appearance. This man was deliberately flattering her—trying perhaps to erase from her memory the thunderstruck fury that he had been unable to mask in the instant of learning her identity? Beneath an unrevealing exterior her mind was a whirling mass of confused impressions and unanswered questions. Dimly, as on the edge of her awareness, she heard Adam acknowledge his cousin's felicitations and inquire into his presence at this particular spot.

Mr. Harding laughed and gestured with a book he had shoved under his arm. "I happened to meet Lady Ellsmere at Devonshire House last night. I don't quite recall how it came up, but we were trying to remember who wrote those old lines about proving all the pleasures."

" 'Come live with me and be my love, and we will all the pleasures prove,' " Adam quoted softly.

"That's the one! Oh, the advantages of a classical education!" grinned Mr. Harding. "Lady Ellsmere would have it that it was one of Jonson's poems, but I found it in this book this morning. It was John Donne!"

"But surely—Marlowe!" April's involuntary exclamation brought the eyes of the two men to her flushed cheeks. "I do beg your pardon," she hastened to apologize. "You are quite correct, sir, that Donne uses a similar beginning to one of his poems."

"Yes, but I've never been able to make up my mind whether he was more interested in the joys of seduction or the trials of fishing!" Adam laughed at his cousin's crestfallen expression. "Try again, Damien. It's beginning to

rain, my dear. We'd best be going. Tell Freddy we'll be
sending out 'at home' cards shortly."

Once again the earl assisted his bride into the carriage,
and followed her after a casual wave to the man who stood
watching the carriage out of sight with no vestige remaining
of the charming smile he had preserved during the
accidental encounter. It was several minutes later that Mr.
Harding roused himself from a grim contemplation of the
empty street and resumed a pleasant expression as he
approached Lady Ellsmere's residence a second time.

Chapter Six

Inside the carriage, April sat pressed into her corner, her gloved hands clasped tightly together in her lap. Her features were frozen in blankness, a slight pucker between her brows the only indication that her mind was not equally blank. At this moment in time she could only wish passionately that that suddenly desirable state of nullity could be achieved. In the scant twenty-four hours of her marriage she had suffered an avalanche of impressions and emotions which left her confused, faintly belligerent, and more than a little disturbed by an inexplicable sense of foreboding. No, foreboding was too strong a word, but she was uneasy in her mind in a way not entirely explained by the natural consequences of a rash act. Setting aside her own initial reactions to a new position in life, a new dwelling, and a number of strangers who would become part of her new life, even setting aside the more vital question of her as yet undifferentiated but predictably difficult relationship with the man who was her husband, she was experiencing a tickling, teasing kind of unease, a general miasma of ill will. Slanting a glance at Adam from the corner of her eye, she could only marvel at his imperturbability.

He appeared in fact to be rather pleased with the results of their morning activities. Although it had been a brief encounter just now, she sensed that he bore his cousin a careless affection and enjoyed his company. She had received the exact opposite impression from the longer interview with Adam's mother. The disturbing factor was not so

much the lack of natural feeling between them—she was not
so naive as to believe that all families were bound as tightly
by the ties of affection as her own had been—but the unaccountable presence of a perverse pleasure she glimpsed in
Adam and to a lesser degree in his mother at causing discomfort to the other. Adam had enjoyed every moment of
the uncomfortable confrontation with Lady Ellsmere. For
some reason it had given him satisfaction to produce a bride
who would not be to her liking.

Disturbing though this conclusion was and prophetic of
unpleasurable future relations with her mother-in-law, it
was not the most destructive element to her peace of mind.
April closed her eyes, the better to bring two faces before her
mind's eye, two faces innocuous in themselves under
ordinary circumstances but remarkable for the similarity of
their fleeting expressions of acute dislike, if not actual
hatred. In her first two days in London she had discovered
that her husband's butler disliked his master intensely and
that her husband's cousin had conceived of an instantaneous
and equally strong disaffection for herself. What was more,
both of these individuals wished to conceal their feelings.
The unreasonable quality of the situation struck her
forcibly. She had not been in a position to observe Lord
Glenville as master of his establishment for long, but she
would have said that he was not much interested in the inner
workings of his household and was inclined to be too lenient
rather than the other extreme in his dealings with his staff.
Surely a difficult master would not have calmly accepted the
poor meal set before them the previous evening. Of course,
there could exist a more personal reason for Morton's
animosity, but why should a well-trained servant continue to
work for an employer for whom he cherished a personal
animus? It made no sense, nor did the existence of Mr.
Damien Harding's instant dislike of herself, but it had
spewed from his eyes when Adam had presented her as his
wife.

April sat very still, aware all at once of the importance of
a thought as yet unarticulated while she groped for it. *Not*

myself; it isn't April Wendover he hates but the *wife* of his cousin! She turned abruptly to her husband to find his considering gaze on her face.

"How . . . how nearly related are you and Mr. Damien Harding, Adam?"

A look of faint surprise crossed his face. "Damien's father was my father's youngest brother. He is my first cousin."

"I see. Is he next in line for the title?"

"No, his brother Freddy is my heir. Why do you ask?"

"No particular reason. It is simply that I know so little of the family. Have you other relatives that I shall be meeting?" April scarcely listened to Adam's description of various female cousins who resided in London; she was more intent on her own heartbeat, which slowed and settled down from the hammering that had begun at a ridiculous suspicion that had flashed into her mind. She relaxed perceptibly. Two people stood between Mr. Harding and the title! And yet she knew beyond doubt that the fact of her existence had come as an earthshaking shock to her husband's cousin, and she was strangely grateful that she had not missed his unguarded reaction, so quickly dissimulated and smothered in obvious gallantry.

Adam was speaking to her. He slewed his powerful body around better to enable him to study her countenance when he had to repeat his question.

"What did you think of my mother?"

"I . . . I found it nearly impossible to credit that Lady Ellsmere is indeed your mother. She seems far too young, and except for the eyes there is little resemblance between you. She must have been spectacularly beautiful as a girl." It was not a particularly clever evasion or alluring red herring — he had caught her unprepared — but April hoped it would be accepted.

She should have known better. There had been no lack of plain speaking between them in the course of their short and stormy acquaintance, and now Adam said impatiently, "Don't, I beg of you, think to fob me off with platitudes. Please answer my question."

April obliged with icy distinctness. "Very well, since you prefer the word without the bark on it, I found Lady Ellsmere frank to the point of incivility, nor did I particularly relish her propensity for indulging vulgar curiosity by asking impertinent questions."

Instantly she was ashamed of the waspish reply and was on the brink of tendering an apology when her husband said with a mildness that brought her eyes to his in quick suspicion, "Well, if we are to speak of frankness approaching incivility . . . " He allowed his voice to trail off suggestively.

"Yes, I know, but you did insist," she offered in a feeble attempt at self-exculpation and noted with surprise not untinged with relief that she had been correct. There was an incipient quiver of the firm lips, though he obviously had no intention of giving way to the amusement aroused by her harsh opinion of his remaining parent.

"You need not trouble yourself about getting along with my mother. We meet but seldom. She will, of course, be invited to the dance we'll give for Diana, but there is no necessity to include her when we entertain my colleagues."

"You did not tell me you were planning to hold a dance for Diana," April said, fastening on to the one vital point in his remarks. She was wondering how to express her gratitude without chancing another rebuff when he rendered any thanks impossible by returning an offhand rejoinder.

"There has scarcely been time to acquaint you with my plans, you will agree, but naturally I am prepared to launch my sister-in-law into society in the style to which you aspire. Can your brief tenure as a respectable matron have caused you to forget the reason for this farcical marriage, my dear April?"

His wife remained silent, struggling to retain her composure in the wake of this wave of sarcasm. Perhaps he sensed her chagrin, for after shooting a glance at her downcast eyes and compressed lips he looked away and moderated his tones.

"I have been used to entertain my various colleagues and

friends at an hotel, but now that I have a hostess I should like to repay past hospitality when you have become more settled in my house. However, that can wait upon launching Diana. No doubt the announcement of our marriage which I inserted in tomorrow's *Morning Post* and *Gazette* will provoke a spate of bride visits as soon as our 'at home' cards go out. She will have the opportunity to meet a number of people in an informal setting before being presented. Not that Diana would seem to suffer from any afflictive shyness, but it can be an ordeal for a young girl to be pitchforked into the *ton* with no prior acquaintance. I hope some of our callers will bring their daughters so she may meet as many young people as possible before her dance." He paused, apparently considering those of his acquaintances who might answer this need, and April studied him from under thick lashes.

She longed to express her gratitude for such wholehearted cooperation in the matter of Diana's presentation but feared to evoke the harsh side of his nature. She was groping for a better understanding of this strange individual to whom she was now bound in the closest of all human ties. In his dealings with herself and with his mother there was a repelling coldness that indicated an absence of any heart, but here he was planning for Diana's smooth entry into the polite world with the care one might lavish on a daughter — and after referring to her as a brainless chit! It was quite incomprehensible.

Adam turned and caught her puzzled regard. Instantly his face lost all expression. "We are nearly home. I shall have to go out this afternoon and shall be fully occupied with government business in the upcoming weeks. You will have to manage the outfitting of your sister and any charges in the house with minimal assistance from me. I shall make banking arrangements for you immediately. Buy anything you wish, but do not bother me with details."

"How do you know I won't bankrupt you with my extravagance or decorate the whole house in puce?" demanded April, nettled at his retreat.

If she hoped to wring an admission that he trusted her taste from her husband she was doomed to disappointment. "You may try to bankrupt me," he said with a glint of amusement in those hard gray eyes. "If you look like succeeding, never doubt that I'll take preventive measures, and if the decor is too outrageous I'll make a bonfire of it and hire someone to do it again. But I really suffer no qualms on that head, my dear April. These last few years must have taught you to hold household if Mattie has not. It will do you good to indulge in a spree of shopping and to know you have the means to indulge your slightest whim."

Utterly incomprehensible! April could only stare into those opaque eyes as she pondered this unlooked-for generosity.

"By the way" — Adam broke the silence that threatened to become permanent as the carriage drew up to the entrance — "I should like you to reserve the gown that is being made up in the tissue silk with the silver threads for our own ball." The keen glance that accompanied this request left her in no doubt that it was, in fact, an order. He jumped down from the carriage and assisted April to descend but left her outside the door.

"I'll have John drop me off at the Ministry, then the carriage will be at your disposal. Don't expect me for dinner." He gave an order to the coachman and reentered the vehicle without any recourse to polite formulas of leave-taking. Before the porter had even opened the door the carriage was halfway down the street.

April headed upstairs to put off her hat and gloves, but she had barely attained the first-floor landing when Diana appeared in the corridor.

"There you are at last! I feared I should have to eat luncheon all by myself in that great gloomy dining room." As the young girl took in her sister's changed appearance, her eyes grew wider. "April, that is a stunning outfit! The color is perfect for you, and what magnificent fur! Is it ermine?" Her tone had grown reverent, and she stretched out a hand to smooth the white fur.

April laughed. "Yes, it is ermine. Come into my room while I remove the pelisse and wash my hands. I won't keep you above a minute if lunch is ready." She had pulled off the gloves and was untying the ribbons of the fur hat as she spoke. She laughed again as Diana seized the hat almost before she had it off and pranced over to the mirror to try it on her golden head the instant April opened the door to her bedchamber. The young girl preened herself and postured with the muff in front of the mirror under the indulgent eye of her sister, who was drying her hands on a linen towel. It was with a decided reluctance that she abandoned the fur hat on the bed to follow April back into the hall.

"Did you not think the ermine excessively becoming to me, April?" she invited, almost running to catch up with that lady's determined pace. "May I have one like it, please? I have always dreamed of owning a fur hat and muff."

April smiled into the eager young face whose brilliant blue eyes had deepened with earnestness. "Certainly you may have fur, dearest, although that particular style is perhaps too old for you." Then as Diana's brightness dimmed and her mouth took on an incipient pout she added in a rallying tone, "Besides, think what figures of fun we should make of ourselves dressing alike as though we were twins."

"Of course, I never meant that we should wear everything alike," Diana muttered with a touch of pique. "I am well aware that I must present a demure appearance in my first season and dress in muslins and crapes when I should really like satins and velvet, but the ermine hat is just perfect on me. Mayn't I have it, April, please? You could get another hat. *Please*, April?"

They were approaching the bottom of the staircase, and April averted her gaze from her sister's beseeching countenance as she laid her hand on the newel post. There was a hint of constraint in her quiet reply.

"Adam chose the hat for me himself, Diana. I could not wound him by giving it away, but I promise we shall find something equally distinctive for you."

Fortunately the proximity of the dining room and the

appearance just then of Morton put an end to the discussion, though Diana's lips had a slightly mulish set. During the course of the meal her good spirits were restored by a lively description of the fabrics and designs April had seen that morning at Mélisande's. She was so eager to begin the pleasant chore of acquiring a wardrobe for her comeout that she scarcely noticed what she was putting in her mouth. In contrast, the new Lady Glenville, conscious of her position as mistress of a good-sized establishment, was judiciously sampling each of the chef's offerings. With the memory of last night's dismal dinner still fresh, she was wary of anything she could not immediately identify but determined to give the man a fair chance before taking some action. Today's mutton pie was edible, though no one could call its creator a dab hand at pastry making. The vegetables were again overcooked, but, in justice, some people preferred all their food cooked until the original color and texture were totally lost. Lord Glenville, for all she knew of him, might belong to this school of thought. The meal ended with an assortment of jellies, probably presented as a concession to the presence of ladies in the house, but since they were universally rubbery, no feeling of appreciation for the condescension was aroused in April's breast. Diana flatly declined trying them. Any delay in the start of her first shopping spree was unwelcome, and she twitched impatiently as her sister lingered over lunch as though she had all the time in the world. As before, the service was perfect, with Morton guiding the most appetizing offerings onto their plates and unobtrusively removing those dishes that failed to appeal.

When at last April signaled that they were finished, Diana heaved a sigh of relief and bounced to her feet before the butler could assist her. After another seemingly interminable delay while the carriage was called for and they got into their outer garments, the two ladies finally set forth on their quest.

When they returned several hours later, April could only be grateful that she had managed to eat a good portion of her lunch before embarking on the ordeal. She'd had need of all the strength she could muster to match the pace set by her young sister in her aggressive pursuit of the latest modes to be found in London. Nine years of living on a tiny income that never quite stretched to cover essentials, let alone luxuries, had left April with a legacy of caution and an ingrained disinclination to accept less than real value for any expenditure. Diana, protected from childhood from knowledge of the true state of the family's finances and indulged to the extent permitted by those finances, first by her mother and then by her sister, was completely unburdened by any such inhibiting check on her ability to spend. Indeed, it had fallen to April's lot to control her volatile sister's orgy of purchasing in a diplomatic manner that would not diminish the child's pleasure in her first real shopping expedition. By the exercise of consummate tact and the liberal use of stalling tactics, she accomplished the feat and at length had the privilege of seeing Diana's bubbling excitement gradually simmer down into an informed satisfaction with the way her wardrobe was taking shape.

There was not time in one short afternoon to do more than initiate the process, of course. As her sister had had to do, Diana was obliged to order her basic requirements to be made up from the designs and fabrics paraded for her selection while her measurements were taken and a list of necessities was compiled. She did enjoy the good fortune to be the exact size and the right coloring to enhance a completed dress in a delicious soft apricot cotton that the original purchaser had decided did not become her after all. Since April agreed with Mélisande that the demurely cut neckline and tiny puffed sleeves with their matching velvet bows were exactly suited to her sister's youthful good looks, and since the designer, with an avid eye to the dimension of the order being amassed by Lord Glenville's ladies, had the shrewdness to offer a substantial reduction in price on an item that represented a total loss to her in any case, Diana had the happiness of carrying it away with her then and there. Clutching her new gown and armed with swatches of several fabrics, she eventually sallied forth from the modiste's establishment to begin the pleasant chore of selecting hats to go with various outfits.

The harmony of their concerted effort had been briefly threatened when it was revealed that Diana's taste in headgear was inclined to be rather too dashing for a girl of seventeen, but thanks to Clothilde's instant reading of the situation and the persuasive and flattering manner with which she guided the girl to more suitable styles, April was saved from seeming to deny her sister her own choices. She knew her earlier refusal to surrender the ermine bonnet still rankled with one who was unused to being denied any request within April's power to grant. It was with sincere pleasure not unmixed with relief that she allowed the purchase of a scandalously overpriced but wickedly becoming sable bonnet and outsized matching muff that Diana fell in love with at sight. For no reason that she could really explain, the idea of turning over to her sister the hat Adam had chosen for his wife had been peculiarly repugnant without even considering his justifiable annoyance at such a glaring circumvention of his intent.

They had emerged from the milliner's considerably lighter in the purse but happy in the possession of no less than five new hats. April would have retired for the day content with the assurance of a task well done, but in the face of her sister's confident assumption that they would continue while breath remained in their bodies and the shopes remained open, she sighed inwardly and meekly trudged onward, trying not to notice that her shoes were displaying an alarming tendency to shrink. Once Jacob had relieved them of the accumulated purchases, which he deposited in the waiting carriage, Diana continued her strolling progress, determined not to miss any of the myriad delights offered by the attractive shops in the area.

A beaded reticule had captured her fancy in one shop, and nothing would do but that she must sample each and every item in a *parfumerie* even though her sister sensibly pointed out that after smelling a half-dozen one was unable to distinguish among them anyway. Diana gaily brushed aside this prosaic reflection and proceeded to select the scent in the prettiest bottle after a lengthy deliberation that April suspected was prolonged by the shop assistant, a thin pallid youth with a receding chin, who was reduced to a state of stammering eagerness by Diana's big blue eyes and the charming air of helplessness she had recently perfected. During the interlude the young man contrived to remain oblivious of the claims on his attention being advanced by a sharp-featured matron in a green velvet bonnet whose available stock of patience and good humor was rapidly exhausted as she eyed the engrossed duo with a censorious eye. When clearing her throat loudly and planting herself in the assistant's line of vision as he turned back from the shelf from which he had selected yet another bottle for Diana's approval had wholly failed to deflect his rapt concentration from his lovely customer, the woman departed in a huff after first delivering herself of an unflattering opinion of the manners exhibited by the current crop of assistants who abandoned their clear duty to wait upon the public in favor of fawning over every pretty face that happened along. If she hoped by this forthright speech to bring him to some sense of his unworthiness, she failed utterly in her object, April noted with a mixture of amusement and sympathy, for the young man did not even become conscious of her voice until she had almost closed the door behind her. He did indeed look a trifle startled at the force with which the door closed, but he then returned to Diana the negligible portion of his attention the irate woman had succeeded in diverting. His engrossed client, still intent on comparing the perfumes in front of her, remained unaware of the incident, but her sister thought it time to put an end to the scene before any additional customer had been turned away from the shop. In a brisk voice, she recommended Diana to make a decision or return another day as she withdrew some money from her purse and looked suggestively at the assistant. His training came to his aid in persuading his client to make a selection. April was unsurprised that the chosen item was almost the costliest in the shop, but she paid without a murmur, feeling that they had cost the owner more in goodwill today than the purchase represented.

Back out on the flagway, an enthusiastic Diana would have continued her perambulations had her sister not decided she had abused her tired feet long enough. She stated firmly that it was time to rejoin the carriage. If Diana was inclined to protest the curtailing of her shopping, she took comfort in the reflection that she would soon have the pleasure of trying on all the new bonnets and the apricot gown for the approval of the maid, Alice, and the temporary cloud was banished from her face.

As they headed for the location of the carriage, however, she arrested their progress at sight of a tobacconist's, declaring that she wouldn't be a minute but there was one more errand she simply must accomplish. Utterly bewildered, April looked again at the swinging sign to see if she had misread it before following the golden head disappearing into the shop. She caught up with her sister as another assistant looked up and came toward them with an ingratiating smile.

April gave a small tug at Diana's sleeve and whispered, "What possible business could you have in here?"

"Adam mentioned last night that he liked to . . . I believe the expression is 'blow a cloud' . . . occasionally, and since he sent me ten guineas this morning for pin money, I thought I'd buy him some cigars." The young girl turned to the salesman who had now reached them and requested his assistance, leaving a silent April with much to occupy her thoughts.

She was struck once again by Adam's consideration with regard to his newly acquired sister-in-law—he had not even mentioned the matter to her during the hours they had spent together this morning—and she experienced a rush of gratitude to Diana for her thoughtfulness. There were occasions when April wondered uneasily if she and her mother had not perhaps spoiled Diana a trifle in their anxiety to make up to her for the loss of her father and the secure life she had so briefly led. And then the girl would make some sweet impulsive gesture that repaid her relatives for all their sacrifices. She was very young yet and intermittently careless of others' feelings, but April was persuaded her sister nourished a fierce affection for those few persons close to her. It could not fail to please that Diana was apparently ready to extend this affection to her new brother-in-law. As she watched the sparkling girl charm another salesman she was glad that Diana was doing something for Adam. She herself was prevented by the awkward nature of their relationship from making any spontaneous gestures toward her husband lest these be misconstrued by him as representing a bid for his attentions. Her face flooded with color at the mere thought of such a situation, and her eyes grew somber. It seemed not all the ramifications of this strange marriage had yet manifested themselves.

Diana's voice jerked her out of a melancholy reverie that suddenly shadowed their happy afternoon. "I said we can go now, April. You seemed a thousand miles away." The girl bestowed her most brilliant smile upon the assistant who was solicitously holding the door for the ladies' departure, then bent a curious gaze on her sister.

"I was merely thinking of my aching feet," April improvised quickly, "and longing for a dish of tea."

Diana's fleeting curiosity was appeased, and for the short ride home the carriage rang with her delighted comments on their accomplishments that afternoon, to which April made suitable replies when called upon to reinforce her sister's opinions.

Both ladies found themselves completely restored by tea and a rest before dinner. They came together in the saloon, where the first disappointment awaited one of them. There had been no opportunity for April to inform her sister that Adam would not be joining them, and Diana, clutching the box of cigars, was crushed that her surprise must be postponed.

"I hate waiting for things," she confessed with perfect truth, a small pout hovering around her lips. This was soon dispelled by her sister's sincerely expressed admiration for the effect of the new gown. She pirouetted gaily and expanded under April's praise of the hairstyle contrived by the clever Alice, which featured a perky bow of the same velvet as the trimming on the dress. April's own smooth hair remained unadorned, and she was again wearing the gray gown. Their exertions had given them a sharp appetite, and they were not sorry to have Morton announce dinner almost immediately.

The meal that awaited them did little to appease their hunger and much to increase the small worry that had lodged itself in the new Lady Glenville's brain on the previous evening. She had been encouraged by the mediocre luncheon to hope the chef was increasing his efforts on their behalf, but tonight's dinner was every bit as unappetizing as that of the previous evening.

"What is this?" Diana asked, eyeing with some doubt the dish being set before her by Morton.

"Salmon poached in white wine and served in a butter sauce with mushrooms, Miss Wendover," replied the butler smoothly as he deposited a similar dish before his mistress.

Diana took a tentative mouthful and grimaced as she swallowed. "It's not cooked!" she declared indignantly as she reached for her water glass.

April studied her own portion and discovered a section of spine with her fork. "Take it away, Morton," she said quietly.

The butler complied in silence, giving the plates to Jacob to remove, while Diana cast her eyes hopefully on the covered dishes residing on the sideboard. Morton served them with veal cutlets that had been coated in a batter and fried. They looked to be a rather dark shade, but both ladies accepted some without comment. Diana set her knife and fork in hers and sawed away for an unconscionable time before she managed to slice off a bit. She chewed it thoroughly for a full minute then had recourse to her water

glass again to aid in swallowing. She remarked with deliberation:

"Well, there's no denying these are cooked. The question
is, when was the deed done?"

"Possibly yesterday," April replied, putting aside her fork
after one bite. "Don't try to eat them, love, you'll break a
tooth. There are several vegetables here, and I see a dish of
stewed pears, which you like. Also, is that a platter of ham,
Morton?"

"Yes, my lady." Morton's thin lips were pinched even
thinner, and he kept his eyes cast down as he served them
with slices of cold ham and offered a dish of spinach and
croutons.

The ladies managed to make a fair meal by concentrating
on the items that had not received the benefit of the chef's
attention. From their accumulated experience they summarily rejected anything in a sauce. Both were loath to
sample the handsome fruitcake that appeared at the end of
the meal until Morton confided in an expressionless tone
that the housekeeper had made it from an old family recipe.
This was discovered to be excellent, and April desired the
butler to relay their appreciation to Mrs. Donaldson.

She had been rather quiet during the dinner, puzzling in
her mind what it were best to do about the continuing
situation of unsatisfactory meals, and at length had resolved
to postpone action no longer. She might not be able to
buy her husband presents without her motives being
misconstrued, but she could rid his house of a cook who
failed to provide his master with even a minimal standard of
nourishment. Consequently, as Morton pulled out her chair
she met his glance squarely and requested an interview with
the chef as soon as he should be finished in the kitchen.

A shade of uneasiness crossed the butler's controlled
countenance and he appeared to hesitate fractionally before
replying. "I regret that Gregory is a trifle indisposed this
evening, my lady. Will tomorrow do?"

April considered his pale composed features for a second
longer. "Is Gregory ill, Morton?"

Again the hesitation, and now Morton's gaze was fixed on a point beyond Lady Glenville's shoulder. "Not to say ill precisely, my lady, but he isn't quite himself."

An unkind suspicion flashed through April's mind. She devoutly wished Mattie were here to counsel her or at least shed some light on the inner workings of the household, but Mattie would not be back for several days. She must handle the matter herself. She straightened her shoulders and forced the butler to meet her eyes.

"Do you mean me to comprehend that the chef is incapacitated by drink, Morton?"

Something that might have been relief flickered in the butler's ice-blue eyes. "I fear that is indeed the case, my lady."

"Is this a chronic problem with Gregory?"

"Not to say chronic, my lady, but more often than not of late he is under the influence of spiritous liquors."

"I see. And why have you not informed Lord Glenville of this circumstance before now?"

His reply was quick in coming, although she thought she detected a hint of discomfort in his impassive mien. "Gregory did not use to be as bad before, and his lordship has never complained about the food. I did not feel it was up to me to get a man sacked."

"Or to see that he kept away from drink? Well, never mind that now, but he'll have to go, Morton, and you will be obliged to visit the registry office tomorrow to engage another chef. His lordship has the right to expect decent, well-prepared food in his home."

Heavy lids concealed the butler's reaction to this speech. He was the well-trained servant in his reply. "Certainly, my lady. Will that be all?"

April nodded and signed to the engrossed Diana that she should precede her through the door Jacob hastened to open. For the first time ever she felt she was indeed mistress of Lord Glenville's establishment.

Chapter Seven

Over the next few weeks, April settled more comfortably into her role as Lady Glenville, wife of a prominent member of the government. She was too much occupied with the demands her new position made on her time and energy to have any leisure for reflection on the state of her own emotions. If she did not know whether she was happy or not, at least she knew that life had suddenly become more interesting than she could ever remember. Her own comeout so many years before had been moderately enjoyable while it lasted, and her brief tenure as a young lady quickly betrothed in her first season had given her a certain status among her contemporaries. In the dark years that followed her father's death and the breaking of her engagement, this short period of gaiety and irresponsibility had grown fuzzy and receded into the dim corners of her memory. Her position today was infinitely preferable to that of nine years ago. Unmarried girls were hedged about by numerous rules and strictures and were under all eyes at all times. As a married woman she had dispensed with these restrictions, and she frankly reveled in her newfound freedom. There were new responsibilities, of course, but nothing could weigh on her as heavily as had the task of keeping her family together under increasingly difficult financial stresses. From this too she was liberated by her marriage to a wealthy peer of the realm.

The first priority, on a par with the acquisition of a wardrobe for herself and her sister, was to refurbish the large and woefully neglected house she now shared with the last man on earth her youthful imaginings could have conjured up. The successful conclusion of her initial decision to replace the undependable chef gave her the impetus to proceed with confidence toward decisions with regard to changes in the furnishings. She had not quite believed that Adam meant to give her a completely free hand in the household, and, despite a resolution to remain calm, her nerves were on the stretch the first time he dined at home after the installation of André, the Gallic chef Morton had obtained from the registry.

It was almost impossible to credit that anyone could remain oblivious to the improvement in the quality of food that appeared on the table. André had the happy knack of cooking each item just to the point that enhanced its inherent goodness, and when he used sauces they were creations to be savored. The earl, however, let most of the dinner hour slide by before pausing with his fork halfway to his mouth, an expression of surprise giving animation to his stern features. "This veal dish is delicious!" His look invited comment.

April swallowed carefully, trying to decide what to say, but Diana solved the problem for her.

"If you'd been home for dinner the past three nights, dear Adam, you'd have discovered that everything André cooks is delicious."

Lord Glenville eyed the teasing face of his sister-in-law with amused tolerance. "I must confess the name of my chef escapes my memory at the moment, but I'd venture a small wager that it isn't André."

"Then you'd lose," giggled Diana. "The *old* chef was Gregory, and the *new* one André."

"Oh, my lamentable memory," sighed the earl. "No doubt I was informed of the change in cooks, but it has quite slipped my mind."

April squirmed mentally under a bland look directed at her. "No, I . . . there has been no opportunity to bring it to your attention. I beg your pardon."

"That's because you spend so little time at home, dear

Adam," inserted Diana in cooing accents. "Otherwise you'd
have noticed long since that the meals Gregory served up
weren't fit to be eaten — at least the dinners weren't. Breakfast was tolerable and one could swallow lunch, but by
evening nothing that appeared on the table was edible."

He heard this in frowning concentration. "I fear I pay
very little attention to what I eat, but is there some inference
I'm to draw from this tale?"

"It seems that Gregory was a chronic drinker," said his
countess, thinking it high time she entered the discussion.

In the pause that greeted this statement she observed that
Morton's attention remained fixed on the tray he was carrying to the sideboard, so he missed the rapier look directed at
him by his master.

"It seems I am the one who should apologize," Lord Glenville said to surprise his wife. "It was a very poor welcome
indeed, my dear, to present you with a problem of this
nature on the instant of your arrival."

April, concentrating on his face and voice, could detect
no hint of sarcasm, and she relaxed visibly, but Diana saved
her from the necessity of a reply.

"What is a wife for if not to run your house?" the girl
inquired with mock innocence, her bright-blue eyes opened
to their widest.

"If you think I am going to rise to that one, young
woman, your optimism exceeds your wit."

Diana giggled again and allowed the earl to change the
subject. The rest of the meal passed in pleasant incon-
sequential conversation, and April's composure was
restored. She had been correct in assuming Glenville was
almost totally indifferent to the quality of food served in his
house. Perhaps he did intend to leave the decorating entirely
in her hands. Perhaps nothing about the running of his
house was of much interest to him.

The earl alluded to the change of chefs later that evening.
Husband and wife were sitting in the main saloon, he
engrossed in an issue of the *Edinburgh Review* and April
occupied with a piece of stitchery. Diana had been enter-

taining them at the piano but had retired early with a slight headache. When April would have accompanied her sister upstairs, Adam had signed that he wished her to stay. After bidding Diana an affectionate goodnight she sank back in her chair and looked questioningly at him over her embroidery.

He apologized once more for not having prevented the unfortunate situation with the chef. "How did you become aware that it was a case of drinking with Gregory?"

"I requested an interview with him one evening to discover the reason for the poor meals. Morton tried to fob me off till morning, and it . . . came out on further questioning that he drank to excess. I hope you do not feel I was too hasty in dismissing him?" she ventured.

He denied this with an impatient wave of one hand. "There was nothing else to do at that point. However, I am at a loss to understand why it had not been brought to my attention before matters came to such a pass."

"Morton said you never complained about the food and he did not consider it his duty to get a man dismissed," April replied somewhat dryly.

Adam's black brows lowered at this. "It was his duty to see the situation did not arise in the first place," he snapped. "I'll have an explanation from him before he's a day older."

April resumed pushing her needle in and out of the cloth in her hands for a moment before putting a casual question.

"How long has Morton been with you?"

"Four or five years. He was a fixture in my uncle's home, but my Uncle Harry was as inveterate a gambler as your father." She winced at this, but he seemed unaware of her reaction. "When he died, Freddy could not afford to keep the estate going. It's rented now to a retired factory owner. He and Damien asked me if I'd take Morton on, since they both keep bachelor lodgings here in town with only a man-servant." He shrugged. "Morton's a queer cold chap, but he and Mrs. Donaldson have run the house between them without bothering me, and I've been content to have it so."

Again there was a short pause, which April was constrained to break. "Our coming has meant a great deal of disruption in your life," she said with a note of apology in her lovely voice.

"The government is my life," he asserted brusquely, "and you won't disrupt that. I've told you before, you may have a free hand in this house."

A tingling silence descended on the pair, but this time April refused to run away. She continued to ply her needle, and eventually the repetitive motion exercised a soothing effect on her nerves. In another moment she would rise and bid him goodnight.

"April, how did we meet?" Adam asked in a musing tone that brought her eyes swiftly to his. A little frown knitted itself between her brows.

"Have you forgotten?" The noncommittal question revealed none of the thoughts churning in her head.

"I wish I could forget!" he clipped out before moderating his tone with a palpable effort. "I meant, what story shall we concoct for the delectation of our public? Ever since the announcement appeared in the papers I've been besieged by well-wishers, and I imagine cards have been left here as well."

She confirmed this, then ventured an objection. "Need we concoct any story at all? Even your mother did not ask how we met."

His smile barely qualified as such and was gone on the instant. "She was too stunned to have all her wits about her that day, but she'll be asking that question at a second meeting. I feel we should agree on the essentials of a story. Obviously I swept you off your feet, our marriage was so unexpected."

"I told Diana we met when Mother was still alive," April said slowly.

"Then why did we not wed at the time?"

Completely expressionless, she stared at him and answered levelly, "My mother would not countenance my marrying the man responsible for my father's and brother's deaths."

Nothing about Adam moved, and his stillness held April

mesmerized until at last he spoke softly to the original question. "If memory serves, your mother died when you were one and twenty. Why did we not marry long since?"

"I . . . I don't know." Although Adam had chosen to ignore her spiteful remark about his past, his wife was too overcome by shame and resentment that she should be experiencing such an emotion to be capable of creative thinking just then.

"Well, use your imagination, woman! Since I've shown myself so impulsive about rushing you into marriage with no hints even to my closest friends, why was I not equally rash several years ago when we were both younger and presumably more ardent?"

"Possibly because you'd forgotten my very existence!" April snapped, disliking the embarrassing subject more each minute.

A gleam of real amusement lightened those still dark eyes. "Perhaps we would be advised to stick as near the truth as we may. Shall we agree that we met long ago under circumstances that rendered any closer attachment impossible at the time, but having met again recently and having made the discovery that the years had not dimmed your attraction for me, I proceeded to pursue the acquaintance with a fervor that swept away your reservations, swept you off your feet and into marriage?"

He took her tight-lipped silence for acquiescence. "Then it only remains to decide when we met this second time. Through mutual friends, I feel sure. Don't you agree, my dear?"

April ground her even white teeth. "Of course. Perhaps you have friends among the parents of my scholars in the village school. Or, better yet, no doubt your father and Mr. Lynley were at Oxford together, and he dandled you on his knees when you were a babe."

The earl's mood had improved measurably in proportion to the decline in his wife's spirits. Now he said, cheerfully ignoring this latest contribution, "It was a house party I think—yes, where better to foster the growth of a whirlwind courtship than a country visit? It was known in town that I went north on business, so if we were to set our mutual friends in Warwickshire around Birmingham that should answer very well."

"No one would be so indelicate as to inquire into the identity of these matchmaking friends, of course?"

"Naturally not, but in any event, their name is Smith, Mr. and Mrs. Martin Smith. Possibly you and Mrs. Smith were at school together. Your dear friend Hepzibah with the dark ringlets married my old classmate, Martin Smith, who had ever an eye for a dark beauty."

"I didn't go to school, I had a governess," April declared dampingly.

"Oh? A pity. I was becoming quite enamored by the thought of a tender reunion with the friend of your girlhood, the sweet Hepzibah."

A reluctant little smile appeared on April's lips as she rose. "You talk a deal of nonsense, my lord, but if this is the Banbury story you intend to foist onto your unsuspecting—or should I say, rather, your *all too suspecting*—friends, I shall try to play my part. And now I'll wish you goodnight." She swept her sewing up in an untidy heap and departed with swift grace.

Adam bowed and remained standing, watching his wife's retreating back through half-closed lids. It was nearly five minutes later that he withdrew his gaze from the closed door and reseated himself. Even then he allowed another few moments to elapse before picking up the periodical he had been reading earlier. He held it unopened, mentally reviewing the recent conversation with April. As in every previous conversation with the woman who had become, so unbelievably, his wife, there had been an elusive element of barely repressed hostility in the atmosphere. Like two fencers they were constantly on guard, ready to repel an anticipated verbal thrust. Understandable, of course, under the circumstances, but unless and until they could manage to conceal this from those with whom they would be associating, their portrayal of newly wedded bliss would be revealed for the charade it was.

His fingernails were drumming an absentminded rhythm on the unopened periodical under his hand as he acknowledged to himself that the fault was mainly his own. It seemed he could not banish his resentment at the whole situation from his thoughts when discussing even the most innocuous of household matters with April. It was apparent that unless goaded to retaliation she tried to avoid crossing swords with him by adopting a propitiating attitude, and strangely enough, he resented this abasement on her part too. In fact, while he was assessing his reactions with ruthless honesty, he might as well admit that everything about his unwanted bride irritated him. He even resented the added attractiveness that was the result of the deliberate changes he had insisted on making in her appearance. Much as he wanted the whole of society to believe he had selected a particularly desirable bride, he did not intend to find her desirable himself. When he caught his gaze lingering on the silken swath of silvery fair hair gleaming under the lamplight as she sewed, and began checking the effect of various colors on those incredibly clear, almost colorless eyes of hers he experienced a tremendous surge of annoyance at his own stupidity. If he didn't wish to defeat his purpose it would behoove him to conquer this incipient weakness. The last thing he intended was to develop a *tendresse* for the woman who had married him to foster her sister's social ambitions, a woman moreover who still considered him little better than a murderer. He would do well to keep this fact clearly in mind when looking at his wife's lovely face or listening to the music in her voice.

The earl pulled out his watch and opened it. Not too late to visit Molly tonight after he had tackled Morton. He could be thankful that at least some things in life remained the same. He tossed the *Edinburgh Review* aside and went out of the room whistling softly to himself.

The following morning, April was alone in the small morning room waiting for Diana to finish arraying herself in preparation for yet another shopping trip when Morton ushered in a caller in defiance of the earl's expressed wish that the ladies remain incommunicado until the matter of their wardrobes had been fully attended to. She had been reading a letter from Mr. Lynley wishing her happiness in his genial though inelegantly expressed fashion when the butler entered. His bearing and voice when announcing "Mr. Frederick Harding, my lady," were so eloquent of proprietorial affection and pride in one whom she had considered totally devoid of all human instincts that amazement held her motionless at first and she was slow in transferring her attention to the man coming toward her with outstretched hand.

Mr. Harding had had ample opportunity to appraise the new countess before large clear eyes turned in his direction. He beheld a delicately fashioned woman of moderate height with extraordinary fair hair and pale coloring. He received the odd impression that she drew herself up as though gathering strength to face a trial, and the eyes that met his were guarded.

For her part April found herself responding to the friendly smile of her husband's cousin as her tentatively extended hand was engulfed in a warm clasp.

"Lady Glenville, this is indeed a great pleasure. I have been out of town for several days or I'd have called earlier to welcome you into the family and wish you joy in your marriage. Morton tells me Adam has already gone out this morning, so I shan't be able to offer him my felicitations just yet."

"Thank you very much, Mr. Harding. You are most kind." April withdrew her hand gently and waved her unexpected visitor to a chair. "May I offer you some refreshment—a glass of Madeira, perhaps?" She permitted herself to relax. The memory of her meeting with this man's brother had sent apprehension coursing through her body when

Morton had announced the caller, but one long look at Mr.
Frederick Harding had relieved her mind of the initial fear
that here was another enemy.

He declined refreshment with a smile, saying that he
could stay but a moment. "I arrived at my lodgings last
night to find a stack of mail waiting me. When I read
Damien's note detailing his meeting with you I could not
wait upon ceremony to make the acquaintance of Adam's
wife. And how is my fortunate cousin bearing up under the
flood of congratulations your marriage must have
occasioned?"

As April returned a light answer, she studied her husband's heir with interest, marveling at the difference in two
individuals who might pass for twins in a dim light. She had
thought Mr. Damien Harding the handsomest man she had
ever encountered until the enmity in his eyes had chilled her
blood and altered her opinion. His brother was only a year
or two older, but lines of dissipation had carved themselves
deeply into his countenance and there were dark shadows
under his eyes. There was a suggestion almost of sagging or
softening in the bone structure of Mr. Frederick Harding's
face, and he was thin to the point of attenuation, where his
brother radiated vibrant health and vitality. This Mr. Harding was dressed as though he never gave his appearance a
second, or perhaps even a first, thought, in contrast to the
dandified image presented by the younger brother. Among
all the comparisons that favored the younger, however,
April had no difficulty in recognizing one element in the
elder that attracted her strongly. Mr. Frederick Harding
possessed too much genuine human kindness to resent the
fact of his cousin's marriage. It stared out from his rather
melancholy blue eyes and allowed her to accept the sincerity
of his gentle smile. Nor could she accuse him of easy flattery
when he remarked:

"Damien wrote that Adam had secured himself a real
diamond for a bride, and I can see this is so, but he neglected to mention that our cousin had acquired an even
rarer jewel, a woman with an understanding heart. For this

blessing all who are close to Adam must be eternally grateful. That he would marry at all was considered doubtful. His early experience had made him intolerant and distrustful of your sex, my dear Lady Glenville, as you may have observed on first meeting him, but it is obvious that he recognized the compassionate heart beneath the lovely exterior."

If it had been possible to die of embarrassment April would have expired on the spot. He could scarcely have hit upon anything further from the truth! She blurted in protest:

"Mr. Harding, indeed you do me too much honor! It is quite undeserved. I beg you will say no more on this subject but rather tell me something about yourself. Are you and Adam close friends as well as relations?"

A shadow darkened Mr. Harding's brow, and he replied soberly, "Adam and I were good friends in our youth, but to my regret have grown apart of late. My strong-minded cousin rather despises me for my weakness. I must acknowledge the justness of this, of course. Unfortunately, we do not all possess Glenville's strength of purpose or single-mindedness."

Bewilderment was added to the squirming embarrassment overwhelming April. Mr. Harding seemed to take for granted that she was intimately acquainted with all the circumstances of her husband's life. "He . . . he is certainly dedicated to his work," she offered lamely in hopes of steering a safe course through conversational quicksands.

"As I noted, single-minded," agreed Mr. Harding, then his attractive smile reappeared. "You will add a new dimension to his life. For years Adam has devoted himself entirely to his career. He is long overdue for some satisfaction in his personal life. He will not have told you how badly hurt he was by his mother's desertion of husband and son. No doubt he makes light of it today, but I was at school with him and I know how deeply affected he was. Even to me he could confide none of his feelings, but I witnessed the change in him. Ah well." Mr. Harding banished his somberness and beamed at the bemused woman staring intently at him. "You must forgive me for harking back to ancient history. I hope I haven't reached the stage of the thrice-told tale."

April murmured a gentle negative and said earnestly, "Thank you for telling me this, Mr. Harding. I'm grateful to you for helping me to understand Adam better." She put out her hand with an impulsive gesture, and her husband's cousin took it in both of his as he got to his feet.

"I'd be honored if you could bring yourself to call me Freddy," he requested smilingly. "After all, we are now quite nearly related."

April returned his smile with interest. "Of course, if you wish it, and my name is April."

"The beginning of spring. The name suits you, my dear April. I—"

"I trust I don't intrude?"

Two heads turned to the doorway, where the Earl of Glenville stood, an expression on his dark-featured face that was less than welcoming.

"Adam, what luck to find you here after all!" cried Mr. Harding. He released April's hand to hurry across the room and grasp his cousin's. "Morton said you'd gone for the day," he added, beaming at the unsmiling earl as he wrung one hand and patted his arm with his free hand. He seemed not to notice the lack of response in the other man.

"I came back for some papers," said the earl, glancing from his cousin's eager face to the carefully blank one of the woman who remained standing in the middle of the room. "Inopportunely, perhaps?"

"Just the opposite," declared Mr. Harding with a laugh. "I was just taking my leave of April and had visions of chasing all over London to find you to offer my felicitations, deplorably late though they are. I've been out of town the last few days, didn't learn the happy news until I read a note scrawled by my brother which awaited me in my chambers."

"How gratifying that you should rush right over to wish us happy," drawled the earl, whose eyes had narrowed slightly at hearing his wife's name on his cousin's lips. "Since you seem to be on Christian-name terms with my wife already, I take it an introduction would be superfluous?"

"We introduced ourselves," returned Mr. Harding with a smiling nod in the direction of the silent countess, "and I sought immediate permission to abandon formality with one who is now so nearly related, which permission was kindly granted. My warmest wishes for your happiness, old fellow. You have won a most lovely and charming bride."

"Come over here, darling, and thank my cousin for his fulsome compliments," ordered the earl in a silky voice April had never heard from him. Obediently, she approached the men, who were still standing just inside the door. Both were smiling, but she didn't trust the gleam in her husband's eyes. To her great surprise he extended his arm and gathered her to his side so they were both facing Mr. Harding.

That gentleman was protesting that he took exception to his cousin's use of the word fulsome, that no compliment to such a lovely lady could be considered in any other light than inadequate to do her justice.

Adam laughed. "I cry quits, Freddy! Your eloquence overwhelms me. She is lovely, isn't she?" April had not yet recovered from the shock of finding herself clamped to her husband's side when another greeted her. Reluctance to verify the sardonic gleam she thought she had detected in Adam's eye when he summoned her to his side kept her standing stiffly in the circle of his arm, her unseeing gaze on Mr. Harding's face while her other senses registered her husband's disturbing nearness. She was therefore unprepared for his sudden swoop as he pressed a quick kiss on her cheek. For an instant as she stiffened involuntarily, his grip on her arm tightened to near painful intensity, then he released her and walked toward the bell pull, saying over his shoulder, "It's a trifle early in the day for liquid refreshment, but you won't let that prevent you from drinking our healths, I know, Freddy." He turned to confront the others again. "You should have offered our guest some refreshment, my dear," he remarked, gently chiding.

"Oh, April nobly upheld the hospitality of the house, but

thinking you absent, I planned only to stay a moment. Naturally I welcome the opportunity to drink to your future happiness."

Morton's entrance just then put an end to Mr. Harding's enthusing, and Diana, looking enchantingly pretty in a modish yellow gown with a triple flounce at the hem, danced into the room as the butler left to carry out his master's request.

"April, look, the most annoying thing!" she declared impetuously, holding out a box. Then, catching sight of her brother-in-law, her aspect became sunny again. "*Adam!* I thought you'd gone long since. I bought these cigars for you days ago and then you didn't come home for dinner so I could not give them to you, and when you did come home last night I forgot all about them. Here, for my favorite brother-in-law," she finished gaily, going up to the earl and placing the box in his hands. "I hope they're the sort you like?"

The earl smiled into the bright face looking anxiously up at him. "They are indeed, my child. I cannot recall an occasion for gifts, but I thank you most earnestly. Morton will put them in my study so I may enjoy one when I'm working." He grasped one shoulder lightly and turned her toward the other man. "Diana, may I present my cousin, Mr. Frederick Harding? Freddy, this is April's sister, Miss Wendover."

"You are the first member of Adam's family that I've met," Diana said with a friendly smile and a flirtatious flick of her lashes when Mr. Harding had bowed over her hand with a graceful gesture and expressed his delight in the meeting. "April has met your brother and Adam's mother, but we have been so busy shopping that I have not yet had the pleasure. In fact," she confided with a quaint little air of importance, "you are the very first person, except for shop-keepers, that I've met in London, so we must be friends."

"It will be my great pleasure, Miss Wendover."

"Oh, call me Diana, do." She wrinkled her perfect nose adorably. "After all, we are cousins of a sort, or at least connections, so why be formal?"

"I shall be delighted to be your cousin, Diana, as well as your friend," returned Mr. Harding gallantly. "This must be my lucky day. I have acquired two lovely cousins."

Morton returned with a tray, and the health and longevity of the bridal pair was proposed by Mr. Harding in a simple and, to April's grateful ears, sincere toast. Almost immediately the earl declared his regret that the pressure of work must take him away as soon as he collected the forgotten papers. His cousin accepted his invitation to accompany him part of the way and took a polite leave of the ladies.

"That reminds me," said the earl, sticking his head back around the doorway briefly, "we have an invitation for Friday that I should like to accept. Have your wardrobes reached a state to include evening dress?"

On being assured by a radiant Diana that they would put forth their best efforts to do him credit, he laughed, promised details that evening, and departed.

"My first party!" breathed Diana, showing her sister an ecstatic face and clasping her hands to her breast. "What shall we wear, April? Will the new blue silk trimmed with blond be suitable?"

Not receiving an immediate answer, she paused in the little dance step she was executing and glanced back to see her sister still facing the empty doorway. "April? Won't it do?"

Large gray eyes focused on the young girl's eager face. "Won't what do, dearest?"

"The blue silk," Diana repeated, and then, as her sister still looked blank, explained patiently, "for this party on Friday."

"Oh!" The older girl seemed to return from some distant place. Her voice became brisk. "The blue silk will do nicely, and I shall wear my rose-colored brocade." She glanced at the tiny watch pinned to her dress and became brisker still. "Goodness, look at the time! Hurry and get into your outdoor things, Diana, or we won't accomplish half of what we planned for today. The Pantheon Bazaar will already be crowded on such a pleasant morning."

Despite her request for haste, April fell back into a reverie as soon as Diana turned to obey her command, and it was several moments after the young girl had departed before she roused and cast a vague eye around for the pelisse and hat she had brought into the morning room earlier. Her thoughts had winged back to the scene just completed, and she replayed it in her mind. On the surface nothing had occurred but a friendly visit from her husband's cousin and heir, but she couldn't dismiss a feeling that it had had a deeper significance. She had been greatly cheered by the discovery that the earl's heir did not share his brother's dislike of the marriage that would in all eyes end his hopes for a possible inheritance. And then in the course of their conversation he had unknowingly imparted a vital piece of information. Now there was an explanation for Adam's cold, almost inimical attitude toward his mother. She had been more than a little disturbed by this flouting of the most basic of human relationships and was glad of a reason to think less poorly of him. She accepted his contemptuous opinion of herself as her proper payment for coercing his acceptance of the marriage but had been rendered acutely uncomfortable by the general dislike and distrust of the female of the species she had sensed in him. Small wonder his opinion of her sex was so low!

But what had he meant by that little performance of devoted husband just now? Obviously it had been staged for his cousin's benefit, but it had struck her as a bit excessive to the occasion at the time and even more so in retrospect. Her imagination was inadequate to the task of conjuring up a picture of the very reserved earl making public demonstrations of affection toward his bride. He certainly had not treated her with any marked degree of warmth in front of his mother or younger cousin. There was a cold-blooded reason inspired by that secretive intellect for this morning's charade, of course.

As she buttoned her new black wool pelisse with its caped shoulders she knew with intuitive certainty that questioning the reason would avail her nothing. Her intuition further told her that her husband had taken a malicious satisfaction in the confusion and malaise his action had produced in her. She bit her lip and concentrated on recalling the incident accurately. Adam had been abrupt and provocative, to put it mildly, in his demeanor toward his cousin, but he had not succeeded in arousing any similar reaction from the mild-mannered Freddy. There was some disaffection between the men — Freddy had alluded to it and Adam had confirmed it by his faintly hostile, or perhaps contemptuous, attitude toward the cousin closest to him in age. April sighed as she crossed to the oval mirror on the far wall to arrange a wickedly becoming hat of shirred blue velvet on her head with unseeing mechanical precision. It was disappointing to find her husband apparently harboring some ill feeling toward the one person she had met in his family who had struck a responsive chord in her.

Diana appeared at the door as April was pulling on her gloves and put an end to her sister's fruitless conjecturing.

"Mmmm, I do like that blue hat. The narrow brim set at an angle shows off your hairstyle better than most. I have a swatch of the blue silk with me. Do you think we shall be able to buy ribbon to match it?"

"We can try, certainly. I hope Morton thought to order the carriage. It is growing very late." The two ladies swept out of the room with an air of purpose about them.

Chapter Eight

Friday morning found the Countess of Glenville taking special pains with her toilette. The earl had agreed with his wife that it would be unseemly for her to begin moving in society without the courtesy of a formal call at the home of Sir Neville Granby, who was now the head of her father's family. Lady Granby had left her card in Hanover Square shortly after the notice had appeared in the papers, and it was essential that the call be returned today, since the earl was to escort his bride and sister-in-law to a musical *soirée* at the home of a colleague that evening.

April stood frowning at the results of her efforts in the long glass, and Mattie paused in her search for fresh gloves to inquire:

"What's amiss? We decided the mauve outfit was still the most elegant for the purpose, and your hair looks fine. By the look on your face a body would think you was off to the dentist's instead of a simple morning call that needn't last above half an hour."

April made a wry little face at the woman regarding her sternly. "I'm not sure I wouldn't liefer visit the dentist than spend a half hour in the company of my cousin's wife. We've met only once when she paid a visit of condolence after Basil's death. She was all sympathy and condescension, but she couldn't refrain from taking a mental inventory and affixing a price tag on every object in the room. It was perfectly obvious to me, though Mother was in no condition to notice, thank goodness."

"Well, if a mere baronet's wife can condescend to a countess, it's more than I ever heard tell of, and you're in no need of sympathy now," Mattie reminded her former charge in a practical spirit. "You'll both behave with civil propriety and that'll be the end of it. You needn't become bosom bows, after all."

"Yes, Mattie," April replied with a suspicious meekness that her tirewoman quite properly ignored. At least the frown had gone. She continued to follow her mistress's movements from the corner of her eye as she rearranged some items in the drawer. The tiny frown reappeared as April put her hand to her throat.

"Oh, I forgot Mother's little pearl brooch." She lifted the top of a silver jewel casket and stared at its meager contents, the frown deepening. "Not here! Now where—oh, I remember, I took it off my gown yesterday after it scratched my finger while I was sewing. I must have left it on the table."

Mattie closed the drawer. "In the morning room? Which table?"

"Never mind, Mattie, you're busy. I'll get it myself; I know precisely where it is." April pulled the door behind her, shutting off Mattie's protests, and ran lightly down the main stairway, her soft house shoes making no sound on the wooden treads. As she came around the corner she paused involuntarily and resumed at a more sedate pace. Morton was talking to someone at the front door, and as April reached the hall she caught a quick view of burnished gold locks beneath a brown beaver before the door closed.

"Someone looking for his lordship, Morton?"

The butler started violently at the sound of her voice and turned swiftly. "Excuse me, my lady, you startled me. It was just an individual inquiring at the wrong house. Did you wish something, my lady?"

April eyed Morton's cavernous figure thoughtfully. His voice was as smooth as ever, his manner as deferential, but she would take her oath he had been more than displeased at her sudden appearance, and he had not turned completely to face her. One arm was concealed from her view.

"No, thank you, Morton. I just came to get something from my morning room."

"Very good, my lady." Morton allowed her to precede him down the hall leading to the back of the house. April was acutely conscious of his presence behind her, and her nerves were tingling for some reason. She stepped swiftly into the morning room, leaving the door open as she found it, and noted the butler's nearly silent passage an instant later. His walk was as unhurried as befitted his station and there was nothing in the hand she could see, but she was unalterably convinced he was concealing something he had received from the person she had glimpsed at the door. Without stopping to consider her actions, she slipped out of the room just in time to see his back disappear into Lord Glenville's study. Silently she followed, but the closed door stymied her for a moment. What excuse could she give for barging in on him? She bit her lower lip and lifted her head proudly. She could say she was looking for a certain volume on her husband's shelves. In any case, why should she have to explain herself in her own home? Yet she stood there un-decided a further second, one hand going tentatively to the paneled door. It moved a silent inch at her touch, and her heart shot up into her throat. Morton hadn't shut the door! Her suspicious mind suggested that he hadn't wanted her to hear the sound of the door closing from her position close by in the morning room. Cautiously she widened the gap a trifle until a slice of the interior was revealed.

Adam's desk was in front of the wall to her left, and there was Morton engaged in unwrapping a small parcel resting on the desk. She could hear the paper crackle slightly as he removed it and folded it with care, though she couldn't identify the contents, since the butler's back was essentially presented to her view. He put the folded paper in his pocket and proceeded to open a box on Lord Glenville's desk and remove the contents to his pockets. What on earth—*Adam's cigars!* Morton was removing the cigars from the box Diana had presented to her brother-in-law and substituting those he had brought into the room. April stared in puzzlement until concern for her own position spying on the man caused her to pull the door gently to and nip back down the hall into the morning room.

The pearl brooch was where she had left it, and she went over to the oval mirror to pin it at the neck of her gown. Her eyes were fixed on her fumbling fingers, but her ears were straining for a sound that would indicate that Morton had left the study and her brain was busily advancing explanations for the butler's conduct. Why would he substitute different cigars for those Diana had bought Adam? Her frown smoothed out as an obvious explanation occurred to her. Most likely the cigars were not, after all, the sort Adam enjoyed and he did not wish to hurt Diana's feelings by refusing to smoke them. Her fingers stilled at their task momentarily. Then why deny the delivery at the door just now? It took only a second to arrive at the conclusion that both master and servant probably thought it more expedient to keep the whole affair dark. Amusement gleamed in the cool gray eyes that met hers in the mirror. Those cigars must have been really obnoxious to have Adam go to such lengths to get rid of them. Still, it was sweet of him to avoid spoiling his young relative's pleasure in her gift. She gave a last look at the pin at her throat, realigned her ruffles slightly, and headed upstairs again, no longer concerned to discover Morton's subsequent movements.

An hour later two fair ladies dressed in the height of fashion sought admission to Sir Neville Granby's residence. The individual who opened the door to them had been trained to recognize quality at a glance, though his perception was not so great as to discern that the sparkling face of the younger concealed a naive satisfaction and curiosity at being once again in the house she could barely recall, and the cool correct manner of the elder was hastily assumed to disguise the churning sensation in the region of her stomach that had resulted from an avalanche of old memories and feelings jarred loose on entering her former home. He permitted himself a minimal relaxation of the muscles of his face, which resembled nothing so much as that of an elderly pug dog, and indicated the visitors should follow him up-stairs to the drawing room, where Lady Granby was receiving.

April's senses were reacting to the changes the Granbys had made inside the house, but as they entered the drawing room she was aware at the same time of a pause in the atmosphere as the butler announced them, and the slight hanging back of her sister—and small wonder! The room seemed at first to be overflowing with humanity, all of whom were strangers. April was adjusting to the necessity of plunging rather than wading into the waters of society when their hostess detached herself from the group in front of the fireplace and surged forward to greet the newcomers.

"Dearest April, at long last! Being a female, I well understand the need to attend to one's wardrobe before going into society, but we had begun to suspect Lord Glenville meant to keep you all to himself." She emitted a titter that rang falsely from someone of such imposing proportions. A whinny would have been more in character, April reflected waspishly, smarting under the thinly disguised suggestion that the earl was ashamed of his country bride. She managed a civil murmur in acknowledgment and presented her sister to Lady Granby.

"So this is little Diana! My, she is growning into quite a young lady," their hostess said archly, eyeing Diana's curtsy and shy smile with a cold blue stare that belied her honeyed words.

The years had not been kind to her cousin's wife, April decided as that lady led them over to meet her other guests. What might have been called a statuesque figure nine years ago by those predisposed to make kindly judgments was now frankly past that description, despite rigid corseting that pushed up a bosom of majestic proportions and whose tight lacing increased her already high color at the least exertion. The blond hair that had been her one claim to beauty in her youth had been prevented from fading by some means that could only be deemed partially successful, judging from the brassy hue of the crimped locks showing beneath a real quiz of a cap. The passing years had also served to heighten the equine characteristics of her long bony face and the nasality of her piercing voice.

The latter characteristic was very much in evidence as she presented her husband's relatives to the expectant group watching their approach with varying degrees of enthusiasm and curiosity. Fortunately, three of the five people present were members of one family, thus reducing the feat of memory to be expected of Lady Glenville and Miss Wendover. Lady Eddington had called with her son and daughter and, as it turned out in the course of the conversation, had been accompanied by the other gentleman, a Mr. Navenby, who was a friend of Mr. Eddington's. The remaining member of the party was Miss Phoebe Granby, the eldest daughter of the house. One look at the latter had served to confirm April's past apprehensions that Lady Granby would never have consented to bring Diana out in company with her woefully plain daughter.

The best that could be said for Miss Granby at the end of a half hour's acquaintance was that she appeared to be a good-natured girl eager to be accepted by one and all. Unfortunately, this led her at times into the error of agreeing with every opinion offered even when consecutive opinions were diametrically opposed. April took pity on her embarrassment after one such exchange and engaged her in quiet conversation until the mottled flush faded somewhat from her lean cheeks. She had inherited her mother's bony facial structure and large frame, but there was no excess weight on Phoebe, the reverse indeed! April wondered that her mother would permit her to be seen in an ill-fitting dress that drew attention to the deficiencies of her figure. She had been aware of Lady Granby's swift appraisal of her own and Diana's attire, guessing that her shopkeeper's mentality had been busy estimating the cost of each item. That these estimates would be wide of the mark was a forgone conclusion, for everything about the furnishings of the room

and her own and her daughter's appearance screamed of
money spent for the sole purpose of display with little regard
for value or aesthetics.

The mantelpiece was crowded with a motley collection of
costly ornaments placed without regard to decorative effect,
and both ladies were expensively but badly dressed, their
choices seemingly unrelated to the coloring or figure type of
the wearer. The coquelicot ribbons adorning Lady Granby's
gown might be all the rage, but poppy red would ever war
with its wearer's highly colored complexion.

April allowed her attention to dwell on the others in the
group, pleased to note that Diana, unaccustomedly shy in
company, was making a favorable impression on Lady
Eddington. The fact that Miss Sarah Eddington was a lively,
pretty brunette with, apparently, a devoted swain in atten-
dance may have made possible her mother's disinterested
judgment, but April was grateful for this evidence of goodwill on the part of one who was likely to become Diana's
hostess on occasion if the initial rapport between the girls
was permitted to develop naturally.

Lady Granby was also quick to note the ease with which
Diana had insinuated herself into the group of young
people, but she viewed this with little evidence of pleasure.
Her own efforts to prevent such an occurrence had begun
when she directed Diana to a chair between the elder ladies,
but after Mr. Eddington had several times leaned across his
mama to include Diana in his conversation, that lady had
laughingly demanded that Diana change seats with her so
she might hear what Lady Granby was saying.

April was well aware that her hostess was eagerly awaiting
a chance to quiz her on her unlikely marriage. She had
determined beforehand to thwart this intention as far as
possible, but now that the young people were enjoying themselves as they described to a rapt Diana some of the delights
to be experienced during the season, she took a sudden
decision to abandon her resolve and oblige her hostess. After
all, what better way to ensure that a sizable portion of the

ton heard the story as she wished it told than by allowing her relative to carry the tale forward? Accordingly, she gently eased the eager Phoebe back into the chattering group and exposed her lines for an attack.

"You must permit me to apologize for not calling somewhat sooner, ma'am, but as you so rightly surmised, Diana and I have been prodigiously involved with updating our wardrobes as well as making a start at redecorating the house. It has been sadly neglected for a period of years."

Lady Granby ignored the tempting red herring. "You had been living in the country until your marriage, had you not?"

"Yes." Lest this simple answer strike the others as too abrupt, April amended, "Naturally our sartorial requirements were a good deal less there."

Having no intention of detouring into a discussion of fashion, Lady Granby headed down another road. "The announcement of your marriage came as a great surprise to us, my dear April. I would have expected you to have consulted your cousin about so important a decision."

"And so I should have had I still been a green girl in the habit of turning to my father's cousin for counsel and assistance," April replied gently, permitting herself a slight stress on the final word. If her hostess chose to interpret this as a subtle reminder that no assistance of any kind had ever been forthcoming from this quarter, then she was perfectly at liberty to do so.

In fact, Lady Granby bridled slightly. "Well, as head of the family, I am sure your cousin always stands ready to render any assistance in his power to one so closely connected."

An incredibly sweet smile spread slowly across the countenance of the Countess of Glenville. "Such a generous expression of family feeling does you great credit, ma'am. I am more grateful than mere words can express. And your kind assurance gives me the audacity to beg a small service of you if you will be so good."

The gratified smirk animating Lady Granby's features at the beginning of this speech was succeeded by a rather wary expression.

"Indeed? And what might that be?"

April laughed merrily. "Only what I am persuaded you would have offered unprompted had you been aware that I meant to present Diana this season. I refer, of course, to procuring vouchers for Almack's for us."

"Of course. Naturally I shall be delighted to be of use." Outmaneuvered on all fronts, Lady Granby surrendered after a glance at the expectant face of Lady Eddington.

April thanked her sweetly, then sat back, highly pleased, and allowed Lady Eddington's expressions of delight at having such a charming addition to the ranks of debutantes to wash over her and assail the ears of her kinswoman. Lady Granby struggled to present a complaisant exterior while her good-natured friend assured her that Phoebe and Diana were bound to become devoted to one another, but at the first opportunity she turned the conversation back to the subject of her cousin's noteworthy marriage.

"I should be failing in my duty, my dear April, if I neglected to drop you a hint that your marriage has been a source of great speculation about town."

Clear light eyes with a hint of violet were directed at her, politely attentive, but their owner made no reply, and, after a tiny pause, Lady Granby rushed on: "Glenville is known to be a misogynist; it was settled among the town's matchmaking mamas years ago that his was a hopeless case. Not even that odious Lady Laleham with six daughters to establish, each one plainer than the next, bothered to send him invitations any longer. Even the cleverest of the designing widows had abandoned the chase with respect to Glenville."

"Really?" April experimented with a tiny smile that she hoped might convey amused understanding, *secretive* feminine understanding.

Lady Eddington's comely face looked almost the same vintage as her daughter's when she laughed, despite the faint lines fanning out from her eyes. "Do not allow your cousin's natural and laudable concern for your welfare to alarm you, Lady Glenville, as to your probable reception in society. You cannot avoid being the object of great interest and not a little envy just at first, but if you do not permit yourself to be alienated by the whispers of the disappointed or the insincerity of the toadeaters, you will soon find the vast majority of people eager to welcome you on your own obvious merit."

This time April's smile held real warmth, but before she could express the sense of her obligation to Lady Eddington for her kind words their hostess abandoned her attempts at diplomatic interrogation in favor of the direct approach.

"Naturally, with your own family connections and those of your husband you need have no fears of your acceptance, but people will wonder how you two met with you having lived in retirement for a number of years and Glenville so impervious to the usual run of feminine charms, not to mention other considerations, *past* considerations," she finished with a meaningful look at the new countess.

"Oh, my acquaintance with Lord Glenville is not of recent date, Cousin Louisa," April replied with seeming candor after a swift glance had assured her Diana was too engrossed to hear her. "Dear me, no, we have been known to each other this age or more. However, I must confess that the *ripening* of our friendship has occurred only lately. It was through the kind offices of mutual friends that the opportunity to renew our acquaintance arose." She gave a reminiscent little chuckle. "As Adam always says, there is nothing that provides a more encouraging atmosphere for the development of those tender sentiments between the sexes than a congenial house party."

Both senior ladies were listening avidly to this cloying performance, but April was spared the ordeal of inventing further details by the eruption just then of the vivacious Miss Eddington from the circle of young people.

"Mama," she entreated, then blushed and stammered, "Oh, I do beg your pardon, ma'am!" when she realized Lady Glenville had been speaking.

"What is it, my dear?" Lady Eddington turned to her daughter with an indulgent air.

"Mama, may Miss Wendover join us this afternoon when we go to Somerset House? Just imagine, she has never been there! If you do not object, Lady Glenville?"

April's quick look at Diana took in her eagerness but noted also the downcast eyes of her cousin, who was sitting beside her. When Lady Eddington stated her entire willingness to extend her chaperonage to Miss Wendover and urged her sister to permit the outing, the latter found herself asking quietly, "Does Miss Granby go too?"

"By all means," agreed Lady Eddington quickly. "Phoebe must come too. You girls will all be able to enlighten each other's ignorance."

The three girls giggled at this sally, and April was rewarded by seeing the pleasure that gave Miss Granby's plain face a momentary glow that rendered her almost attractive. Lady Granby shot her a look of mingled surprise and reluctant gratitude as she gave her permission for her daughter's inclusion in the party bent on inspecting the latest works by members of the Royal Academy.

The details of the excursion were arranged in short order, and the visit was terminated just in the nick of time as far as April was concerned to secure her release from Lady Granby's inquisition before she was forced onto the uncertain and untested resources of her imagination to supply further details of Adam's supposed courtship. She apologized to him mentally for her lack of cooperation on the occasion when he had raised the subject and took care to coach Diana in the bare essentials of the story on their return to Hanover Square. Beyond an expression of surprise that it should be thought necessary to improvise a tale to explain her marriage, Diana did not pursue the topic. April had no difficulty in attributing this welcome indifference to her sister's preoccupation with her own first venture into society and thankfully refrained from fuller explanations. That these would be necessary sooner or later she accepted with a fatalistic calm. Diana was curious about her sister's marraige, and April had put her off with deliberately vague answers up to now.

She could not quite account for her extreme reluctance to relate the whole truth to her sister. It wasn't that she feared to destroy the romantic illusions of a young girl regarding love matches. The fact that Diana had, not so very long ago, been urging her to marry Mr. Lynley, well knowing the lack of anything warmer than friendship in her sister's regard for the man, was sufficient proof of that young lady's practical turn of mind. She would not be shocked to learn that April did not love Adam, but she would be shocked to learn that the sister who had preached Christian ethics and guided her behavior from childhood was herself capable of seizing an opportunity in such a contemptible fashion and forcing a man to marry her. Also, for some inexplicable reason, she was loath to reveal the part Adam had played in their lives in the past, though she wouldn't give much for the chance that someone else would not spill the tale into Diana's ears on some occasion. Diana liked Adam unreservedly, and April hated to see this ease and liking diminished for both their sakes. One of the unexpected benefits of the marriage had been the natural shifting of some of her authority to a man's broad shoulders. The strong-willed Diana meekly accepted Adam's pronouncements on various subjects where she might have rebelled against the same decisions made by her sister. Well, it would not do any good to worry herself into a frazzled state over circumstances that did not rest with her. She must play it by ear and try not to concern herself overmuch with possible evil consequences in the future.

With an effort she switched her thoughts to the quite satisfactory results of their morning call. She had been a trifle nervous about that first meeting with her cousin's wife, and her nerve had nearly failed at the sight of strangers in her drawing room, but everything had turned out for the best. The presence of others had put some curb on Lady Granby's quest for minute details of the marriage, and Diana had been exposed most advantageously to an attractive group of youngsters who had made definite overtures of friendship. No doubt Louisa Granby would prefer to keep social contacts between the families to a minimum in order to spare Phoebe unfavorable comparisons with Diana, but it would not be possible to isolate Phoebe from all such comparisons in any case. Unless she was vastly mistaken, the girl had conceived a spontaneous admiration for her pretty cousin which would not suit her mother's book at all.

It was unfortunate the child was so plain, but she seemed to be of a sweet disposition and could be rendered more presentable if someone possessing better taste than her mother took her in hand. Her soft hair of an attractive shade between blond and brown could be dressed to better advantage, and her lean form could be disguised with a more suitable selection of designs and more attention to the fit of the garments. A few minutes of speculation, however, served to convince her that it would be no easy task, situated as she was, to contrive for Phoebe's benefit. The biggest hurdle would be to overcome her mother's inherent and understandable mistrust of the unwanted relatives who had succeeded in escaping the obscurity to which they had been relegated for the past nine years. The more she thought about it the more she allowed that she had been divinely inspired to secure the promise of vouchers for Almack's under circumstances that compelled Lady Granby to conceal her feelings and act as everyone would expect.

Diana, noticing the little smile that curved her sister's lips, paused in rhapsodic recounting of the conversation that had obtained among the young people, gratified to find that April endorsed her opinion of Mr. Eddington as a gentleman of superior address and pleasing appearance. In due course the carriage arrived in Hanover Square and discharged two ladies equally well pleased with their morning activities.

Chapter Nine

The Earl of Glenville, large and impressive in black-and-white evening dress, stood with his back to the green marble fireplace and surveyed his ladies with the eye of a connoisseur as they entered the small saloon. Diana was a bit ahead of her sister, but his glance passed over her to absorb his wife's appearance in a lightning assessment before returning to study the young girl with flattering interest. His all too rare smile shone out, untinged for once by mockery.

Diana blossomed like a spring flower under the warmth of her brother-in-law's fluent compliments, pirouetting slowly with innocent coquetry to present him with a more detailed view of the glory of her first evening dress. April watched the performance in silence, a prey to mixed emotions. The nagging anxiety that she and Diana might not come up to the earl's expectation had vanished with his first words, and she was grateful for the pleasure his praise gave her sister, but she found it necesssary before greeting him with quiet civility to suppress an unreasoning disappointment at the minimal share of the compliments that fell to her lot. His flattering words might be addressed to both; his attention remained on Diana. If April had not been so greatly heartened earlier in the evening by Mattie's gruff declaration that she hadn't realized just how good-looking her mistress was, her courage would have faltered at her husband's apparent indifference. Fortunately there was just enough feminine pique generated by his cavalier attitude to stiffen her spine and enable her to maintain an air of cool unconcern during

127

the drive to Mount Street, where the Jeffrieses' hired town house was situated.

Adam had not been generous with information about their host. April knew only that Jason Jeffries was an opposition member of Parliament from somewhere in the Midlands and that Adam had known him since their days at Eton. The fact that they were the only guests dining with the family before the musical entertainment scheduled by Mrs. Jeffries rather pointed to a close friendship between the men, but April had been made too conscious of the negligible position she occupied in her husband's thoughts to wish to demonstrate her very real curiosity about his associations lest she invite a snub.

The warm welcome accorded them on their arrival confirmed her speculations in the carriage and marked the pleasantest encounter so far in her brief London sojourn. Mr. Jeffries greeted Adam with the casual ease of long acquaintance, and his wife, a plump and smiling brunette, put her hands on the earl's shoulders and kissed him unselfconsciously before turning a magnificent pair of hazel eyes to April with an expression that radiated goodwill. When introductions had been made she confided merrily that she had been dying to meet Lady Glenville and that her *odious* husband, and here she flung a saucy look at the amused Mr. Jeffries, had refused to satisfy her very natural curiosity about his friend's new bride.

"All the provoking creature would reply every time I inquired was that Adam said you were 'difficult to describe.' Is that not just like a man?" she pouted engagingly.

April produced the required social laugh and was relieved when Mr. Jeffries took over from his garrulous wife by declaring gallantly that he would now on his own authority be able to describe Lady Glenville as a prize far beyond the desserts of her inarticulate husband. He led her to a chair and seated her with a flourish, repeating the action for Diana, who dimpled adorably.

Their host then indicated a tray holding glasses and a bottle of champagne. "I wish I might have had the honor of offering this toast at your wedding," he said, looking at April with simple friendliness as he poured the bubbling liquid into the waiting glasses, which his wife distributed, "but at least you will permit me now to wish you the same felicity in marriage that Jane and I have found. To Adam and April."

April concentrated on the contents of her glass, unhappily aware of the obstruction in her throat and the man at her side, so close his shoulder touched hers but still as alien in spirit as on the night they had met. Though thankful for the sincerity of the good wishes being tendered them, she was made more miserably conscious than ever of the falsity of the situation. Strange, but she had never before considered the effect of the marriage on others, people like these kind friends of Adam's who genuinely wished him, and therefore her, well. Troubled gray eyes sought his involuntarily and blinked at the look they encountered. The moment stretched unendurably. She felt the heat rise in her cheeks but was incapable alike of preventing this betrayal or wrenching her glance from the incomprehensible intensity of her husband's regard.

Rescue came in the form of two small children who entered the room at that moment in the company of a middle-aged nurse. They were beautiful children, but the accompanying illusion of docility disintegrated instantaneously when they spied the earl.

"Uncle Adam! Uncle Adam!" shrieked the elder, a boy of about six with his mother's hazel eyes and his father's thin, regular features in miniature. He outdistanced his sister easily and launched himself upon Lord Glenville, who broke into laughter and tossed him high in the air. The unexpectedness of this action elicited a gasp of alarm from April and Diana, but the victim merely squealed with delight and demanded, "Again, Uncle Adam, do it again!"

"Do me, Uncle Adam, do me!"

April's eyes were drawn to the owner of the insistent little voice, a golden-haired cherub clinging to the earl's knees and imploring his attention with piping treble and huge blue eyes. As the man put down his protesting passenger to gather the small girl into his arms, his face came into his wife's line of vision, its hard planes softened by an expression of such tenderness as she had never thought possible from her knowledge of him. Her fascinated gaze was riveted to him as he raised the little girl slowly over his head for an instant before drawing her into a close embrace. The child squirmed in an agony of pleasurable fear. "Do it again, Uncle Adam, please!"

He pretended to consider. "Well, that depends. Who does Missy love?"

"Mummy!" replied the little girl promptly, casting him a sly look from under gold-tipped lashes.

"Anyone else?"

"Papa!"

A gentle shake was administered to the tiny temptress. "Anyone else?"

"And Uncle Adam!" she crowed with a squeaky giggle.

"That's better." As the earl again raised the enchanting little bit of femininity overhead, it was clear from the indulgent looks on her parents' faces and the dancing impatience of the small boy that this was a familiar ritual enjoyed by all.

"It's my turn now, Uncle Adam!"

"In a minute, Jonathan," said the mother. "We mustn't forget our manners. Come make your bow to Lady Glenville and Miss Wendover."

Despite his disappointment at the postponement of his treat, the boy performed a creditable bow and said a polite how-do-you-do to the ladies before returning his attention to the earl, who stood with the little girl in his arms watching the introductions.

"Missy's afraid to be tossed," pronounced her brother with more than a trace of satisfaction.

"I'm not afraid!"

"Then let Uncle Adam toss you."

Adam intervened quickly as two little hands clutched his lapels in a tightened grip. "Missy, I'd like you to meet Lady Glenville and Miss Wendover." He brought the child to the two women, but when Diana would have taken the small hand, Missy pulled it back and ducked her head against Adam's shoulder. April was careful to make no overtures to the little girl as Adam sat down beside her on the sofa with the child on his lap.

"Missy's almost four, but she's afraid of everyone," Jonathan informed the assembled company. "Nurse says she's shy." After this brief detour he went back to his primary objective. "You promised to throw me again, Uncle Adam."

"I will before you go to bed."

Mrs. Jeffries was telling the ladies (quite unnecessarily) how the children adored Adam, and had begun relating an amusing incident concerning him when April felt a tiny movement at her hair. She turned her head slowly to see a chubby hand withdraw. One blue eye stared daringly back from the safety of the earl's arms.

"You may touch my hair if you wish," she whispered with a smile, bending her head invitingly. After an instant she felt another little movement as Missy satisfied her curiosity by stroking the silken length with feather-light pressure.

April smiled again and this time was rewarded by an answering smile that revealed tiny white teeth. Seeing the earl's attention on this interchange, Missy explained solemnly, "Pretty hair," then, more comprehensively, "Pretty lady."

"Out of the mouths of babes." Mr. Jeffries sent a companionable grin in the direction of the bride and groom. Adam's eyes were still fixed on his wife's countenance, but he made no reply. She could only hope the color in her cheeks would be attributed to Mr. Jeffries's gallantry. It was a relief to be able to focus on Missy, whose exploring hand was reaching for the pearl pin fixed at the bodice of her gown. Unthinkingly, she extended her arms and the child went into them, all shyness forgotten in her eagerness to examine the pin.

Thanks in part to the numerous possibilities offered by the existence of the Jeffrieses' attractive children, an easy conversation ensued for a further few moments, all of which saw Missy comfortably settled in April's lap. Each time the latter glanced up she was conscious of her husband's enigmatic regard, however, so she was not too reluctant to have the interlude brought to an end with the announcement of dinner. Jonathan was allotted the promised tossing, then Nurse swept her reluctant charges off to their beds after affectionate goodnights were taken of their parents and Uncle Adam. April was honored to be the recipient of a shy hug from Missy, and the little one even summoned up a valedictory smile for Diana.

Dinner was a most relaxed and enjoyable meal. Conversation ranged over many topics, with subjects of general interest interspersed with periods when the ladies left the gentlemen to discuss political points while Mrs. Jeffries eagerly sought details of the ongoing renovation of the earl's house, which she recalled as being excessively gloomy on the one occasion when she had visited it. When the talk swung around to the latest fashions, April found her attention at first wandering and then caught up in the men's discussion of the chances of getting the latest of Sir Samuel Romilly's reform measures through the House of Lords. Mr. Jeffries was more optimistic than Adam that the peers might finally relent and repeal the death penalty for the theft of five shillings from a shop.

"Never!" Adam stated positively. "They've defeated it before and will assuredly do so again even if Lansdowne, Grey, and others speak for the bill. Each new report of a workers' rally, a meeting of radicals, or even a window broken by a street urchin sends them scurrying back to their holes."

"At the moment perhaps, but reform of the criminal code is inevitable. Romilly managed to get the penalty for pickpocketing reduced a few years ago, and sentiment around the country is strongly for reform."

"One cannot argue that transportation is not preferable to hanging," April said at this point, "but it is still dreadfully severe. A lad from the village where I lived was convicted last year in London. His parents know they will never see him again. He is their only remaining child, and their hearts are broken. It is pitiful to see them suffer so, and all for the theft of a few shillings."

Adam responded in all seriousness. "The system of penalties itself is a crime against justice and encourages witnesses to lie and juries to disregard their oaths and refuse to convict in the face of indisputable evidence. Many judges, too, arrest the course of justice by refusing to impose the sentence prescribed in the statutes. Jason is undoubtedly correct in reading the sentiment for reform around the country, but he is mistaken if he thinks those jumped-up merchants in the Lords will relent during this session or the next. The bishops are even more reactionary. I have great difficulty in comprehending their particular brand of Christianity."

"Romilly will keep hammering away at them, and he gains support daily," Mr. Jeffries repeated before abandoning the topic in favor of questioning Adam on the recent happenings in the Ministry.

April, marveling at the intellectual compatibility existing between a member of the government and a staunch Whig MP, couldn't help the silent reflection that the state of the country couldn't be expected to improve materially until the number of such reasonable men increased considerably in and around the government.

In due course the ladies filed out of the dining room, leaving the gentlemen to the peaceful imbibing of their port, although Mrs. Jeffries, with a beguiling wrinkling of her small, nearly *retroussé* nose, declared that the word "port" was merely a euphemism to cloak their transparent intention of filling her dining room with the noxious fumes of the vile cigars they professed, quite incomprehensibly, to enjoy.

"We shall open wide both windows, my love, despite the imminent danger to our lungs from the damp night air," her husband promised soothingly, thereby convicting himself out of his own mouth on his wife's charge.

She directed a look of mingled resignation and affection toward him before leading her guests to a small anteroom off the combined drawing rooms, explaining as they settled comfortably around the fireplace, "We shall be more at ease here while awaiting the arrival of the rest of the company. I think there can be nothing so destructive to a conversation as a room full of empty chairs."

The interval while the men remained absent was pleasantly taken up by speculating on the forthcoming wedding of the heir to the throne. Mrs. Jeffries assured her guests that the visit of Princess Charlotte to Brighton the previous month had gone famously, although her father's gout was still troubling him. She had it on the authority of one of the other guests that the Prince and his daughter had met with every evidence of filial affection on her part and paternal benevolence on his, and the result had been his freely given consent to her marriage to Prince Leopold. "It really is a love match, you know. After that other unfortunate affair and her subsequent confinement to Cranbourne Lodge she'd no doubt have accepted any suitor to achieve the status and freedom of a married woman, but by all reports she simply dotes on Prince Leopold. I must say I find his person rather severe, though attractive enough. I should be surprised indeed to find he possessed much in the way of a sense of humor. The Germans are so dreadfully dull on the whole, do you not agree?"

The other ladies, being newly arrived in town, were unable to voice an opinion on this important subject, but they displayed a flattering eagerness to learn as many details of the royal romance as Mrs. Jeffries could supply. Diana, just a couple of years younger than Princess Charlotte, was particularly keen to hear even secondhand reports on one who was destined to become her sovereign one day.

When the men ultimately joined them, the three women looked up in some surprise, so absorbed had they become in palace gossip. There was just time for a lingering cup of coffee before the guests were due to arrive. The earl, looking more relaxed and human than April had ever seen him, inquired as to the entertainment they were to expect. Mrs. Jeffries named the cellist and violinist whom she had engaged to play, and added with a smile, "And you will give us the pleasure of a song or two, will you not, dear Adam? I vow you are the main reason my musical evenings are so well attended. No other hostess can boast of producing such a fine voice from among her friends."

"After that highly exaggerated but most acceptable tribute I am desolated to have to refuse you, Jane, but my throat has been a trifle scratchy all afternoon and I fear it is worsening. I would not be an asset to your program tonight, I fear—very much the opposite, indeed."

April scarcely heard Mrs. Jeffries's polite murmurs of sympathy and disappointment. She was storing up in her mind yet another unexpected discovery about the man she had married. This had been an evening of surprises. She had barely assimilated the startling but unmistakable evidence that the man she had considered quite cold and inhuman had a definite soft spot for children, at least for two specific children, when she was confronted with another unsuspected aspect of his personality. That he enjoyed music was no surprise—his attentiveness when Diana played and sang had been repeated too often to be counterfeit—but she would not have guessed in a thousand years that his natural reserve could dissolve to the extent that it would permit him to perform before an audience. Mrs. Jeffries's disappointment was as nothing compared to that which swept through April as she searched her husband's countenance in an unsuccessful effort to discover whether or not his easy excuse had been genuine.

The sound of the door knocker below brought the company to its feet as the first guests arrived. As they passed into the larger rooms, Jason Jeffries mentioned to his wife that he had run into Damien Harding that afternoon and had invited him to drop in. Damien had planned to attend a boxing exhibition with a friend but said he'd come by if his friend were agreeable to a change of plans.

"Very good," said his spouse. "Freddy is coming, you

know." She turned to April. "Have you and Miss Wendover made the acquaintance of Adam's cousins yet, Lady Glenville?"

April had time for only the sketchiest reply before the main doors were opened and the earliest of the guests announced. The next half hour was spent in responding to numerous introductions to people she despaired of remembering at a later date. Among the hordes was only one familiar face, that of a girl she recalled from the days of her own comeout, once remarkable for her extreme silliness, and now to all appearances a sober young matron. In the press of new arrivals she was allowed time neither to re-animate the acquaintance nor dwell on the change in her erstwhile friend. Adam remained at her side giving a totally believable performance as a devoted husband. She felt there must be a permanent flush on her cheeks at the many ingratiating comments from the people presented to her. She glanced at her sister to see how that young lady was bearing up under the ordeal.

Diana was deliciously flustered by all the flattering attention being showered upon her and had need of all her innate self-possession to maintain a demure facade. April squeezed her hand and smiled encouragingly at the girl and thus missed the arrival of the two men she most hoped to avoid in London. It was Adam's casual-looking but insistent hand nipping her waist that alerted her, and she directed an inquiring stare toward him. At sight of Mr. Damien Harding's handsome face a foot away, the smile on her lips stiffened, but it was the man beside him who caused it to fade slowly away. Only the comforting pressure of her husband's hand at her waist enabled her to conquer an instinctive physical shrinking.

"You remember Lord Allerton, my dear," he was saying in a voice devoid of all emotion after having greeted his cousin warmly.

"Yes indeed. How do you do, sir, and you, Mr. Harding? May I present my sister, Miss Wendover. Diana, this is

Adam's other cousin, Mr. Damien Harding, and Lord Allerton."

If April hoped in the crush of arrivals to be able to slide by with no further contact, she was doomed to disappointment. Mr. Harding was greeting Diana with the same effusiveness he had displayed on being introduced to herself, and Diana's wholehearted response left her sister face-to-face with the detestable Allerton for some seconds while someone engaged Adam's attention on his other side. Allerton's initial astonishment upon seeing her, which she had no hesitation in ascribing to the marked improvement in her appearance, gave way to a narrow-eyed scrutiny which April found no less offensive. By exercising a stern self-command she was able to meet his glance with the cool composure of an actress when it returned from the thorough survey of her slim person attractively clad in glistening folds of pale-rose brocade.

"I nearly failed to recognize you, Lady Glenville," he offered with more haste than wisdom.

"Indeed."

With the single word uttered in freezing accents, the conversation languished and died. Lord Allerton seized the hand Diana had extended to him like a drowning man grasping for a raft and held it longer than was strictly acceptable.

"This is a great pleasure, Miss Wendover. Glenville is a fortunate man indeed to have surrounded himself with feminine loveliness. If I had only been permitted to make your acquaintance the day after your sister's marriage when I met her in the inn I might now claim the privilege of a friend to request the pleasure of your company for the entertainment this evening."

"Oh, did you meet April at the inn?" the girl asked, a trifle puzzled. "She and Adam weren't—"

"Diana, I require your assistance in pinning up this torn flounce before the music begins," April cut in quickly, conscious of the sudden alertness of both Mr. Harding and Lord

Allerton but unable on the spur of the moment to invent a
more convincing excuse.

"How did you tear your flounce?"

"Someone trod on it," was the curt reply as April placed a
firm hand under her sister's elbow and led her away, saying
over her shoulder, "I beg you will excuse us for a moment,
gentlemen?"

When the two women reached the ladies' retiring room,
April waved away the offer of assistance from the maid and
spoke to her sister in a quiet intense voice.

"There is no time to explain fully, Diana, but it is imperative that no one should learn the exact date or place of my
marriage. If Lord Allerton or Mr. Harding or anyone else
should refer to the subject again, be vague but allow them to
think we married before arriving in town. Do you understand?"

"Of course, but why should you wish to deceive people?"

"I cannot explain at the moment; we must be seated
before the entertainment can begin. Here, allow me to
straighten this bow on your sleeve a trifle before we return.
There, that's better. You have conducted yourself very
prettily tonight in the face of so many introductions,
dearest. Are you enjoying yourself?"

"Oh yes," Diana replied sunnily as they made their way
back to Adam's side. "Everyone is most kind." She twinkled
at her sister. "Why did you not tell me Mr. Damien Harding
was so handsome? Such an air of distinction, such address,
and his manners so exquisitely polished! I really believe I
prefer older men after all."

They reached Adam at this point, so April was spared the
necessity of commenting on this ingenuous and unwelcome
disclosure. The presence of Mr. Frederick Harding in
company with his cousin and the situation of his brother and
Allerton at a distance that precluded conversation went a
long way toward restoring April's serenity. Seated between
her husband and his heir, she was able in time to relax her
taut nerves and enjoy the musical program. It had been a
close-run thing, though, and she would have no hesitation in

wagering her entire wardrobe against the chance that either of those men would allow the subject of her marriage to drop without making an attempt to discover all the particulars. The earl had looked at her searchingly upon her return with Diana but had refrained from comment. It wasn't until a break in the music while Mrs. Jeffries introduced a friend who had agreed to play a selection on the harp that he leaned closer and whispered:

"What happened? Why did you disappear so suddenly?"

She lowered her voice to a thread of sound behind her ivory fan. "Did you not hear? Diana nearly revealed that we were not married at the time we met Allerton at the inn. I was obliged to remove her and warn her against any future disclosures."

Before Adam could respond, her attention was claimed by Freddy, and shortly the music recommenced, severing any opportunity for further communication. She had seen the tightening of her husband's finely chiseled mouth, however, and knew a selfish comfort in having enlisted a fellow sufferer in her anxiety. Thanks in part to a fundamental conviction that Adam was more than a match for Allerton, she was able to put the awkward incident clear out of her mind for the remainder of the evening except during the short interval when she discovered Diana in private conversation with the two men. How right she had been to heed her instincts in delivering a prompt warning to the girl! They had not let any grass grow beneath their feet in seeking her out. It was impossible to tell the nature of the conversation from the expressions on their faces, and in any case Diana's instant popularity among the younger guests served to curtail the tête-à-tête. She had the pleasure of seeing the men bow and remove themselves fairly soon, and neither approached her sister during the remainder of the evening.

With his quiet charm, Freddy set about making her feel at home in society later when refreshments were served. He seemed to know everybody and guided her into conversation with an ease born of genuine interest in others. While in the supper room with its lavish buffet, April was approached by her former friend, whose idea of bridging the gap of years was to bring her up to date on the number and ages of her own progeny and those of mutual friends from that long-ago season. During the enforced catalogue, Freddy melted away with the acquired ability of the male to avoid boredom, and when, her head stuffed with birth statistics, April at length negotiated her release after a promise to call and meet the children, it was to find him wending a slightly unsteady course toward her again. His quiet manner was unchanged and his speech unimpaired, but she noticed a trembling in the fingers that held a wine cup and a hint of rigidity in his bearing that caused her to suspect he had been dipping rather deeply in the interim. A look of disgust on Adam's face when he sought her out a few moments later gave rise to some conjecture on April's part as to the frequency of such behavior, but she dismissed the notion in the pleasures of their first social engagement. Later when she bade Diana goodnight at her door they agreed that it had been an altogether happy baptism in the waters of society.

Chapter Ten

It was close to five o'clock when the Earl of Glenville entered his house, heartened by an unusual sense of homecoming. The day had seemed endless, packed with irritating problems and petty skirmishes that took on additional weight because he was feeling well below normal. With heartfelt relief he stripped off his gloves and allowed Morton to divest him of greatcoat, hat, and cane.

"Ladies in, Morton?"

"Not yet, my lord, but Lady Glenville ordered tea for five-fifteen. They have gone driving with Mr. Frederick in the Park."

"Thank you. I'll be in my study until then."

Morton had been making a discreet survey of his master's person during this exchange, and now he asked, "Are you feeling quite yourself, my lord?"

"Frankly, Morton, I feel like something left for dead on a battlefield. Must have a cold coming on."

"Can I get you anything, sir? Shall I ask Mrs. Donaldson to brew you a posset?"

"No. I refuse to quack myself. Nature brought it and in due course Nature will take it away."

Following this clipped pronouncement, the earl disappeared into his study, where he remained until he had finished writting a letter begun the previous day. A mild commotion in the hall a few minutes before had proclaimed the return of his wife and sister-in-law with attendant guests. He frowned as he sealed the letter and franked it. Rarely

had he felt less disposed to do the pretty to the assortment of
tame cats April and Diana had collected about themselves
in their brief exposure to society, but the promise of a hot
cup of tea lured him upstairs. Or so he told himself as he
headed for the main saloon, from which drifted animated
snatches of conversation and trills of feminine laughter
interspersed with the odd masculine guffaw. He was not prepared to admit that he missed the occasional peaceful hour
spent drinking tea with his wife that had become almost
routine before she and Diana had achieved their current
popularity, but he didn't mind acknowledging a certain impatience at having his house constantly overrun with
humanity, especially since the examples of such tended to
run heavily in favor of the idle young sprigs of fashion whom
he found mildly intolerable at best and totally irrelevant at
all times.

For a moment his presence in the doorway went
undetected by the merry group scattered about the tea
table. He was relieved to discover the only guests were his
two cousins, but the initial relief was quickly succeeded by a
twinge of irritation as he noted Freddy's golden head bent
attentively toward April. As usual his gaze lingered on the
silvery fall of satin-smooth hair caressing his wife's cheek as
she reached for her cup.

It was April who first became aware of the blue-coated
figure that had entered the room so quietly.

"Adam! I did not hear you come in. Would you like some
tea?"

Whether more influenced by his wife's spontaneous smile
of welcome or the unwelcome presence of his cousin sitting
close beside her on the green settee Adam did not attempt to
assess as he set a course for the empty chair near the settee
and deliberately leaned over to salute her cheek with his lips
before responding to the bright greetings of the others.

"Let me prepare your tea, Adam," said Diana, jumping
up immediately. "You look to be in urgent need of it."

"Too right, old man. You look like the end of a wet

week," was the unfeeling comment of his younger cousin.

April had reached the same basic conclusion after a covert study of her husband from under her lashes while she pretended to be absorbed in the contents of her cup. Now she rested a concerned glance on his face.

"It's my belief that you would benefit by a spell in your bed, Adam. You have been battling that cold for days." She watched his mouth tighten as he nodded thanks to Diana and accepted his cup.

"Nonsense. I am perfectly capable of functioning normally and refuse to be rendered bedfast. I'm probably over the worst of it by now in any case." He changed the subject determinedly.

April preserved an unconvinced silence while the conversation flowed around her. To her eye, Adam looked worse each day. His throat continued to be scratchy, as evidenced by the hacking cough that overtook him at intervals. His eyes were red-rimmed, and she was persuaded that he was a frequent victim of the headache. In fact, he presented all the appearance of a person with a feverish cold, except that until the present at least he had not run a temperature. She noted that he avoided the tempting scones and iced cakes on the tray but rapidly drank two cups of tea. His appetite at dinner, the only meal they partook of together, had diminished alarmingly of late, and this too was worrying.

Aware of her silent scrutiny, the earl turned and addressed her with determined lightness. "How go the riding lessons and dancing lessons? Will she be likely to put us to the blush at our ball?"

April laughed out suddenly, and a rare twinkle came into the cool gray eyes as they surveyed her sister's indignant face. "There is much less likelihood that she will disgrace us on the dance floor than on horseback, thank heavens. I have gleaned from among a plethora of complaints that Diana would be more inclined to profit by her instruction in horsemanship if only the noble beast might be persuaded to refrain from habits of twitching, sidling, dancing, snorting or sudden lifts of the head, and most vital of all, could be bred to a much smaller stature!"

Diana tossed her golden curls and pouted at the general amusement. "Well, they *are* too tall, and it cannot be denied that the stupid creatures are disastrously prone to sudden movements that are unnerving to the rider."

"Do not be discouraged, Diana," soothed Freddy. "You are experiencing the difficulties that beset most novice riders, but you'll find you will soon accustom yourself to the animal's peculiarities and will grow much more confident in the saddle."

"Lord, yes, you'll be leading the hunting field in a year," predicted Mr. Damien Harding, with what Diana could only consider a gross overestimation of the probable rate of her progress in the equestrian arts. "In fact," he added breezily, "I'll invite you here and now to hunt with me this fall."

"And I'll decline on her behalf here and now." The earl turned to his sister-in-law and said with mock seriousness, "Diana, you are never under any circumstances to put your life in jeopardy by joining Damien on the hunting field or in any shooting sport whatever. In a hunt he is sure to part company at the first fence, and the cawker doesn't even know how to carry a gun safely. He nearly killed me when we went out pheasant shooting last fall, but the pheasants had never been so safe."

April's eyes had flown to her husband's younger cousin, so she caught the flash of real anger that distorted his handsome face for a bare instant before he got it under control and produced a protesting laugh.

"Hey, now, that's libel or slander or something. I haven't fallen at a fence in years, and anyone could have tripped over that root and discharged his piece. It was an accident that could have happened to anyone."

"And I wouldn't be sitting here at this moment had I been two inches taller," retorted the earl, "as the hole in my hat can testify. Do I exaggerate, Freddy?"

That gentleman grinned at his discomfited brother. "Not a bit of it. Damien is a menace even with a harmless fishing rod, but judging from that exquisitely tied cravat, he's putting to good use the time he saves by keeping off the field of sport. A real pink of the *ton*, my little brother."

His little brother's rude rejoinder drawing attention to the crumpled state of his senior's own neckcloth and the haphazard style of his attire developed into a lively exchange that provoked laughter from Diana and the earl. April kept a smile pinned on her lips, but she heard none of it. The artless disclosure by the earl of a near miss at the hands of his cousin had rocked her more than was warranted by the facts of the matter. Her initial unfavorable impression of Mr. Damien Harding had undergone a slow revision in the wake of his persistent efforts to be pleasantly attentive and accommodating toward his cousin's bride, but in a flash all her instictive wariness had returned stronger than ever. She was hard pressed to hold up her end of the conversation during the remainder of the tea party.

The earl grew less animated presently, and he indulged in one or two bouts of coughing that left him looking drained and exhausted. His heir regarded him with sympathy on making his adieux and advised him to take things easy for a time until he had shaken off his cold. "The Ministry can run without you for a few days."

Damien added his advice. "Stay home and enjoy the benefits of your gorgeous wife's nursing skills. It's an ill wind, after all."

Adam dismissed them both summarily and cut short the earnest representations of his wife and sister-in-law on the wisdom of retiring early to bed with a tray for dinner. He joined them in the dining room at the appointed hour and exerted the utmost effort to conceal the fact that he could scarcely face any food with equanimity. With all parties constrained to avoid the topic of the earl's health, conversation was necessarily of a rather artificial nature, and the end of dinner was greeted with relief by everyone. April and Diana were scheduled to attend a small card party at the Eddingtons', and as they took their leave of Adam, April mustered the courage to express the polite hope that he would have an early night and feel more the thing in the morning.

It was soon evident that her hopes were not to be realized. Adam was no better the next day or on the days that followed. The scratchy throat and coughing continued unabated, and his eyes remained irritated — these symptoms were impossible of concealment. Likewise it became obvious that he had lost weight, which was not surprising, since he was eating poorly. April suspected that the sight of food nauseated him, but he denied this, as he denied any problem with headaches. He persisted in reporting to the Ministry each day and flatly refused to consult a doctor, though April had it from Freddy that one of the Regent's own physicians, Sir Everad Howe, was highly thought of around town. Her ears ringing from Adam's pithy description of this physician's skills, she still found the nerve to venture another name, but her husband was adamant. Miserable though it admittedly was, he was only suffering from a cold and had no slightest intention of involving any of the charlatans of the medical profession in his affairs.

Perforce, April subsided, but the truth was that as the first week of Adam's illness gave way to the second she began to question that what he was suffering from was indeed a head cold. For one thing, he never developed a fever, and for another, his symptoms did not seem to worsen rapidly and then gradually ameliorate as in the natural progression of a feverish cold, nor did his nose stream. When she noticed a distinct tremor in his facial muscles her mind started to query what else might produce a similar effect on the human constitution, and although it chilled her blood to consider it, she could not rule our poison with complete confidence. Her instincts had been too active about the enmity she was convinced Morton bore the earl for her to dismiss the possibility out of hand. Suspicions, however, were not evidence, and she could not see how such an end could be achieved when she and Diana ate the same food and were served the same dishes at dinner. Adam always breakfasted early and alone, however, so one morning she joined him unexpectedly, answering his surprise with a tale of rising early to finish writing out the invitations to Diana's ball. She watched Morton closely but could discover no concern for her presence on the butler's part, and he served her the same food his master was doing scant justice to.

Adam never lunched at home, so April thought she was safe in ruling out that possibility as the source of any poisoning. Doubtless he ate with freinds, and Morton would not have access to his food supply during the day. She was reluctantly being forced to the conclusion that her suspicions arose from an intellect disordered by fears based solely on prejudice when the idea struck her like a *coup de foudre*.

The cigars! She found she was trembling physically as her mind raced back over the details of the scene when she had witnessed Morton receive the package of cigars from an unidentified caller with blond hair. The exchange had looked strange at the time until a reasonable explanation had presented itself to her. Fool that she was, she had never checked the truth of that explanation!

April had been changing for dinner when the idea hit her, and her subsequent actions caused Mattie to question her mistress's sanity. She halted her dresser in the process of brushing her hair, cast down the amber beads she had been about to clasp around her neck with such force the string broke, scattering beads all over dressing table and floor, rose from the bench in one precipitate motion, and rushed from the room without a word to the astonished woman, whose scolding was interrupted in midstream by the slamming of the door.

After pelting down the stairs as though all the fiends in hell were at her heels it was a decided anticlimax to find the saloon deserted. April's agitation of spirits was so great she could not stand still, and Adam found her pacing the floor when he entered a few moments later. She searched his surprised face for signs that the symptoms had worsened, but to her infinite relief he appeared a trifle brighter tonight. Without stopping to consider a tactful approach, she blurted out:

"Adam, did you ask Morton to order other cigars to switch with the ones Diana bought you?"

For a moment the earl eyed in astonished silence the tense

Dorothy Mack

figure facing him with fingers laced tightly together against her amber gown. When no explanation for this extraordinary question was forthcoming, he said quietly, "No, Diana bought my favorite type of cigar. Why do you ask?"

It was here that April made the mistake that was to have such disastrous consequences. She continued to stare at her husband's curious, watchful face, her own blank with shock as the implications of his reply reverberated in her brain. Her legs felt incapable of taking her weight of a sudden, and she dropped into a chair. When she had assumed Adam had ordered a switch in cigars, Morton's lie with regard to the person at the front door had seemed unimportant, but now she berated herself for not challenging him on it. Why had she not realized that even if Adam had ordered a switch in cigars they would not have been delivered to the front door?

The mental picture of crisp blond locks beneath a rakishly tipped hat brim crowded out the question Adam had asked her. She recalled now Freddy's recent admission when she had idly wondered why she had not seen him driving his phaeton in the park that he had sold his fine chestnut pair to bail Damien out of a scrape. Subsequent delicate probing on her part had elicited the information that Damien was never more than one step ahead of the tipstaffs. He was an inveterate gambler, with the addict's irrational faith in his star. Adam, who had made good his cousin's losses periodically for years, had finally lost all patience with his worthless promises of reform and had warned him last summer that he had towed him out of the River Tick for the final time. Since then, according to his tolerant brother, Damien had made a real effort to reform his way of life, but he had been forced to apply to Freddy for assistance on one or two occasions when he fell into dun territory again. With stomach-turning conviction, April could imagine Damien's increasing desperation since Adam's ultimatum. Within his power, Freddy would always come to his brother's rescue, but Freddy's financial position was none too healthy either. If Adam were to die without issue, however, Freddy would inherit his consequence and his fortune, and Freddy would never deny his brother. She knew in her bones that it had been Damien Harding at that door passing over poisoned cigars to his former servant for the purpose of murdering his cousin! He had failed to kill him with a faked hunting accident but had been forced to hurry into a new attempt by the unexpected acquisition of a bride, who could not be allowed to produce an heir who would cut him out of the succession. Put into words, it was absolutely appalling, but all the facts fitted.

"April, are you feeling faint?"

Adam's voice, seeming to come from far away, brought April's dazed glance up from her twisting fingers. How could she possibly tell him his favorite cousin wanted him dead badly enough to do the deed himself when she hadn't a shred of actual proof? The enormity of the accusation and the impossibility of making it rendered her speechless. When Diana came into the room a second later, April was still gazing helplessly into her husband's puzzled eyes.

"You two look like statues in a tableau," declared the young girl with a giggle. "How are you feeling tonight, Adam? I do think you look a little better."

"Thank you, I am feeling stronger today. And you are blooming with health and spirits as usual, I see."

Perhaps it's all a ghastly mistake, April thought, staring intently at her husband. Adam does look somewhat recovered. Perhaps it never was poison at all. Diana turned to include her in the dialogue, and her sister gathered her scattered wits together and made a conscious effort to take part. During dinner she was not put to too much strain, thanks to Diana's bubbling spirits, which, as frequently happened, prompted her to assume control of the conversation.

It wasn't until the women rose to leave the table that April's surface attention was jerked back to the subject occupying her deeper thoughts to the exclusion of all others. In an unusual move the earl got up and walked to the door with them, explaining that tonight was the first night in several that he had felt well enough to enjoy an after-dinner smoke. "Bring some brandy to the study, Morton," he directed as they exited the dining room.

"*No!*"

April clutched Adam's arm. "Do not try to smoke a cigar tonight," she begged, moderating her tones. "I am persuaded they are bad for you while your throat is so irritated. Wait until you are quite recovered."

"I am touched by your solicitude, my dear," replied her husband in a smooth voice that gave away none of his thoughts. "Your wish must be my command. Since I am to be denied my smoke, may I request that you play for me tonight, if I am correct in assuming you and Diana have no engagement this evening?"

April was slightly taken aback. The earl had never asked her to play for him before. "Yes, of course, Adam, if you wish it, but would you not prefer to have Diana play and sing as usual?" He repeated his request, subjecting her to an intent study from unreadable dark eyes. She took her place at the pianoforte in some confusion.

Diana expressed herself as pleased to have an opportunity to finish sewing beads on the matching band she intended to wear in her hair when she wore her new yellow ball dress. She settled down contentedly to enjoy the delightful sounds April could coax out of any piano. The only luxury they had been able to bring to the cottage from the sale of their father's property had been the pianoforte, because it belonged to April and their mother had flatly refused to allow her to sell it to pay Sir Charles's debts. During those dreary years in the village, music had been Lady Wendover's only pleasure, and it would not be extravagant to say it had been her daughter's salvation when troubles pressed heavily upon her. Since they had been residing in Hanover Square their days had been filled to overflowing with activity; time to devote to music had been severely curtailed. Despite her general malaise and worry about Adam tonight, April felt a sense of peace and well-being steal over her as she began to play softly. In a few minutes she had forgotten the presence of others in the room as she gave herself over to the wholly satisfying pursuit of beauty. She never bethought herself to ask the others' preferences, and Diana and the earl were content to listen to the works she selected. There was almost no interaction among them until the tea tray was brought in. When April rose to join her husband and sister, Adam thanked her quietly for bringing him great pleasure. The implied compliment was more welcome than paragraphs of hyperbole, and she retired shortly thereafter in a glow of contentment that lasted until the door of her bedchamber closed behind her.

The fear and horror that music had set at a distance for a short time crowded in on her again as she made her preparations for bed in a mechanical fashion. It was almost impossible to credit that the very civilized Damien Harding might actually be capable of attempting to do away with his cousin, and if she, who disliked him, had difficulty accepting such a depth of depravity, how could she hope to convince Adam of such an evil intention on the part of one bound so closely to him by ties of blood and long association? The plain answer was that she could not, not without proof, and there was no way to obtain proof. The only truly convincing evidence, she thought bitterly, would be her husband's lifeless corpse. Morton would deny everything, of course. The best she could hope for was to have the cigars analyzed, but she could not persuade herself that Adam would accept her word against Morton's even then. He already thought her an adventuress; there was little reason for him to accept her word of honor. The problem seemed insoluble.

After a night of tossing in her bed with no more than fitful periods of sleep, April arose heavy-eyed and unhappy but determined on her course. The one essential action was to exchange those suspect cigars and have them analyzed. Her duty was clear. If Adam refused to believe her, at least she would have done her best. She refused to dwell on the likelihood of Damien's trying another method when this one failed. Whether her husband believed her or not he would be on his guard. But would she ever know another moment entirely free from fear? That question didn't bear examination.

Purchasing the cigars presented no difficulty. April left Diana browsing in Hookham's Library in the company of the Eddington ladies whom they chanced to meet there while she hastened out and made the purchase. This was accomplished in a matter of minutes, but making the substitution proved to be another matter entirely. Adam was in his study when she and Diana returned from shopping. Though he joined them briefly for tea, he intended returning to do more work before changing. The ladies were dining with Jane Jeffries, since Jason Jeffries and the earl had made plans to go to Cribbs's to see the latest bruiser to capture the public's fancy. April hoped to be able to slip down to the study before the carriage was due to arrive, but Mattie took so long over her dressing that Diana was ready first and came into her sister's room to peacock around for her old nurse's approval. This effectively canceled any early-evening attempt at effecting an exchange.

There was nothing to be done about it — she must possess her soul in patience, April told herself as she accepted her blue velvet cloak from Mattie's hands. But it was imperative that she make the switch tonight. Adam's cough was a trifle better these past two days; he might take it into his head to enjoy a smoke at the boxing match. She would be unable to prevent him from taking some cigars with him on his way out should he desire to do so, but she was resolved these would be the last.

The evening would have been most enjoyable had April been capable of keeping her mind directed at the affairs of the moment. Jane Jeffries was an easy-mannered, companionable woman with few ambitions to cut a dash in society. Being endowed with a sunny nature, she enjoyed herself everywhere she went, but her husband and children filled her world completely. Jonathan and Melissa again came to bid their parent goodnight and deigned to remember "Uncle Adam's ladies." To be sure, Jonathan was unable wholly to conceal his disappointment at not finding the earl among those present, but Missy, free from the shyness that had previously afflicted her, more than made up for her brother's forced politeness by running over to April and demanding to see the pretty pin again. Fortunately April was able to gratify this desire, and there followed a rather one-sided conversation as Missy explained that Nurse said Lady Glenville was Uncle Adam's wife like Mummy was Papa's wife and that Miss Wendover was Uncle Adam's sister like Auntie Rose was Papa's sister.

"Do you have any little girls like me?" she inquired after this informative discourse had been delivered.

It required a prodigious amount of effort on April's part to produce the necessary negative and accept Missy's sincere commiserations on the lack without betraying herself. Looking at the eager little face raised to hers, April had known with sudden painful intensity that she wanted desperately to have a little girl like Missy—or a little boy—it didn't matter which as long as the child was hers.

And Adam's!

The incredible thought took sudden and complete possession of her mind. She sat perfectly still, so stunned by what had just transpired that she could not fully take it in, didn't wish to take it in.

"April," Diana was saying, "Missy wishes to know if you would like to have a little girl."

The smooth silvery head nodded to the curly golden one. "Yes, Missy, I think it would be lovely to have a little girl just like you or a big boy like Jonathan."

Mrs. Jeffries laughed. "And now while my awkward infant is preening herself on her importance in the scheme of things, I think we shall dispatch her to her bed and go on in to dinner."

April and Diana were home by eleven-thirty, but the day would not be over for April until she had accomplished her self-imposed task. There was no call to arouse Mattie's suspicions by seeming desirous of curtailing her evening routine. Morton, whose pantry was near the study, never went to bed until Adam came home. Since she could not chance discovery by the butler, it was going to be necessary to wait until the whole household was asleep, which could

mean hours of tedium and anxiety. There was no question
that her resolution might fail, but she must guard against
falling asleep, especially after a nearly sleepless night
yesterday.

To this end, once Mattie had retired, she searched
through a small pile of books in a drawer and finally
emerged with a tattered copy of *The Castle of Otranto*,
which she had read when she was Diana's age. Comfortably
settled in the new velvet *bergère*, she was away in the land of
Otranto with the fair, doomed Matilda when she was alerted
by muted sounds from the adjoining room. Her eyes flicked
to the French ormulu mantel clock. One o'clock and Adam
was preparing for bed. She would give him an hour to fall
soundly asleep, even though there was little danger that a
quick careful trip downstairs would disturb him. She
resumed her reading, but now the story failed to grip her
completely, and her eyes kept wandering to the hands of the
clock, which had slowed to a crawl. All sounds from the next
room had long since ceased and she was growing a bit
chilled even with her legs securely wrapped in a woolen
shawl.

Throwing off this covering, April jumped to her feet and
headed purposefully for the drawer in the bedside table
where she had placed the cigars bought earlier today. Only
today! Weeks seemed to have passed since she had embarked
on this undertaking. Gripping the box in her left hand, she
opened the hall door with infinite care and went back for
the lamp burning on the rosewood table beside the velvet
chair. As she picked it up and headed again for the door,
the box containing the cigars caught the edge of the book on
the table, knocking it off. Had the book simply landed on
the rug, the noise would have been minimal, but it glanced
sharply off the pedestal foot of the table with a crack that
froze April in her tracks. She stood there immobile for
countless seconds while the lamp flickered in her shaking
hand and her heartbeats magnified alarmingly. There had
been one creaking sound from the other room, followed by a
reassuring silence, and eventually life and the ability to

move flowed back into her limbs. Swiftly now she went through the door and along the corridor toward the main stairs.

The light from the lamp was adequate to illuminate her path, but she was unprepared for the unfamiliarity of her surroundings under this condition, and after one nervous glance around at the shadowy shapes that were not immediately recognizable, she returned her eyes to the path ahead of her and kept them so directed. Her bare feet padded steadily down the wooden stair treads but faltered at first when they struck the cold tiles in the main hall. She increased her speed, anxious to attain the comfort of the thick turkey carpet that covered the floor of the study.

Unfortunately the door to this room was firmly closed, necessitating a careful repositioning of the cigar box under her right arm to free her left hand for the task of opening it. This was accomplished with scarcely any sound, and she slipped into the room, leaving the door slightly ajar behind her. It was a matter of a few seconds to deposit the lamp on the desk and remove the cigars remaining in the box. No doubt it was an excessive precaution, but she counted these carefully before taking an equal number from her own box. As she arranged them in the empty container she was vaguely conscious of the flickering light glancing off the gold inkwell reposing on the desk top and picking out the gold lettering on the spines of books on the shelves behind the desk. In a compulsive gesture she counted the cigars once more before replacing the top to the container.

Suddenly there was a prickling sensation in her spine that radiated rapidly to all parts of her body, arresting the hand that was reaching for the lamp. A dreadful coldness made her shudder, and it was agony to turn her head, but turn her head she must. Reluctantly, her heart pounding frantically in her throat, she peered into the deeper shadows and thought she discerned a figure standing silent and motionless just inside the door.

For a painful eternity neither figure moved a muscle. The silence was so complete April had the queer notion that she could detect their two separate breathing rhythms, hers shallow and irregular, his harsh and deeper. When she could stand it no longer she opened her lips and managed to produce a faltering whisper.

"Adam?"

The figure at the door, as though released from a spell, removed his hands from the pockets of a dressing gown and moved forward.

"So it was you," said her husband.

Chapter Eleven

The earl continued to walk slowly toward the woman whose hand retreated from the lamp and fell at her side as she watched his approach with strained concentration.

"So it was you who tried to poison me," he repeated, sounding as if each syllable were jerked out of him.

"You *knew* about the cigars?" whispered April in agonized unbelief. "Then how could you allow—"

"No, I didn't know until yesterday, though I had begun to suspect it was a case of poison. What happened—did your nerve fail you at the last moment, or did you suffer a belated attack of conscience?"

The bitter sarcasm of his words and the icy sternness of his expression, made malevolent by the wavering shadows, struck fear into the marrow of his wife's bones, but still she could not credit her ears. "You cannot believe that I did this terrible thing!" she protested strongly.

"Who else then? Wasn't it enough of a revenge to force me into marriage? Did you feel you could not sufficiently avenge your father's and brother's deaths except by achieving mine? Why did you not go through with it, or are these cigars even more lethal than the others? Perhaps they are intended to finish the job?"

Her head came up proudly. "I bought these cigars today. I meant to have the others analyzed—I knew you wouldn't believe me if I told you I suspected that you were being poisoned, so I meant to get at least that much proof before confronting you with my suspicions."

These words produced a vibrating silence that lasted so long April thought her nerves would snap.

"And whom did you intend to accuse?"

It had come, the moment she had dreaded, and under circumstances more horrible than she had ever imagined. She must convince him that she spoke the truth! Summoning up all her dignity, she forced herself to speak in reasoned tones. "The morning of the Jeffrieses' musicale I saw Morton speaking with someone at the front door. He was disconcerted at my discovering him and said it was a case of someone coming to the wrong house. I suspected that he was concealing something behind his back, and when he passed on down the hall after I had gone into the morning room, I followed him in here. He had left the door pulled to but not shut. By pushing it open a trifle I could see that he was exchanging the cigars Diana had bought you for others. It seemed strange behavior, but I assumed you hadn't liked the cigars and did not want to hurt Diana's feelings. I didn't assign much importance to Morton's lie about the person at the door until much later, after I had begun to suspect it must be the cigars that were making you ill. Last night when you confirmed that you hadn't ordered a switch, I knew I was right." Here she paused fearfully and swallowed dryly. Adam's unbelieving expression had not altered during her recital, and it was supremely difficult to say what must alienate him further, but it had to be done. Her voice shook slightly as she continued, "I had caught a quick glimpse of the man at the door that morning, just his hat and the back of his head, but he had blond hair. It was Damien!"

She rushed on, aware of his sharply indrawn breath, aware of his mounting fury but committed now. "It *was*, I tell you! I hadn't been in this house twenty-four hours before I realized that Morton hates you. Sometimes he gets such a look on his face when watching you that it frightens me, and I saw the same look of utter rage on Damien Harding's face when you announced that I was your wife. How could it be personal? He didn't know me—it was the fact of my existence he hated, because I might produce an heir. You said he is always in debt, forever outrunning the constable. If Freddy were to inherit your wealth, no doubt he would take care of his brother's debts." At his impatient movement of one hand she let out a sobbing breath but still persisted, "I can see you do not believe me—I was afraid of this—but it is true! He tried it once before and failed in that shooting accident, and he has just tried again! Can't you see—"

"Enough!" thundered the earl. Though he had not closed the distance between them physically, April felt menaced by his barely controlled anger, and she shrank back against the desk.

"I have never heard such a farrago of lies in all my life! It wasn't bad enough that you should use the medium of an innocent girl's gift to achieve your evil design, but to choose one who has been like a brother to me all my life upon whom to foist your guilt is beyond anything! Damien knew nothing about those cigars! No one knew about them but you—*and Freddy!*"

"And *Morton!*" flashed April defiantly. "Do not forget Morton. He saw them and told Damien about them. Why should *I* wish you dead? I achieved my object when you married me!"

"Perhaps you'd prefer to be a rich widow instead of a nominal wife to a man you've hated these nine years. Do you think I've been blind to the attachment growing between you and Freddy? With one husband conveniently disposed of you could marry his heir and never even have to change the name on your calling cards or bother about decorating another house!"

"You're mad! Completely mad!"

April regretted the words the second they left her lips, and she wrenched away from the desk which had been taking her sagging weight in a blind attempt to escape from the threat of violence that had been swelling like a balloon in the atmosphere surrounding them. She had taken only one step when strong fingers biting into her arm arrested her flight. Adam's other hand seized her free arm, and he dragged her shrinking form so close she could feel his breath in her hair.

"Mad, am I? The real madness would be to believe this faradiddle you've concocted. Why light on Damien if you must have a scapegoat? Why not Freddy? As my heir, he stands to profit much more substantially than Damien by my death. And his hair is also blond. Why must this mythical man at the door be Damien if all you saw was the back of his head? Why could it not just as well have been Freddy?"

She was silent for a split second of paralyzing doubt, then the rough shake he administered loosened her tongue.

"Freddy is incapable of such an act," she said with quiet conviction.

The sneer in Adam's voice was cruelly evident. "Freddy is incapable of *any* act. He's even incapable of getting on with his life. Ever since his fiancée died of pneumonia six years ago he's been trying to drink himself into the grave, and one of these days he'll succeed. But you would know all about the tragic story, would you not, the two of you are so close. Have you promised to make it up to him after you are his wife?"

"Adam," she pleaded desperately, "don't say any more in this vein. You know it isn't true. This has all been a great shock to you, but you will see things more clearly in the morning. Let it rest until then."

Her propitiating words served no other purpose than to increase the heat of his simmering anger to a full boil. "Let *what* rest? The trifling question of who is trying to kill me, the cousin I have known all my life or the wife who isn't a wife, the woman who has assured me on more than one occasion that I am guilty of the deaths of her relatives, the woman who sought my name and fortune as her due but expected to give nothing in return? Am I to let this rest while you try again? You may succeed yet if you are clever enough and persistent enough, but you will never go to Freddy unsullied. If I'm to be saddled with a murdering bitch for a wife, at least let her *be* my wife!"

As he spoke, Adam released one of her arms to enable himself to take up the lamp, but as he started to drag her bodily toward the door, the meaning of his words belatedly penetrated April's brain, and she was galvanized by a more intense terror than any that she had yet experienced.

"*No!*" she screamed, and tried to break away. She wrenched her arm free from his grasp and sprang instinctively toward the door, her soft draperies floating in the breeze thus created. Her action in its unexpected vigor nearly succeeded. The earl managed to regain possession of one wrist before she reached the entrance, but he was compelled to replace the lamp on the table. Her nails were digging into his fingers in a furious attempt to loosen his grip; one hand was not going to be adequate to the task of preventing her escape.

The ensuing struggle took place in semidarkness in an atmosphere of menacing silence on the man's part that was later to form the most frightening aspect of the recurring nightmares that haunted April's sleep for weeks. He was deaf to all her pleading, unmoved by her cries, and finally, untouched by her pain. His actions were never those of a thwarted lover; not once did he try to woo her with kisses or seduce her ultimate acquiescence with caresses. Inexperienced though she was of a man's passions, there was never any doubt in April's fear-maddened intellect that his intention was purely and aggressively punitive. Once he had succeeded in getting both her hands imprisoned behind her in one of his, and not before suffering several deep scratches on his own wrists, he twisted her down onto the rug, more or less on her back, with her arms beneath her. He paid no attention to her writhing attempts to free her arms or the harmless and ineffectual thrashing of her legs as he efficiently swept aside an excess of fabric in her bridal-night regalia. April's panic was augmented to near frenzy by the fact that he never glanced at her face and never responded with so much as one syllable to any of the pleas she gasped out. He proceeded in the same grim silence to force his eventual way between her tightly gripped legs while controlling her arms with bone-crushing pressure. It was not until days later when her shocked brain could bear to examine the events leading up to the final act of violation that April realized that she had contributed immeasurably to her own pain and suffering by the strength of her instinctive resistance. She had fought him fiercely and mindlessly until the very end, even sinking her teeth into his shoulder when his weight descended on her, giving no quarter and thereby securing no amelioration of the inevitable tearing agony of such a violent possession.

When he finally withdrew and removed his smothering weight from her quivering body, she was in no state to appreciate her release. The intolerable weight was gone, but the pain remained, and her wild sobbing continued unabated. She was unaware that he had pulled down her nightclothes to cover her limbs as he got first to his knees and then to his feet. Nor did she hear the clink of glass as he found a bottle and glass and poured himself a generous measure of brandy.

His back remained to her as he drank the brandy down in two gulps, but, though he might not be forced to look upon his victim, he could not prevent the keening of her low, continuous sobbing from assailing his ears. After a moment or two he said over his shoulder, "Would you like some brandy?"

There was absolutely no diminution in the rhythm or volume of the weeping, and he turned reluctantly. Except that she had drawn her legs up at the knees and curled her body slightly into itself with her hands over her face, she was as he had left her. He approached with the glass and repeated the offer with the same lack of result. Growing anxious, he knelt beside her and proffered the glass more insistently. The only reaction was an accentuation of that protective posture.

"Come, you cannot remain here all night." He set the glass down on the desk and returned to the huddled figure, intent on helping her to rise. At this tentative touch on her shoulder she shied violently away, and the sobbing intensified.

"April, this has to stop! You'll make yourself ill if you continue."

At this point he scarcely expected his words to have any effect, nor did they. Leaping to his feet, he seized one of the candelabra on a side table and lighted the candles at the lamp's flame. He walked rapidly out of the room, shielding the flames, and headed for the stairs, where he deposited the candelabrum on the landing. He moved back to the study, feeling his way along the wall. Another light was going to be needed if he was to accomplish his end without chancing an accident in the dark that would bring the whole household down upon them. Consequently he lighted another candelabrum and placed it on the floor midway down the hall.

When he returned for April, he noted that the tempo of the abandoned weeping had subsided, at least he hoped it had. He picked her up from the floor, not knowing whether to be grateful or alarmed at her lack of resistance, and proceeded to carry her up the stairs to her room. Her hair streamed across her wet face, from which every vestige of color had drained. Her eyes were closed and her dark lashes rested on her cheeks in wet clumps. Her breathing shook her body periodically. She was slightly built, but in his debilitated physical condition even her light weight proved to be an enormous strain by the time he reached her bedchamber door, and his task was not aided by the stygian darkness that prevailed beyond the top of the stairs. By the time he reached the door, which was, thankfully, not latched, his breath was coming in gasps and his arms felt as though they were being pulled out of their sockets. He lowered her onto the bed and sagged down onto it himself for a few minutes until he could recover his breathing and control the spastic twitching in his limbs.

April lay quietly now, seemingly insensible of his presence, and Adam admitted a very real concern. He felt like death himself, but this girl—his wife, he reminded himself bitterly—was near to complete collapse, and he feared to leave her alone. Dismissing personal considerations, he rolled off the inviting surface of the wide bed with a groan and gazed down at the still form sprawled diagonally across the bed. There was not enough moonlight coming in through the blinds to make out any details of her appearance, but pushed by an instinct of urgency, he looked around for candles and flint and succeeded in kindling a light.

April still hadn't moved from her former position, but when he brought the light closer he saw with relief that her eyes were open. She closed them at sight of him and flung a hand across her face for good measure. He abandoned the idea of taking her pulse, knowing his touch would agitate her.

"April, are you all right? Shall I bring Mattie to you?"

Her eyes remained covered, but she answered him in a low voice that he strained nearer to hear. "Don't bring Mattie — just go away."

"Are you sure?"

"Yes!" Just go *away!"*

This time her voice was stronger, and, after one last assessing look at the crumpled, swollen-faced, and disheveled figure of his generally exquisite wife, he blew out the candle and went into the hall with no further words.

He retrieved both candelabra on his way back to the study and replaced them on their table, drank the brandy April had spurned, poured himself another glass, and drank that off too. As his eyes fell on the box of cigars his wife claimed to have bought that day, his mouth tightened unpleasantly, but he gathered it and the lamp up and, abandoning the empty glass where he had set it down, removed himself from the room and made his way back to his own bedchamber.

A glance over at the open door leading to his wife's room told him that she hadn't moved since he had left her. Never would she have allowed it to remain open had she been aware of the circumstance. There was still a vague worry that she might become ill during the night after the hysterical collapse he had witnessed, and he had no intention of closing the door. He listened intently for a moment, and then, reassured by the silence, dragged over to his bed and eased his weary body onto its welcoming surface. There wasn't much point in getting right into it; his chances for achieving a restful oblivion for what was left of the night had vanished with his first look at April after he had raped her. He examined the word gingerly and found, whether attributable to the numbing effects of the brandy he had drunk or a deplorable lack of conscience, that he had as yet no real feeling about committing an act he would have had no hesitation in condemning in anyone else. Had anyone ever told him he would be as capable as the next man of such disgusting behavior he would have demanded an apology. In the last hour he had learned something about himself that gave him no cause for satisfaction. Before tonight he would have denied on the rack that any woman could arouse him to a degree of anger that could produce such bestial retaliation. What was there about the Wendover family that they should all have such power to destroy his life? He had never wished to feel anything for or against April Wendover. He had been determined to keep his emotions inviolate when she had invaded his life, and look where he had come in less than a month!

His fingers traced and retraced the carving on the bedpost behind him. He knew more about the shapes and designs on this post even in the dark than he had learned about April since she had been living in his house. How could a cool civilized woman who looked so delicate and innocuous plot a murder? And how could this same delicate creature fight him with the single-minded intensity, if not the strength, of a jungle cat as she had done tonight?

He groaned and rolled over on his side, but the thought could not be suppressed. Would-be murderess or not, how could he, Adam Harding, alleged gentleman, with all deliberation have inflicted such humiliating and painful punishment on this same delicate creature? An hour later he still couldn't answer his own questions.

A small rustle from the next room brought his thoughts

forward. It was really too chilly at this hour near dawn to remain on top of the covers, especially for someone clad as lightly as April. He slid off the bed and crossed to the doorway. He recalled promising in all good faith that he would not cross the threshold unbidden, and a wry grimace twisted his mouth at the unlikelihood of ever receiving an invitation to enter this room, but she should not be allowed to grow chilled in her present state. Slowly, almost against his will, he approached the bed. She was still lying on the diagonal on top of the coverlet, but she had curled up again in that oddly protective posture, and she looked so small and so young that the whole situation struck him suddenly as impossible. He shook his head unbelievingly. None of it could have happened!

He bent closer and stiffened for a second at sight of the dark stains on her frothy, light-colored dressing gown. A muscle twitched in his cheek, and he averted his eyes as he gently lifted her to pull the bedclothes out from under her and replaced them, tucking them closely around the softly breathing girl. Before straightening his back he yielded to one last impulse and lightly brushed strands of soft hair back from her face. After another long look at the sleeping girl he went back to his own room, and this time he closed the door behind him with deliberation.

Chapter Twelve

The next few days were the worst of April's life. She had grieved for her father and Basil and the loss of her own future; her mother's death had revived all this feeling plus an added dimension of loneliness; but the period following the rape was characterized by a nightmarish quality of undifferentiated anguish.

She awoke slowly to bright sunshine accompanied almost instantaneously by a sense of hovering calamity. The sun streamed in the large window, causing tiny dust motes to dance in its path. As April lay watching them, small busy sounds impinged on her consciousness—Mattie selecting her clothes for the day. She changed positions in the bed and drew in a gasping breath as her wounded body protested. With the pain came memory rolling over her with relentless pressure. Her head fell back onto the pillow, and sweat broke out all over her body. She gripped her lower lip with her teeth to suppress a groan.

"So, you're awake at last? Will you be wanting the ivory wool carriage dress for the morning? It's easy enough to get in and out of for fittings."

The eyes of the woman on the bed flew open and focused for an instant on the uncompromisingly honest face of her oldest friend before long lashes swept down in defense against the shrewdness encountered in Mattie's snapping black eyes.

First things first. She swallowed hard and produced a weak voice. "Don't bother getting anything ready, Mattie. I

. . . I don't feel quite up to shopping this morning. I think I'll sleep awhile longer. Please convey my regrets to Diana."

"Are you sickening for something?"

April averted her eyes from the concern on Mattie's face as she bustled over to examine her former nursling more thoroughly. She spoke quick words of reassurance. "No, no, but I didn't sleep well last night. I shall be quite myself presently." The untruthfulness of this intended reassurance struck her completely dumb.

"Why are you wearing a dressing gown in bed?"

Blankly April stared down at one shoulder encased in light-blue silk. "I . . . I must have been cold. Mattie, you take Diana shopping this morning," she urged, anxious to fix the woman's attention elsewhere. Mindful of the concerned appraisal being accorded her, she yawned ostentatiously, snuggled deeper under the covers, and determinedly closed her eyes.

Mattie's hesitation was palpable. Her instinct told her she should remain with her mistress, but Miss April was not a child and she clearly wished to be relieved of her maid's presence. After a long moment while the figure on the bed listened with all her senses, Mattie rustled over to the hall door and said shortly, "I'll have a tray sent up in an hour."

April's faint expression of gratitude was more for the promise of privacy than for a breakfast tray, which held no appeal at all.

At last the closing of the door released her from the necessity of pretending she was suffering from nothing more than a lack of sleep. For a bit longer she lay still, postponing the time of assessment. The bed was comfortable and protective and quite warm. She had been so cold.

The dark lashes swept up. How had she come to be *in* the bed? A frown of concentration wrinkled her brow. Adam had carried her upstairs and put her on the bed, but then he had gone away. Then how—? She shook her head once, aware as she did so of an ache behind her eyes. What did it matter how she had gotten here? What did anything matter any longer?

Experimentally she moved her legs, sat up, and swung them over the side of the bed. A hiss of pain escaped her as she took her first step, and she clenched her teeth against it. Her hand went out to the bedpost to steady herself, and her eyes winged to the blue marks on her wrist. Her mouth set grimly as she noted the matching bruises on her other wrist, but after one look, she dropped her arms to her side and headed for the mirror to assess the damages.

She could walk unaided, but she felt like a rag doll that had been torn in two by a child who had grabbed a leg in each hand and gleefully ripped away. There was a beading of perspiration on her upper lip by the time she reached the mirror. At first she was relieved to find she had changed so little outwardly; the same pale face stared back at her from under tangled lank hair. After the first assessment, however, she turned away from her image and tears sprang to her eyes. She was afraid to look further, afraid the degradation she had undergone might have left a visible mark for the world to see and judge.

April was trembling and sweating, standing with down-bent head, unable for the moment to command mind or body to decision or action. A tear ran down the side of her nose, and she flicked it away with an angry jabbing finger. Enough of that! She had wept a lifetime's allotment of useless tears last night. She wanted a bath; she must have a bath! Her head came up decisively, then her eagerness receded as quickly as it had arisen. It would be necessary to wait until Mattie had gone out with Diana. She couldn't face Mattie yet.

Suddenly the proximity of her bed seemed like heaven's gate to April. She stumbled toward it and burrowed into it, closing her eyes and willing her jangling nerves to quieten. In a while she slept.

The arrival of a maid with a breakfast tray woke April from her nap. Though she avoided the toast and eggs, the coffee was welcome and kept her from fretting over the necessary delay in securing the hot water for a bath. In the meantime she wrenched off the blue dressing gown and matching night rail and changed to a heavy robe of lavender velvet, which she tied tightly about her waist. After one dry-eyed look at the evidence of her ravaged virginity she consigned the stained garments to the fireplace, watching with bottom lip firmly gripped in her teeth until the loathsome items had burned beyond any recognition. Thus the woman who had squeezed every penny until it squeaked for nine difficult years!

Still dry-eyed, she climbed into the tub when it was ready. The hot water was marvelously soothing to her aching muscles, and she lay back unmoving and almost unthinking until the cooling temperature forced her into action. By the time she had washed her hair and toweled it dry before the fire, April was feeling much more herself, enough at any rate to have overcome her first quavery desire to seek comfort from Mattie or Diana by revealing the whole sorry chapter of events. She knew as she dressed in the prettiest of her new morning gowns, a long-sleeved, softly tucked cotton in pale green that flattered her coloring, that she could never oppress the two people in the world who loved her with the burden of such knowledge.

As she brushed her drying hair in front of the mirror she peered at her sober reflection with disinterested curiosity. Who would have thought that a woman could undergo a violent, life-changing experience accompanied by a surcharge of all the vilest emotions and emerge looking substantially the same except for a lack of natural color? She remedied this lack with a delicate application of the contents of the rouge pot on lips and cheeks and studied the results. She had been wrong in thinking her outward appearance unchanged. Her eyes were smoky dark and dull-looking, and the rouge only accented the shadows beneath them. Annoyed, she wiped it off and flung down the hairbrush after a check of the mantel clock.

Almost noon. Diana and Mattie should be back shortly. Lunch was generally served at twelve-thirty, and she found herself listening for their arrival as she wandered around the large room, her feet sinking into the silver-gray carpet. The apartment had taken on a different character with the addition of carpet and light-blue hangings and bed covering. The ceiling too was painted blue, with the delicate plaster designs picked out in a fresh white. The walls were striped in silver and blue, and until today she had thought the effect light and charming. At the moment it resembled nothing so much as a prison. Perhaps she would go to the morning room and look over the early post—anything to postpone the moment when she must admit her husband into her thoughts.

Glad to have something positive to do, April tucked a lace-edge handkerchief into her pocket and set off for the morning room. She met the footman in the hall and returned his quiet greeting pleasantly but was unable to meet his eyes. It was all she could do not to break into a run and race for the privacy of her sanctuary. It was necessary to monitor her pace the entire distance, and she shut the door behind her in trembling relief. What was the matter with her? Jacob knew nothing; not another soul in the world would ever learn what had happened between the earl and herself last night. She must stop acting as if she had a communicable disease! She was guilty of no crime except the initial one of marrying Adam against his will.

After a few minutes of railing against her own cowardice, April had calmed down enough to seat herself at her charming painted desk, where she fixed her attention on the everyday chore of going through her mail. As usual, the major part of her post consisted of invitations and dressmakers' bills. She caught herself up short making a little moue of distaste. Why the sudden dissatisfaction? Was it not precisely for this reason that she had come to London? Firmly cutting off all tendency to indulge in tardy regrets, she embarked on the task of replying to the various hostesses seeking the pleasure of their company and was thus employed when Diana bounced into the room.

"Here you are, lazybones!" teased the girl, glowing with good looks and good spirits. "Can't you stand the pace at your advanced age?"

April was spared the necessity of concocting a suitable reply by Mattie, who appeared in the doorway behind Diana. "Your sister doesn't look a day older than you do, Miss Impudence, she just has more sense, that's all."

April smiled affectionately at her old nurse for her blind championship and made an easy response to Diana, who wrinkled her nose at Mattie before unwrapping a parcel she wished to show her sister.

Aware that she was being subjected to prolonged scrutiny by the person who knew her best in the world, the Countess of Glenville applied herself to the chore of giving a convincing performance as a carefree young society matron. She must have succeeded, for Mattie's brow cleared presently and she bustled off to check on the maids, reminding the sisters that lunch would soon be served.

One hurdle overcome, thought April as she headed upstairs with Diana and the results of the morning's buying spree. She walked a bit stiffly, conscious of various aches in her body but hopeful that Diana's overriding interest in her new life would blind her to any slight changes in her sister. Mattie was much more observant, however, and she was at a loss how to conceal the vivid bruises Adam's fingers had made, not only on her wrists but on the soft flesh of her upper arms also. The best she could come up with was to plan to be dressed before Mattie came to her room for the next few days and to continue to wear long-sleeved garments exclusively.

The rest of the day passed quietly. One of Diana's admirers took her driving in the Park at the fashionable hour, and April was grateful for the solitude this won for her. Her nerves had been tightening up as the hour for tea drew near, and she found herself straining to listen for sounds in the hall that might herald her husband's arrival, though she ventured to hope he would have the grace to absent himself today. When, during the late afternoon, Morton delivered a message that the earl would not be in to dinner, she relaxed perceptibly and was able to cast her mind forward to the necessity of dressing before Mattie arrived to assist her.

She accomplished it, just barely, ignoring Mattie's surprised glance at the clock as she came into the room in time to see her mistress struggling with buttons down the back of her gown.

"Why the rush?" inquired that lady with raised eyebrows.

"I . . . I was not sure if I would care for this gown and so decided to try it first," April improvised, pretending to look through her jewel box as Mattie took over the buttoning operation.

The dangerous moment passed, the long dinner hour wound to its conclusion, the uneventful evening with only her sister's undemanding company eventually ended, and April successfully diverted Mattie's attention to something in the wardrobe while she slipped out of her gown and into her nightclothes. The blackest day she had ever known had been lived through, and she climbed wearily into bed with a faint sense of satisfaction lightening the depression in which she was becalmed, only to awake hours later from the first of the nightmares. The content of the dream was too elusive to be grasped and explored; the details faded the instant she tried to fix them in her mind, leaving only the suffocating sense of dread to contend with and overcome before sleep was again possible.

The essentials of the pattern repeated themselves during the days that followed, though not again did April try to excuse herself from her social commitments. To the contrary, indeed. She plunged into activity in a feverish desire to tire herself so greatly that she could overcome the dread of falling asleep at night. In this quest she was successful as far as achieving the desired fatigue to enable her to drop off to sleep, but the dreamless oblivion she sought continued to elude her efforts. Each night she came tremblingly awake, full of half-remembered tears, sentenced to hours of desperate wakefulness before her restless mind permitted her tired body the necessary repose.

Sometimes she was able to recapture the calm necessary for sleep by lying very quietly and willing her tense limbs to a state of relaxation. Sometimes she gave up the effort and sat up reading till nearly dawn. The worst times were those nights when she could not settle to a book and indulged in a compulsive pacing of the floor until sheer exhaustion claimed her. On these nights she gave thanks for the warmth and comfort of the silvery carpet under her feet, and especially for its sound-deadening properties.

April was frequently aware of the hour of Adam's homecoming. He did not allow his valet to put him to bed, so any sounds issuing from the next room during the night were an indication that the earl had returned. The first time she heard his arrival was the night after the assault, and she froze in her tracks, terror flooding back over her in a cold tide while her eyes strained for any faint sounds that might indicate an approach to the door. Time lost all meaning as she remained standing, poised for instant flight but unsure whether her limbs would obey her brain's command. The idea of returning to her bed and feigning sleep occurred to her, but still she stood motionless while a chill that had nothing to do with the room's temperature crept over her body. It was an effort to remove her eyes from the door long enough to check the time. The light from her bedside candle was barely adequate to reach the mantelpiece, but she thought the clock read two-thirty. Her uncertainty and fear were mercifully brief. In a matter of five minutes all sound from the other room faded into the consuming silence.

On shaky legs April sped to her bed and achieved the security of its solid surface. She huddled under the covers with a sense of calamity averted and tried to compose herself for sleep.

The first meeting between husband and wife did not take place until the third day after the violent scene in the study. They had little to say to one another and that little confined to labored exchange of commonplaces, but Diana's presence served to dispel some of the natural constraint under which each could be judged to be functioning. Theirs was the manner of slight acquaintances striving to perform a mildly distasteful social duty with the grace expected of them. There was only one moment when either let slip the mask of well-bred formality. When dinner was announced, the earl extended his hand in an automatic gesture to escort his wife into the dining room, only to draw it back as she flinched away from him involuntarily. For an instant both hastily averted faces displayed the same rise in color before April placed none too steady fingers on her husband's rigid arm and allowed herself to be led into dinner. As he seated her the colorful Paisley shawl draped artistically across her arms slipped momentarily, revealing fading purple marks on her upper arm beneath the short puffed sleeve of her gown. April, who was studiously examining the table appointments, missed the twitching of a muscle in Adam's cheek as he moved away to his own place at the head of the table.

Diana, appearing to notice nothing amiss, took up the slack in the conversation. The ladies were being escorted to a private ball that evening by Freddy Harding, so the embarrassment was not prolonged beyond dinner. As the time passed, however, even the young girl's happy preoccupation with the excitements of the world opening up to her was pierced eventually by the continuing pall cast over the occasional meetings of husband and wife. Adam rarely acted as escort to the parties, routs, and dances that occupied the time of a new debutante, but April's presence was required except on the rare occasions when Diana attended an affair under the chaperonage of another matron.

About a week after the incident in the study, there was a ball given for the daughter of one of Adam's colleagues to which he did escort his ladies. It was a glittering affair lasting far into the night. By now Diana had acquired quite a train of admirers, and she enjoyed her customary popularity, taking her pick of the eligible dancing partners throughout the evening. At one point while partnering her brother-in-law she glanced over to a group of dowagers against the wall and pointed out that his wife wasn't dancing. Adam made no comment, but when the dance ended he delivered the girl to her sister, excusing himself immediately with no conversation expended on April. Diana stared after him in surprise, which was converted to indignation a moment later as the earl deftly cut a stunning redhead out of a crowd and proceeded to conduct an elegant flirtation with her on a settee directly opposite his wife's position.

"Well, of all the *uncivil*—"

"Shush, dearest!" begged April, smiling in sympathy with Diana's indignation but maneuvering around so she blocked her sister's view of this tableau. The smile widened but didn't reach her eyes. "Did you by any chance suggest to Adam that I might require a dancing partner?"

"Yes, I did!" sputtered Diana.

April chuckled and cut in calmly before Diana could elaborate on the insult, "Well, that should teach you a valuable lesson, my love. Gentlemen don't take kindly to feminine attempts at directing their conduct. Now smile— here comes your next partner, if I am not mistaken."

Diana whirled off on the arm of the gentleman in question, and April herself was solicited to dance at that moment. When in due course her partner waltzed her past the spot where Adam was still being entertained by the vivacious red-haired beauty, she was careful to be completely engrossed in her own amusing conversation.

The incident was not allowed to sink into oblivion, however. Diana was decidedly cool toward Adam on the drive home, despite April's attempts to smooth the situation with chatty observations on the party they had just left. She abandoned her unsuccessful efforts to pour oil on troubled waters after the earl bade them a formal goodnight at the foot of the stairs. It was obvious from her expression as they climbed the stairs that the young girl was more troubled than indignant by this time, and April decided it was imperative to air the grievance before relations between Diana and her brother-in-law deteriorated. In the ordinary way the child was no grudge bearer, but she was fiercely protective of her milder-mannered sister when the occasion demanded, and April would not put it beyond her to say something injudicious that would damage the rapport she shared with Adam. This cordial, almost affectionate relationship between her sister and her husband was the only good thing to come out of this marriage, and she dreaded to see it threatened.

As they approached Diana's bedchamber, she studied her sister's face with a discreet sideways glance and, reading the indecision there, made her own decision.

"What's troubling you, dearest?" she invited softly.

For a moment Diana remained still, her fingers tight on the door handle, then she faced her sister with resolution written on her lovely features.

"More to the point, what is troubling you and Adam? Have you quarreled or something?"

"Something of the sort," she admitted with drastic understatement, "but you must not allow any . . . differences between Adam and me to affect you. Believe me, Diana," she added earnestly, "it would distress us both to see you worrying about us, and it is totally unnecessary in any case."

Diana regarded her sister steadily. "Do you love Adam, April?"

"Why I . . . I feel for Adam all those sentiments that are most appropriate to the married state, respect—"

"Please answer one question truthfully, then I promise I'll not pry further," begged Diana, holding up a hand to stop this faltering speech. "Did you and Adam marry for love?"

On the point of delivering an untruthful affirmative for the sake of her sister's youthful illusions, April read the curiously pleading expression in those intensely blue eyes and paused. Was Diana pleading for reassurance or was she begging to be treated as an adult capable of dealing with the reality of the situation?

"No," she confessed quietly, "we did not marry for love."

The tenseness seemed to go out of her sister's shoulders. "Did you marry for my sake?"

April hesitated fractionally. "In a way, but you mustn't feel respon—"

"It's all right, I understand. It's just that I learned something tonight and I was afraid it might wound you, but since you and Adam married for convenience I don't suppose it matters after all."

Apprehension held April's faculties suspended for an instant. Could it be that the true story of the marriage had become one of the *on dits* of the season despite the care they had taken to conceal it? She cleared her throat of hoarseness. "What did you learn?"

"Do you recall the redhead Adam was flirting with for ages tonight?"

April smiled wryly at the likelihood that she might have forgotten the creature but confined her reply to an affirmative nod of her head.

"Her name is Lady Ellis. Sarah Eddington told me Adam wanted to marry her a long time ago, but it was before he inherited his uncle's title and she threw him over for Lord Ellis, who was already a baron. Sarah says people claim he never got over her, and it did look tonight as though he . . . he might still love her." Her voice trailed off, and it was with relief that she heard April's warning that Alice was coming toward them ready to put her mistress to bed.

The sisters bade each other a hasty goodnight, and April continued on down the hall to her own room. So there was another woman, apart from his mother, who had treated Adam badly in the past! There was no reason to question that the vivid Lady Ellis had once been the object of Adam's affections, but that she still retained her former position in those affections, his wife, not being an impressionable seventeen, took leave to doubt. It had been perfectly apparent to her that Adam had indulged in that public flirtation tonight for the sole purpose of punishing his erring wife. In fact, she seriously questioned whether he was capable of loving any woman. Small wonder, though, that he had reacted so strongly against herself on scant evidence! After all, she had already convicted herself of being an unprincipled opportunist in his eyes. With his history she was no longer surprised that it had been such a short jump to believe her also capable of murder. He was well and truly disposed to suspect all women of duplicity!

She sighed prodigiously as she removed her jewelry, having sent Mattie to bed early to nurse a cold. How the fates had conspired against this marriage! And to think that she had, just hours before his cruel attack, begun to wish, under the influence of a winsome child's attentions, that she were in fact his wife! The irony of having one's wishes granted in this world was not lost upon her as she slowly slipped out of her costly gown. She had wished for a husband who would provide her with expensive clothes. Well, she now had the clothes and the husband, and the dream had turned to dust and ashes at his touch. Perhaps the most disturbing element of all was that knowing what she now did about his past dealings with the women he had loved, she could not even hate him wholeheartedly for what he had done to her. If she had been what he thought her she would have merited the treatment he had meted out. Her heart ached for the pity and waste of it all.

Chapter Thirteen

If April was deeply unhappy in the period immediately following the rape, her husband didn't escape scot-free of emotional repercussions himself. Far from having a cleansing action, the release of his retaliative fury left him physically drained, depressed, and rather defiantly determined not to acknowledge any regret even in the privacy of his thoughts.

His first action on appearing in the breakfast room the next morning was to ask Morton outright whether he had substituted other cigars for those Diana had given him. Under his basilisk stare the butler preserved an apparently unthreatened composure. His thin colorless eyebrows rose fractionally.

"Naturally not, my lord, since such a request was not made of me." He cast a professionally assessing eye over the table and turned an expressionless countenance back to his employer. "Is there anything else you require, my lord?"

Adam continued to regard his butler under lowered brows for another moment, then dismissed him with a wave of his hand, staring in frustration at the stooped back disappearing from the room at an unhurried pace. Well, what had he expected, for heaven's sake? That the man would reveal his guilt, even supposing for the sake of argument that he *was* guilty? His clenched jaw grew even more rigid as he denied the existence of any faint hope that April had been telling the truth; after all, her innocence would mean Damien's guilt! He pushed the almost untouched plate away and concentrated on black coffee. *Damn her for a lying jade!* How dare she cast aspersions on one who had been an integral part of his life for as far back as memory reached! Not content with complicating his life in the present with her unwanted presence, she had contaminated his past with her accusations.

The coffee was too bitter for his taste, and he pushed it away too. Nothing tasted right anymore, thanks to those filthy cigars. Well, the one constructive action he could take would be to get them analyzed, not that he was particularly interested to learn what she was trying to kill him with. His face expressing thoughts more bitter than the rejected coffee, the earl took his bad temper and the remnants of his hacking cough off to the Ministry, where he put in an unprofitable day and offended at least two unsuspecting persons who had the temerity to question one of his decisions.

His mood was marginally improved by a brisk canter in the Park late in the afternoon. The imminence of nightfall made this a practical compromise between his desire to gallop off on an endless ride and the necessity to fulfill a dinner engagement with several members of Parliament in less than two hours.

The benefits of fresh air and exercise did not outlast the long dull dinner, however, and it was with minimal enthusiasm that he went on to the Cocoa Tree with his companions. Gambling held little allure for him at any time, and tonight the thought of concentrating on the turn of a card or the numbers that appeared on dice cubes was positively repellent. He bore the tedium in silent but growing restlessness until eleven o'clock, when, casting diplomacy and courtesy alike aside, he took abrupt leave of his party, but not without having to endure a few pointed and puerile comments on the tendency of newly married men to become spoilsports.

Once outside in the air, his restlessness increased as he debated his next move. His own house had no appeal, yet he hesitated to inflict his presence on any of his friends who might be happily engaged at another of the gambling hells in the area. After a few aimless steps he reversed his direction, setting a course for the one person who could always be relied on for uncritical acceptance of his moods.

Molly rose nobly to the occasion. Her lovely face glowed with pleasure when he entered her boudoir, and she exclaimed with relief at the improvement in his appearance as she helped him off with his coat. At her innocent mention of his alleged cold, a shadow darkened the earl's countenance. He shot her a quick questioning look, then dropped into an upholstered chair.

"Tell me what's been going on around here, Molly," he requested, breaking in on her eager flow of chatter about his improved health.

She looked faintly puzzled, but stopped hovering over him after he refused Madeira, brandy, and a cigar, settling herself on the pink chaise to begin a chronicle of the day-to-day events of her quiet life. Her puzzlement grew as she continued with a tale of some beautiful peacock satin that Mr. Norris, the draper, had set aside because he thought it perfect for her coloring. The earl never took his eyes from her face, but she had the oddest impression that nothing she said was reaching him. It was almost as though her words fell one at a time into an invisible chasm somewhere in the three feet of space separating his chair from the daybed. Disturbed, she paused and glanced uncertainly at him. The silence lengthened, then the earl's eyelids flickered.

"Go on," he invited.

"What is it, my lord? What is troubling you?"

"Nothing. Why do you ask?" he evaded, removing his eyes from her face at last. Her glance followed his to the lean-fingered hand that fiddled incessantly with a small china ornament on a nearby table.

"Because you are very unlike yourself tonight and because you have not heard a word I've said to you," she answered daringly.

The earl's laughter sounded forced to her ears, and she

watched him warily as he set down the ornament and rose from his chair to tower over her.

"Is this more like me?" he teased, bending to kiss the side of her neck, exposed by the low-cut bodice of her figured-lace gown. For an instant she was still under his familiar touch, then her body relaxed and her arms reached for him. His went around her, and she made room for him on the chaise.

A few minutes later Molly slowly removed her mouth from under his to protest laughingly, "You are nearly suffocating me, my darling. May I suggest that the bed would be much more comfortable?"

To her surprise there was no immediate rejoinder from the earl. Nor did he resume kissing her. He shifted his weight to ease her breathing, but his own sounded uneven, and his next words, low though they were, rang harshly in her ears.

"It's no use, Molly, I . . . *can't!*"

The handsome brunette froze as the blood seemed to stop beating in her veins. The coals in the fireplace hissed loudly in the silence that succeeded his blunt admission. Then all her loving instincts prompted her to tighten her arms protectively around him. Her voice was calm and reassuring.

"Do not let it worry you, my lord. You have been very ill just lately. This will pass; it means nothing."

Very gently he disentangled himself from her embrace and stood up, raking his fingers through his dark locks. He didn't look at her.

"You don't understand, Molly. Something has happened. I wish I could explain, but—"

"You do not have to explain anything to me," said the steady voice at his back. "And you need not concern yourself about a temporary incapacity, either. Let me pour you some brandy."

He did not protest as she left the chaise and occupied herself at a table against the fireplace wall. Presently she glided over to him, glass in hand, and eased him back into the chair he had abandoned. "Here, you'll like his brandy, you selected it yourself," she said lightly, and resumed her position on the chaise.

The earl eyed her appraisingly over the rim of his glass. It was he who ended the silence a short time later. "You've been good for me, Molly, and I'm grateful, believe me."

"You have nothing to be grateful for," she insisted in low tones. "You've always treated me well, and your generosity is astounding." She closed her lips as he waved away her protests. There was a terrible tingling along her nerves like a warning of creeping death. She had dreaded this moment from the instant he had announced his marriage. She hid her clenched fists in the folds of the black lace gown and waited in quiet hopelessness for the blow to fall.

He looked at her fleetingly, then focused his attention on the liquid in the glass. After a moment when she had nothing further to add, he raised his head and said as though the words were pulled from him individually:

"Last night I raped my wife."

This admission, unlike the former, drew no immediate reaction from the woman on the chaise, and Adam glanced up from the brandy to encounter faint bewilderment in the soft brown eyes. Seeing that he expected a response, Molly said hesitantly, "There can be no question of rape between husband and wife, surely?"

"You do not understand, Molly. I was furious at discovering . . . at something I found out. I wanted to hurt her, I think I almost wanted to kill her. Well, I did hurt her—desperately." His voice, impatient at the beginning of this impetuous speech, lost its force, and his self-disgust was perfectly evident to the woman regarding him with compassion.

"If you forced yourself on her, no doubt in your anger you did cause her some pain, but she is your wife, after all. Perhaps you do owe her an apology, but surely it is unnecessary to castigate yourself to this extent."

"You still don't understand, and why should you," sighed the earl, "when you know nothing of the real situation between April and myself. The marriage had never been consummated." He saw her eyes widen at this but continued without pause. "I had assured her, in fact, that I had no intention of ever touching her, and then last night I lost my head and my self-control and deliberately raped her. She is smallish and slightly built, but she fought me like a tiger right to the end. So it *was* rape," he finished.

Both were silent. Molly had lowered her eyes to hide her reaction to an odd note in his voice that might almost have been pride when he had described his wife and her resistance. The earl took another sip of his brandy and then addressed the down-bent head. "Well, do you still think it wasn't rape? Do you believe a man would ever be justified in doing what I did?"

"I think perhaps it would depend on what *she* had done," she temporized, and added at once as he opened his lips, "I understand that you feel you cannot tell me that." Now she seemed to be searching for the right words to express herself. "It is clear that your wife hurt you very badly." Large brown eyes searched hard gray ones until the latter were veiled by lowered lids. "Are you quite certain she is guilty of . . . whatever it is you said you had learned?"

Again the words seemed to be dragged from the earl. "She denied it, of course, but she was lying."

"I see."

"Dammit, Molly!" he exploded. "She *must* have been lying! Nothing in the world makes any sense if she was telling the truth!"

"Except that if she was telling the truth she had not hurt you." Now it was Molly who had difficulty in enunciating the words that would sound like a defense of her rival. For it had become appallingly clear to her in the course of this extraordinary conversation that the earl had fallen in love with his wife. It was equally clear that he was unaware of his feelings as yet, and she was *not* going to seal her own doom by saying one more word that might reveal this state of affairs to him. Consequently, for the first time in their long association she was more than willing to see her lover leave her presence, though she stared at the door in flat despair when he departed full of brandy and confusion. The happiest period of her life was coming to an inevitable end. Nothing would ever be so satisfactory again, but for Charlotte's sake and for her own she had best start thinking about a future that would not contain her love. And with this sensible resolution taken, she threw herself on the big empty bed and gave way to a storm of weeping for the hopes that had never been fulfilled.

The earl made his way home on foot, whiling away the time in compiling a list of his wife's iniquities. In addition to impinging on his consciousness to a degree he deplored and trying to kill him so she might marry his cousin and enjoy his fortune at the same time, she had now managed to emasculate him. It hadn't been enough to fight him to the point of collapse rather than submit to his possession, she had even succeeded in preventing him from enjoying another woman. Molly's presence in his life these last years had served as a balance to his unwavering pursuit of his political career. He had always enjoyed his relationship with her, and what was even rarer when he considered the so-called "respectable" women he met in society, he *liked* her and admired her essential honesty and simplicity. And now April, with her deceptive softness and her damnable duplicity, had insinuated her image between himself and Molly and rendered him impotent. Lord, how she'd laugh if she knew this!

He reached his bedchamber and the conclusion that he was indulging in ridiculous fantasy at the same time. April had no interest whatever in him as a man. She'd been relieved early in the marriage when he'd intimated that he'd be content to find satisfaction elsewhere, and his behavior on the previous night would have rendered him forever repellent in her eyes.

The restlessness that had driven him earlier in the evening had seeped away, leaving him feeling the effects of a sleepless night and a totally frustrating day. It took no more than five minutes for him to seek the comfort of his bed.

The future looked no less dismal the next day, but at least

he was gradually regaining his normal good health. He made a firm resolution to table his personal problems, and, by determinedly refusing to allot any time to them, he managed to get through the next few days without attracting undue attention to his depressed spirits.

The first meeting with his wife brought the events of that night vividly before his mind's eye once again as he took in every detail of her appearance with an avidity he attempted to conceal behind a precariously maintained air of bland unconcern. His last sight of her, crumpled and disheveled, her slight form lost among incongruous wrinkles of what had seemed to be an acre of filmy material as she slept in an exhausted sprawl across the bed, had intruded into his memory at unoccupied moments ever since. He assured himself that there was nothing personal in his reaction; he would feel the same regret on seeing a beautiful painting slashed or a temple desecrated. One slanting glance reassured him that this particular artwork had been completely restored as April entered the room with her customary graceful glide, a figure of slender elegance in a floating creation of seafoam green. He would have said she was intrinsically untouched by the ugly experience could he have ignored the way her eyes shied away from any contact with his and the instinctive knowledge that her composure was a very fragile edifice supported solely by grim courage.

They circled around each other like boxers in the first round, but he resisted the urge to dwell anew on the incongruity of a murderous soul being contained in that exquisite exterior. It was only when she recoiled from his touch that he had difficulty in controlling an impulse to force her to submit to his possessive handling once again. The sight of the bruises he had inflicted marring her white skin sobered him instantly, however, and he realized how imperative it was that he confine his necessary contacts with April to the bare minimum. If society wished to question the success of the marriage, then society must be allowed its diversion. It was more vital that he retain his control over his own conduct, and he couldn't guarantee this control if he was forced into frequent contact with the woman who despised him enough to connive at his death.

Two long weeks passed in this manner, with Adam spending very little time at home. He indulged in a spate of social activities that served the sole purpose of wearying him sufficiently to allow him to fall asleep at night. For some reason he didn't query, he kept away from Molly during this period also.

Thanks to hours spent riding and driving in the fresh air, he had regained his health and strength, not to mention his appetite. The chemist to whom he sent the cigars reported that they were laced with arsenic. He was furious at the weakness that permitted final confirmation of his suspicions to shake him at all, but at times he could barely keep his hands off April's lovely throat. Merely looking at her caused his temperature and his spleen to rise to an unhealthy degree. Though he avoided looking at her whenever possible, it had not escaped his attention that his wife was not in her best looks of late. She was thinner, and there were dark shadows like bruises under her eyes. The eyes themselves, those clear pools of luminous gray that he had once found so mesmerizing, held an appealing hint of tragedy in their depths. There was no question, the woman was an accomplished actress! Had he not known how impossible was her story he would have been taken in by that air of wounded innocence she projected so convincingly.

He was becoming increasingly irritated by her persistence in presenting what he could only call a haunted appearance, and when Jason Jeffries asked him at a rout party one evening if April had been ill, sending a concerned glance after the slight figure, Adam determined to nip any such rumors in the bud. He had told her that first day that he intended her to cut a dashing figure in society, and he was prepared to enfore his edict if he had to beat those die-away airs out of her personally!

Chapter Fourteen

Spring was making tentative advances into the city when the Earl and Countess Glenville gave a ball in honor of their young sister. The affair was expected to be one of the highlights of the annual round of frenzied activity known as the season. Diana's excitement had been rising with each day that brought the dreamed-of event nearer. Shopping for the perfect gown for the occasion turned into a marathon ordeal, since the younger Miss Wendover's tastes ran to the kind of highly visible, dashing styles that no conscientious guardian could approve for a girl in her first season.

Battle was joined early and continued until April abandoned cajolery and tact in favor of exerting her authority. Deprived of the daring design of her dreams, Diana proved almost impossible to suit, and her sister nearly despaired of finding fabric special enough to awaken her admiration in time to have the gown finished before the date of the ball. They were cutting the margin perilously close when Diana admitted that a length of ivory silk discovered in a little shop off the Oxford Road and woven with a tiny pattern of flowers did not absolutely disgust her. She conceded that it might make up into a tolerably attractive gown if April meant to persist in taking up such a gothic attitude as to insist on her wearing pale uninteresting colors for her formal comeout. When Mélisande suggested that it be fashioned as an overdress to be worn with a slip of palest blush satin discreetly ornamented with embroidered roses at the hem, her reluctant interest was caught. After April agreed to a neckline a whole inch lower than those approved so far and made no objection to the purchase of pearl rosettes to use as fastenings, a mild enthusiasm awoke in her breast and she was even able to participate in the more mundane details of preparing for the ball in a manner which, if it could not be described quite accurately as helpful, was at least amiable.

There was a ballroom on the ground floor at the back of the Hanover Square residence, which was certainly an advantage in planning an affair on a grand scale. That it would require extensive redecoration before appearing to advantage had been obvious from the start, but April, taking Adam at his word, had had no hesitation in setting matters in train almost immediately with scant regard to cost, and by the week of the ball nothing remained to be done but the washing of the countless lusters from the three chandeliers and numerous wall sconces and the final polishing of the handsome parquet floor. The designs on the pilasters and ceiling had been regilded, and the fresh paint smell had departed from the room in good time. The new curtains of seafoam green at the long windows hung perfectly, and dozens of spindly gold-painted chairs had been cushioned in matching fabric. The peeling panels of painted designs spaced around the walls between the pilasters had been replaced with mirrors that would reflect and multiply the shifting sea of colors in the ladies' gowns and jewels. Several banquettes done over in orange-pink velvet formed areas of eye-catching color at intervals. April had decided to use masses of flowers in the pink and orange color range as well as lacy greenery to bring the huge room to life. Though it was too early in the spring to stroll outside, gardeners had been hard at work bringing the neglected grounds into order, and strings of lanterns were to hang from the trees to illuminate the scene for those inside.

Mrs. Donaldson, with Mattie's able assistance, dealt with the caterers, but April, who preferred to have as little contact as possible with Morton, turned the problem of supplying the wines and other liquid refreshments over to her husband with the information that she did not plan to concern herself further in the matter. This represented almost the sum total of conversation between husband and wife for nearly a week, as Adam continued to be more often absent than present at dinner unless they were entertaining. It was, therefore, something of a surprise to find him in the saloon three days before their ball.

His critical eye was upon her as she entered the room and checked for an instant when he rose from a chair near the fireplace. She resumed her pace at once, trying to return his measuring stare with one of her own.

"You look terrible," he said by way of greeting.

"How kind of you to notice," she replied coolly, seating herself with careful attention to the fall of her skirts. "Hasn't today been unseasonably balmy? I do hope it will continue so for our ball."

"It is not my intention to discuss the weather with you. Cancel whatever engagements you have made for the next three days and take to your bed if necessary to repair the ravages of whatever is making you look like a ghost. And eat something for a change. You look as if a puff of wind would blow you away."

April had been unable to control her surprise at this attack, but by the time he had barked out his orders, she had the polite mask back in place.

"Whatever you say," she murmured obediently.

A sound that fell somewhere between a growl and a sigh of exasperation escaped the earl. "And don't be so damned meek—we both know that pose for the fiction it is. I said in the beginning that I had no objection to my wife's being the talk of the town for her style-setting. I have a rooted objection to the talk being caused by purple shadows under your eyes and a haggard air about you."

Diana's fortuitous appearance canceled any further criticisms the earl might have planned to level at his wife, and she was spared a reopening of the subject later by the arrival of the carriage immediately after dinner to take the ladies to Almack's subscription ball.

The earl had been quite correct in one accusation, at least. His wife was not meek. Although his verbal attack had come as a nasty surprise, it had not served to cow her spirits, nor was it allowed to influence her activities over the next few days. She and Diana went about their accustomed routine with no thought to their lord and master's possible disapproval. He would have been pleased to see that one command was being obeyed, however. April's appetite had improved of late, and she was sleeping better. The night-mares had not ceased entirely, but she was able to get back to sleep after a shorter interval of wakefulness these days. She was too occupied with the various details of their up-coming ball to spare much time for personal problems.

Diana's ball gown was completed and much admired by her sister and its creator, who predicted that all the young ladies would be envious of her appearance that night. Mélisande assured Lady Glenville that her own gown was nearing completion and would be ready the next day. April thanked her politely, having long since forgotten about the special design Adam had selected for her to wear at Diana's dance. She was unprepared, therefore, to handle the storm of protest that arose when her sister first cast her eyes on the gray silk creation with its elaborate overall pattern of silver threads. The gown was cut very plainly, relying for its effect on the beauty of the fabric with its shimmer of silver and sparkle of hundreds of crystal beads sewn into the pattern. April's gown, Diana hotly declared with what was no less than the truth, clearly outshone her own and would cast her into the shade at her own ball. She was deaf to her sister's protestations that nothing a matron past her first youth might wear could in any way detract from the combined appeal of youth and beauty. With tears of temper filling her eyes, she accused her sister of trying to spoil the most important night of her life by stealing the limelight. Per-fectly appalled to be thought capable of such an act, April promised to wear a less spectacular dress, smothering any concern over Adam's reaction in the deeper concern that Diana's party should be perfect for the girl. It was no personal sacrifice at all events; she had dozens of gowns now, any one of which would do. In fact, if she were to confess the shaming truth, she was not best pleased to find the shadows under her eyes fading after a couple of restful nights. It would have been soothing to her bruised pride to have been able to deny her heartless husband this small satisfaction. Far from being flattered that he was still determined to have his "murdering bitch" of a wife do him credit in public, she felt reduced to the status of a snuffbox or some such object selected to complement a costume.

Fortunately there was little time to spare for unprofitable musings of like nature. The day of the ball was upon them, and there were the usual last-minute crises to threaten the success of the affair. The florist's helpers dripped water all over the polished floor, thus incurring Morton's wrath, and the caterers delivered the wrong kind of rout cakes, which he summarily returned with a blistering message. The staffs of the caterer and florist clashed head on with the resident servants on several occasions, setting tempers to fray. April's diplomatic skills were worn thin by five o'clock, when Mattie ordered her to her room to rest until it was time to dress. She dropped onto her bed and fell fast asleep until Mattie's hand on her shoulder roused her.

"I'd have let you sleep a bit longer," her tirewoman said with gruff affection, "but I expect you wish to see Diana finish dressing tonight."

"Thank you, Mattie, you're a dear. I do want to make sure Alice doesn't pull her hair back too severely. A *dégagée* style suits her best."

April's own toilette was achieved in record time, barring five minutes spent arguing with Mattie about the silver dress. Her simple hairstyle never wanted arranging as such, and as a peace offering she allowed Mattie to select a gown for her. Her mother's pearls, the one item aside from the little brooch that had not been sold, gleamed around her throat as she gave a quick glance in the mirror to approve Mattie's choice of dress, a pretty lavender satin that tended to imbue her eyes with a hint of that shade. Together they hurried down the hall to bestow their loving approval on the girl they had raised together.

The two women could be pardoned their partiality as they gazed with pride on a radiant Diana, for she was the epitome of youthful appeal and eagerness, her golden prettiness enhanced by the ivory and pink of her gown. Its sleek lines produced the illusion of added height, and the pearl Adam and April had presented to commemorate the occasion added the perfect finishing touch.

Not quite the finishing touch, evidently. When they entered Diana's bedchamber she was attempting to decide which of five posies sent to her would best complement her appearance while poor Alice tried to effect a becoming hairstyle on a head that wouldn't stay still. They had decided against a wreath of flowers in favor of a simple ribbon in the same blush pink threaded artfully through an abundance of golden curls falling from a Grecian knot. Mattie took over the final arrangement of the curls from a rattled Alice, who was almost as excited as her mistress, and under her no-nonsense approach Diana obediently sat still for this operation, only begging her sister to tell her which of the flowers to choose. April obliged in the full knowledge that Diana would overrule her, and was proved correct. It seemed the posy she had selected had been sent by a gentleman with rabbity teeth and an importunate air, two characteristics that rendered his gift quite ineligible in Diana's eyes. The final choice devolved on a very pretty bouquet of pink rosebuds in an ivory holder. The pink ribbons complimented the gown, and its presenter, Mr. Lawrence Eddington, was one of Diana's favorite beaux. April was secretly relieved that the honor had not gone to an all-white posy containing Mr. Damien Harding's card. The fact that the latter was one of her sister's most persistent gallants contributed not a little to Lady Glenville's general worries. That his motives were totally corrupt was not open to question — impecunious men of four or five and thirty did not dangle after new buds of seventeen, even ravishingly pretty girls like Diana, unless they were notable heiresses. Knowing he had not made a hit with his cousin's bride and unsure of her influence on Adam, he pursued Diana as a means of harassing herself while keeping close to the situation in Hanover Square. She gathered up her sister's netted reticule and the charming ivory silk fan with its painted pink roses that had been a lucky find in the Pantheon Bazaar, and urged the girl into the hall. After a hasty hug and a knowing grin for Mattie, who was determinedly holding back sentimental tears at the picture her nursling made tonight, Diana joined April in the hall and proceeded gaily down the stairs, having long since lost any vestige of nervousness in society.

At the door to the small saloon, Diana gave her sister a playful push, whispering, "You go in first, April, then I'll make an entrance for Adam."

Perforce, April entered the saloon alone, her eyes automatically seeking her husband's, her spine suddenly stiff as though braced for a blow. She did not have to wait long for Adam's reaction. Those dark brows flew together and his lips became a straight line before parting, but his words were deceptively mild.

"Where is the gray silk gown?"

"We . . . I decided it was a bit too spectacular for anything less grand than an event at Carlton House."

"Well, you may now *un*decide. Go and put on the gray."

She faced him squarely, her head high, aware that Diana had come into the room behind her. Her sister's big entrance was spoiled anyway, so she might as well be hanged for a sheep as a lamb. The angle of her chin elevated a trifle. "I prefer this gown. It is more comfortable for dancing."

"Do not try me too far, April. Either you go upstairs and put on the gown I ordered or I'll put you in it myself."

By this time Diana had assimilated the situation.

"But Adam!" she wailed, and her sister quaked for her temerity. Adam held up a restraining hand, not even glancing at the guest of honor.

"Later, Diana. Well, madam, do you desire me to act as your abigail?"

April swung around on one foot and flounced out the

room without another word. Fury drove her up the stairs at twice her normal pace, but it was anxiety for Diana that caused her to call loudly for Mattie, who came out of Diana's room almost on her heels.

"What's the matter?"

"Get out the gray silk, Mattie," she ordered shortly, already ripping open the buttons she could reach before she entered her boudoir. "And take that look of satisfaction off your face," she added with the remnants of temper. "I'll need the silver sandals too."

In less than five minutes she was hurrying back down the stairs arrayed in the most beautiful gown she had ever seen and unaware of how it became her, since she had not spared the time for a glance in the mirror. She was impelled by a fear that Diana might have thrown a tantrum over the dress, exposing herself to the rough edge of Adam's tongue in the process. If he *dared* to ruin that girl's big evening he would have more to deal with than he bargained for, she vowed! By the time she burst through the saloon door, sweeping past an astounded footman, she was in a fine rage.

"Excellent! Every bit as lovely as I hoped," Adam said smoothly to take the wind out of her sails. "I had intended to recommend a touch of rouge, but I see something, exertion perhaps, has given you a fine healthy color. May I pour you a glass of sherry?"

April's eyes had gone immediately to Diana, who though a trifle subdued, was smiling easily. She barely heard her husband's comments as she searched her sister's face for signs of a recent storm or one to come, and was reassured. For a moment she stood there feeling remarkably foolish. Obviously Adam had acquired the knack of turning Diana up sweet if he had averted a scene tonight. His patient repetition of the offer of a glass of sherry rescued her, and she clutched at it, glad to have something to occupy her hands for the moment. She flicked an uncertain look at the earl, but his reaction to her change of costume had passed, leaving her strangely dissatisfied. Now he was being the suave host as they waited for Morton to announce dinner.

She sipped her sherry in mute discomfort, wishing her paralyzed brain would dredge up even one acceptable topic of conversation.

Dinner passed off very smoothly, with Diana and Adam shouldering the burden of conversation while April concentrated on achieving a state of relaxation. By the time Morton had cleared the table she felt able to greet their guests with a semblance of ease. As they rose from their chairs, Adam said casually:

"One moment, my dear. Before we head for the ballroom, I have a little something for you to wear tonight." He was taking a jeweler's box out of an inner pocket as he spoke, and now he strolled toward April, who stood still, blinking in surprise.

"Oh, how absolutely *gorgeous!*"

The exclamation was Diana's. April was too dumbfounded to speak as her husband drew a delicate necklace out of the case and motioned for her to remove her pearls. Huge gray eyes questioned him, but there was nothing to be read in his face. He laid the necklace against her throat and fastened it. Womanlike, April headed for the nearest mirror and stood staring in awestruck admiration at the exquisite thin chain of diamonds supporting a center pendant consisting of a teardrop-shaped diamond that must have been worth a king's ransom. It was the most perfect thing she had ever seen, and she struggled to find the words to express her pleasure in the gift.

"Adam, I don't know how to thank you—I—"

"I'll show you," he said lightly. Before she knew what he was about, he had taken her chin in one hand and was pressing his mouth to hers. Shock kept her perfectly still under his touch at first. Memories and fears, along with strange new sensations, sent the blood pounding through her veins, but before she could react in any way it was over. Adam had released her and stepped back. April's eyes were glazed, but she noted the dark color under his skin before the sound of Diana applauding the event brought her attention to her surroundings.

"Bravo! Perhaps someone will kiss me tonight. I do hope so!" declared the irrepressible girl.

"Diana, you *wouldn't!*"

"That's quite enough out of you on that subject, minx!" Adam's laugh sounded forced, but he continued in a nearly normal tone to describe in detail the unpleasant fate in store for any young gallant who attempted to take such a liberty with his sister-in-law. "For tonight, all your kisses belong to me," he finished, saluting her briefly on the cheek.

"Pooh! Tame stuff—kisses from an old married man!" scoffed Diana, voicing an opinion that was definitely not shared by her silent sister.

But the girl's nonsense had relieved the moment of embarrassment, and they went into the ballroom in unusual harmony, which was increased by the warmth of the earl's approval of the renovation and decoration of the beautifully proportioned room. The members of the orchestra were already bustling about on the dais arranging their music stands, and there was barely time to inspect the refreshments in the supper room before the first of the guests were upon them.

It was nearly two hours before April and Adam felt free to mingle with their guests, as they were constrained to keep visible to greet latecomers for whom this event might be the second or third stop of the evening. Diana had been released earlier to enjoy the dancing, and she was doing just that, April concluded as she drifted toward a group of young ladies without partners who were chattering vivaciously to demonstrate how little they regarded this circumstance. Glancing about for reinforcements, she noticed Adam disappearing into the card room with the Duke of York. A lifted brow brought Freddy to her side, however, and they reached the girls just as two gentlemen approached from the opposite direction. Three men and four girls meant one young lady would remain partnerless, and with a sigh April realized it would be Phoebe Granby who would suffer this indignity. Not only was her unhappy prediction confirmed, but one of the gentlemen stepped on Phoebe's gown, tearing a ruffle, as she bent to retrieve her dance card.

"I always said William Dixon was a clumsy lout," April pronounced mildly as the offender, all unknowing, led a giggling brunette off. "How fortunate you did not get landed with him for a partner, my dear child. Come, let us go upstairs. Mattie will see to that ruffle."

"Oh, please, you must not bother about me, Lady Glenville. I shall be able to pin it myself in the ladies' retiring room," Phoebe protested, quite distraught at the idea of inconveniencing her hostess.

April had noticed the girl's trembling lip, however, and was busy weaving her toils, seeing this accident as a heaven-sent opportunity to do something for the unfortunate Phoebe. Louisa was nowhere in view—probably she was settled in the card room trying to win back the cost of her daughter's dress—and her cousin was resolved to try her hand at improving Phoebe's appearance. Thus she slipped a hand under the girl's arm and piloted her toward the main wing.

She talked a spate of cheerful nonsense that finally succeeded in drawing a shaky laugh from the embarrassed girl by the time they reached April's bechamber, where she rang for Mattie. While awaiting the maid, April sought in her mind for a tactful approach to what she planned to do and decided there wasn't one.

"Phoebe, do you trust me?"

A startled look leaped into the girl's light-blue eyes. "N—naturally I trust you, Lady Glenville."

"Good. Then I am going to ask you to put yourself unconditionally in my hands for the next few minutes and we'll try to see what can be done about that gown to make it fit better. Will you let me try?"

Slow color mounted in Phoebe's cheeks, leaving her skin with a mottled effect, but she nodded silently.

"That's a good girl—ah, there you are, Mattie. Take a good look at this gown. There is a torn ruffle, but that is nothing. Do you think if we took a tuck here and here perhaps, it would fit better and show off her neat waist?"

Mattie made a lightning assessment and declared herself capable of fixing matters in twenty minutes. "Can't do anything about that color though."

April was unhooking the gown before she finished speaking. "No, but I can tone down her own coloring. Sit here, Phoebe." She placed the bemused girl on the bench at her dressing table and handed her bright-pink gown over to the maid, who had already possessed herself of the work box.

While Mattie set strong stitches, April dulled Phoebe's high color with a careful application of powder. After a critical appraisal of the results, she ordered Phoebe to close her eyes, telling her what she didn't see she couldn't confess to her mother. It took only a moment to darken and define the pale brows. "There, that brightens your features. Now for that hair. You have lovely hair, Phoebe, but it is crimped too tightly. If you do not object, I propose to brush some of the curl out and give you a fuller style." She was removing the pins as she spoke, so it was just as well that Miss Granby was too cowed to voice any objection. After a vigorous brushing, April started to form larger, softer curls, which she anchored securely, letting several fall free over the ears. Rummaging through a drawer, she emerged with a length of white ribbon. "With your permission, child, I am going to substitute this for the wreath of roses you were wearing." An almost imperceptible nod being accepted as permission, she carried out her intention, calling over her shoulder to Mattie that Miss Granby was now ready to be redressed.

The girl said nothing at all when her hostess had done up the last button and positioned her in front of the mirror with a flourish of triumph. April flashed a look of consternation at Mattie. Had her juggernaut tactics offended Phoebe? Her lips parted to offer a sincere apology, which was forestalled when two brimming blue eyes turned to her in mute gratitude.

"Very nice you look indeed, Miss Granby," said Mattie, easing the situation for both.

April hugged the girl, who shyly thanked Mattie for her assistance, then bustled her downstairs. The first young man they encountered on entering the ballroom was Mr. Eddington. In answer to the countess's speaking look, he grinned and politely requested the honor of standing up with Miss Granby. As the two walked off to enter a set forming near the center of the room, April was well rewarded by his casual remark that he'd never seen Phoebe looking better.

It was time to circulate. Her glance roved along the sides of the room where small groups of chaperons were conversing and lighted on a still-lovely woman wearing an elegant purple gown and a frankly bored expression beneath her feathered headdress. As she wended her way toward her mother-in-law, stopping to acknowledge the complimentary remarks of several people in her path, she schooled her own features to an expression of pleasure. The two had met at two or three large gatherings and achieved a moderately amiable *rapprochement* under the curious eye of the *ton*. Lady Ellsmere, with her air of world-weary skepticism, was never going to be a prime favorite with her daughter-in-law, but it was an act of Christian charity to rescue her from the garrulity of General Smythe-Thomas, who looked settled to recount the entire history of his military career.

She had cause to be grateful for her own rescue ten long minutes later as the earl came toward them with an old friend of his mother's in tow.

"Mrs. Anselworth was just saying, ma'am, that she has not set eyes on you for an age, so I brought her over to enjoy a comfortable coze, and since the orchestra is striking up for a waltz I propose to solicit my wife's hand for our first dance. Your servant, General. As you see, I have not depleted your court, merely added some new blood."

"Adam, what a thing to say!" April protested laughingly as he swept her onto the floor.

He held her off a trifle and stared down at her with a glint in his eye. "Did I mistake the piteous looks you were casting about the room? Shall I return you to the general?"

"Wretch!" She subsided, smiling at his absurdity.

"Was he recounting the details of his last military campaign?"

"I'd have preferred that! No, it was the inside story of his life—stomach, kidneys, liver, and the rest. It seems the general has always suffered from an excess of—"

"Enough! Fascinating though anything to do with the general must always be, right now I would rather have you tell me where you disappeared to for half an hour."

"It's a long story," replied his wife, "which I'll tell you some other time."

"Does it have anything to do with the fact that the maypole Granby girl's appearance is suddenly improved out of all reason?"

Astonished at his perception, April looked more closely at him than was her habit and saw a smile lurking in his dark eyes.

"My fingers have been itching to undo some of Louisa's work," she confessed with a self-congratulatory air. "Phoebe is a sweet girl and more could be made of her."

"If she needs a partner, I'll stand up with her for the next set."

"Thank you, Adam." She gave him an unclouded smile reflecting her satisfaction in her night's work and her pleasure in the dance.

An answering smile appeared on his face, then faded. "Moonbeams and stardust and mountain lakes," he said slowly to mystify her.

"I beg your pardon?"

"That is what you remind me of, looking as you do tonight."

There was a new and unfathomable element in the intense regard Adam bent on her that quickened April's pulses and drove down her lashes in an instinctive need to protect herself from some unidentified threat to her peace of mind. She did not even attempt to reply. Adam too fell silent, but he drew her pliant body closer and gave himself over to a sensual abandonment to the beauty and rhythm of the waltz music. April was content to follow his lead; in fact, at that point in time she would have been content to continue moving in this weightless floating fashion forever.

But no dance lasts forever, and inevitably the music wound to a close. April and Adam found themselves in the corner near the orchestra with the earl's back to the room. For a second after the music stopped he continued to hold her loosely, and she held her breath as he seemed to be pulling her nearer without actually moving. It flashed through her mind that he intended to kiss her again, and of course she could not permit such a breach of good taste, but still she stood there, waiting.

"Now, now, this is a respectable party. That sort of thing won't do outside of the Cyprians' Ball," admonished a jovial voice.

The earl and countess jerked toward the speaker as if pulled on strings. Mr. Damien Harding's face had assumed a teasing expression, but April had seen icy rage in his eyes before he had quite mastered it, and fear struck through her like a knife blade. She turned unconsciously pleading eyes to Adam, but the stiff formality of the past few weeks was back in full sway, all traces of recent softening gone.

"How are you, Damien?"

"How nice of you to ask, cousin. I've seen almost nothing of you lately, old chap."

"I've been busy. Jason Jeffries and I are going to drive to Exton to watch a mill tomorrow night. Come with us if you like."

"Unfortunately I am already engaged for tomorrow evening. And speaking of engagements, I have not yet had the pleasure of dancing with the beautiful bride, though the guest of honor favored me with a waltz. May I request the pleasure of the next dance, Cousin April?"

April excused herself on the grounds of neglected hostess duties, uncaring if her excuse sounded fabricated. If she was to conceal her feelings for Mr. Damien Harding it was necessary to put the greatest possible distance between them at all times.

The rest of the evening was devoted to conscientious

carrying out of her role of hostess. The magic that had hovered over the affair earlier had dissipated and she was unable to recapture the mood, but at least for Diana the party was a resounding success, and she went reluctantly to bed in the small hours of the morning basking in the glow of her triumph.

Chapter Fifteen

Neither of the ladies rose very early on the day after Diana's ball. Having had the foresight to order Morton to deny them to morning callers, they gave themselves over to the rare indulgence of a leisurely breakfast abovestairs at a deplorably late hour while they engaged in the enjoyable activity known as talking over the party. When Diana had finally related all the most original and eloquent of the compliments paid to her by her numerous partners and happily criticized the gowns of most of the females of her acquaintance, she bethought herself to mention the improvement in Phoebe Granby's looks and was regaled by the story of her cousin's transformation at the hands of her sister and Mattie. She was less confident than April that the improvement could be sustained in the face of Lady Granby's blatant poor taste but agreed to try to aid and encourage Phoebe whenever possible.

"Everyone mentioned how lovely you looked last night, April. I'm sorry I made such a fuss about the silver dress," she admitted, shamefaced. "I'm a selfish beast at times. I think perhaps you spoiled me a bit."

Her sister laughed and hugged her shoulders briefly. "Perhaps a bit," she agreed, "but I would not trade you for anyone else's sister."

"Adam thought you looked beautiful too," Diana added, slanting a glance at her sister's still face. "He scarcely spoke to Lady Ellis all evening and couldn't seem to take his eyes off you."

"Playing matchmaker, Diana? You'll catch cold at that ploy."

The bitterness in her sister's voice silenced the younger girl, who sought a quick change of topic.

During the afternoon they had the felicity of being complimented by numerous callers on a most successful ball. Adam was not in to tea or dinner, and the ladies were promised to the Eddingtons for a theater party that evening. April found it a trifle flat surrounded by youngsters, agreeable though they all were. The play was lively, however, and well worth seeing.

It was the following morning before April saw her husband. For no particular reason she decided to go down for an early breakfast, garbed in her most becoming morning gown of soft lavender muslin. On the threshold of the breakfast parlor she halted in consternation.

"*Adam!* What has happened to your arm?"

The earl leveled a somber glance at her concerned face. It seemed an inordinately long time to the expectant girl before he replied in a wooden voice, "Someone tried to kill me last night."

April swayed and reached out to grasp the back of a chair as her husband jumped up and came toward her.

"Don't worry," she said, holding him off with one hand and meeting his eyes squarely. "Murderesses never faint."

"Ah, please don't!" he begged, his mouth twisting in a grimace of pain. "I know you didn't do it."

"Not personally, of course," she agreed. "I have an alibi, but I might have hired someone to do the actual deed."

Husband and wife confronted one another across a gulf of misunderstanding, Adam's eyes reflecting the pain in April's heart.

"I know you had nothing to do with it or the other," he stated quietly. "I owe you an abject apology for suspecting you, and for . . . for—"

"*How* do you know?" she interrupted, pride keeping her stiff and emotionless.

"It was . . . Damien."

Her eyes never left his face, but some of the stiffness drained out of her body. "You have proof?"

He nodded grimly. "Damien's corpse."

This time April really did sag, and the earl pushed her onto the nearest chair with the arm that was not resting in a white sling. Her head came up after a second or two and their eyes met.

"Adam, I am so terribly sorry. What else can I say?"

"Nothing." He sighed as he settled wearily back into his own chair. "It is the best way. The scandal would have been impossible to avoid."

"How did it happen? How badly hurt is your arm?"

"You heard me invite Damien to go with us to a mill? He declined, you will recall, on the score of a previous engagement. After the fight, Jason wanted to get back to town, and there was a full moon, so we set out. About halfway across Hounslow Heath we were ambushed. The assailant, who was masked, got off one shot, which winged me. Before he could shoot again, Jason shot him, and he fell. The team bolted, and it took me a few minutes to get them back under control and return to the spot. Jason insisted on bandaging my arm with our handkerchiefs before we took a closer look at the highwayman, as my groom had already pronounced him dead. Perhaps you may imagine my feelings when we unmasked him and discovered his identity."

"Yes, I think I know how fond you were of Damien."

He gestured impatiently. "That was only part of it, as you *must* know! *You* were the rest of it, you and the way I treated you. April, can you—"

"How will you explain Damien's death to Freddy?"

He hunched a shoulder and fixed his gaze on his fingers toying with a spoon. "We took his purse and watch and a signet ring he always wore, got rid of the mask, and left him for someone else to find. It should look as though he had been set upon by highwaymen."

She winced, and he said harshly, "I know, it's damned

callous, but what choice did we have if Freddy and the world are to remain in ignorance of the truth?" His eyes challenged hers, and hers fell.

At that moment the door to the pantry opened and Jacob entered, carrying a large tray. April and Adam watched him in silence as he deposited the dishes on the table. The earl waved him away when he had finished.

"Where is Morton?" April wondered as the door closed behind the footman.

"Packing his gear. Did you think I'd keep in my employ a man who tried to kill me?"

"You kept a wife who tried to kill you—or so you thought," she returned steadily.

The color drained from beneath his dark skin, leaving him as ghastly as she was. The scar on his cheek stood out redly, and his eyes were two black holes with no life behind them.

"April, I . . . you must know how greatly I regret what happened in the study. Can you ever forgive me?"

"How *could* you believe I would do such a horrible thing after all you had done for Diana and me?" she cried, tears starting to her eyes.

"I didn't *want* to believe it!" he replied in desperate earnest. "But there was Damien, whom I'd known all my life, and of course I knew how you hated me and blamed me for your father's and brother's deaths."

"You knew I *hated* you?" she echoed in disbelief. "Why I . . . I—" Suddenly April tore her gaze from her husband's tormented face, gave one nauseated glance at the food spread on the table, and turned even paler. "I don't believe I care for breakfast after all," she whispered, and bolted for the door before Adam could intervene.

He rose halfway out of the chair, then sank back in defeat. Nothing had changed at all. For a moment last night when he had recognized the face under the mask, wild intoxicating elation had surged through his veins at the realization that April had not tried to kill him. The truth had been horrible enough to sober him in the next instant, of course. Jason's shock had to be dealt with without revealing all the circumstances surrounding the attempted poisoning. And the situation itself had demanded an instant decision as to the best way to avoid a scandal. Thank God, his own groom, Delsey, had been with him since he was a young stable boy and was completely loyal.

It had been a grim ride home, and thoughts of the blow ahead for Freddy had weighed upon him, but not so heavily as the weight that had been removed by the proof of his wife's innocence. At last he would be able to stop denying his love for the woman who had married him against his will and invaded his heart with the insidious stealth of a fog creeping in over the city. He had fought it, denied her attraction, refused to admit that he was lost from the moment she had faced him from a dressing-table bench in a quaking fear and still defied him to try to turn her into a fashion plate.

In the beginning, confident of his indifference toward women, he had relegated her to the negligible position in his life befitting a wife in name only, but she had refused to occupy that position and had climbed by insensible degrees to a permanent perch in his heart before he was aware of what was happening. And when he did become attuned to the possible benefits of such a situation it was to discover the woman who fascinated him was conniving at his death. How he had despised himself and railed against the weakness that made him desire her while knowing her for the unprincipled adventuress she was! All that was in the past now. He was free to love her, but after what had happened between them it was entirely possible that her original antipathy, based on misunderstanding of his role in her past, had become immutable loathing.

Ignoring the food on the table, he poured himself a cup of coffee and drank it scalding hot without noticing taste or temperature. He deserved to lose her if he gave way to despair. He had expected too much too fast this morning. She was shocked, naturally, by the events he had related, but he could not believe a woman who could cherish the burden

of a dependent sister and unself-consciously cuddle someone's else's child on her lap could remain forever unfor-
giving. There had been moments when their eyes had locked
in a long searching look void of animosity, moments when
an expectant electricity seemed to spark between them. He
thought, he *hoped,* the feeling had not been all on his side.
He must curb his impatience and try to insinuate himself
into her affections. She felt guilty about coercing him into
marriage—this had been evident in her eagerness to disturb
his life as little as possible under the circumstances, to fall in
with his plans and comply with his wishes. There was a solid
conviction in his mind that if he played on that sense of
guilty obligation she would submit to his possession out of a
feeling of duty, but, dammit, he didn't *want* a dutiful wife!
Better to wait forever while there was the slightest chance of
winning her love.

The earl was so busy over the next week or so that there
was relatively little strain placed on his good resolutions with
regard to his wife. There were all the details connected with
Damien's death to arrange. Freddy had accepted without
question the circumstances as they appeared to come to light
and had been grateful for his cousin's emotional support. As
Damien's debts began to surface after his death, he had
cause to be grateful also for Adam's willingness to discharge
his brother's financial obligations. Adam took care that
Freddy never knew the full extent to which his brother had
been under the hatches. Small wonder Damien had been so
desperate.

He saw relatively little of April for over a sennight. When
they did meet, he found her a trifle guarded but cordial.
With great thankfulness he observed that the haunted look
had vanished from her eyes. He took consolation in the hope
that it had been the result of distress at being wrongly
judged rather than fear of being physically abused by a
vengeful husband. She made no overtures toward establish-
ing a warmer relationship, nor had he expected any, but it
did seem as if her eyes held a welcome when he came into a

room these days. With this he tried to be content for the present.

Several weeks had elapsed since he had last visited Molly, and something must be done in that quarter. The years of using Molly as an emotional crutch had ended with the realization that his wife's image filled his life. Even if she never came to love him, his own feelings for April were too strong to permit him to seek consolation elsewhere.

He dropped in on Molly one afternoon not long after Damien's funeral to tell her of the financial arrangements he had made for her and Charlotte. She received him with a pleasure that dimmed when the reason for the visit was explained, but Molly possessed an inherent dignity that stood her in good stead. She thanked him most sincerely and surprised him very much by acknowledging that she had known at their last meeting that he had fallen in love with his wife. The occasion was saved from the usual awkwardness attending such partings by Molly's revelation to her protector that Mr. Norris, the draper, having decided to retire to a modest establishment outside of York to become the nonparticipating partner in another business venture, had proposed to her and was patiently awaiting her answer. He knew the whole story of her past and was prepared to welcome Charlotte as a daughter. She successfully hid the pain that filled her at the earl's patent pleasure and relief on receiving this news. They parted with perfect amity on both sides, and the earl wasn't to know, as he ran down the stairs with a light step, that his discarded mistress, with silent tears coursing down her cheeks, was regarding her secure financial future and long-desired respectable marriage in the light of a lifetime banishment.

The period following Damien's death was viewed by April as a much-needed respite from the state of emotional turmoil that had evolved in the frightening manner of a snowball sent rolling downhill over the relatively short span of her marriage. She was released at last from the gnawing fear that Adam was targeted for death while she herself stood by

powerless to avert the catastrophe. It was nearly as great a
relief to know herself vindicated in her judgment and freed
of the weight of unjust suspicion that had had a crushing
effect on her spirit.

At times she had to force her features into a semblance of
somberness befitting a family in mourning. This might have
been more often necessary had not all her patience and
sympathy been called upon to help ease the shock and
sorrow that Damien's death had produced for Diana. The
young girl had unreservedly admired the handsome cousin
who flattered and amused her and occupied a prominent
place in her court. She was disconsolate for a time and clung
to her sister literally and figuratively. April knew that it was
a reaction to additional loss in a young life already marked
by loss rather than a lover's despair, but the girl needed a
good deal of comfort and reassurance at first. Her own
sunny nature reasserted itself after a time, aided by the pull
of all the distractions offered to a popular young lady during
the London season. Gradually she began to take a renewed
interest in the activities of her friends, and her dependence
on her sister lessened.

At last April had opportunity to consider her own
emotions and long-suppressed, only partially acknowledged
dreams. What she discovered was not entirely to her liking.
It was amazing how quickly one could accustom oneself to
passive blessings such as the absence of fear, and begin to
seek greedily after more positive gratification. All she had
requested of life for the last few years was the opportunity to
give Diana a London season, and she had achieved this goal
in a luxurious style inconceivable just three months ago.
What was wrong with her that she could not convince herself
of her perfect contentment with the privileged existence they
were leading? What more did she wish from life?

For a considerable period April shied away from this
question, refusing to admit unconscious longings into her
conscious mind. This determined avoidance dated from the
morning Adam had told her of Damien's last attempt on his
life. When he had tried to defend his earlier suspicion of his

wife he had mentioned as an accepted fact her hatred and blame of himself for causing the death of her relatives. Freddy had long ago told her Adam's side of that unhappy period, and she had not even thought of the earlier acquaintance after the first week or so of their marriage. In her utter shock at hearing him cite her hatred as fact she had almost blurted out — what? A simple denial of hatred? Or a declaration of love? Whether through cowardice or reticence, she had fled the scene before baring her soul, and for a time successfully managed to suppress the memory of that moment.

It refused to be buried for good, however, and as April and Adam began to resume the pattern their lives had begun to take before the poisoning episode, her thoughts returned with the regularity of homing pigeons to the scene in the breakfast parlor. What would have followed had she finished that sentence? It required very little cogitation to decide that anyone would be pleased and relieved to know himself not hated or held responsible for another's death. It required an increase in courage, however, to examine the other possibility. *Had* she been about to declare her love for her husband? *Did* she love him? Once she finally admitted the question to consideration the answer was abundantly clear as far as her feelings were concerned. Of course she loved her husband!

She didn't know when the process had begun, but if she'd used the intelligence she'd been born with she'd have long since recognized the cause of her terror over Adam's vulnerability with regard to his murderous cousin.

At first the mere acknowledgment of her love was sufficient to produce a quiet happiness. She went about in a private haze of contentment that fed on Adam's presence and attentions, wanting nothing save his continued good health and good humor for its nourishment. After a time, though, she couldn't prevent herself from seeking signs of increased interest on his part, and thus began the distressing period in which her spirits alternated from the dismals to soaring into the boughs, wholly depending on Adam's

attitude. In her more rational moments she was wryly aware
that her moods, if not her behavior, were on a level with
those of her seventeen-year-old sister. Diana, however, delighted in achieving the complete subjugation of all the
hopeful males in her train, while April would have been
more than content to settle for the exclusive attentions of
one specific man for the rest of her life.

Adam *was* attentive and seemed to seek out her company
more than formerly, but always her burgeoning hopes were
kept in check by the knowledge that except for the period of
their estrangement, it had ever been his object to convince
the *ton* that theirs was a love match. She found to her
dismay that she had passed beyond the age of innocent
coquetry without having gained the confidence (or wit) to
throw out serious lures to the man she wanted. Not that she
was unhappy, far from it, but there was and perhaps would
always be an unfulfilled yearning to matter to her husband
on the deepest level.

This was the state of affairs existing between the pair
three weeks after Damien's death when Adam and April
were bidden to an intimate dinner and conversable evening
at the Jeffrieses'. It had not been deemed improper for
Diana, who was after all not even related by marriage to
Damien, to resume her social activities at this point.
Tonight she was attending Almack's under the less than
wholehearted chaperonage of Lady Granby, who had been
prevailed upon by her daughter to invite her pretty cousin to
spend the night so the girls might continue to enjoy the event
by recapitulating the highlights into the wee hours of the
morning.

The earl and countess arrived early in Mount Street, as
was their custom, in order to enjoy a visit with the Jeffries
children. To her brother's satisfaction, Melissa was content
to go to April after one quick toss by Uncle Adam, leaving
him a clear field for rougher play. After ten noisy minutes
that sated even Jonathan's lust for action, the earl dropped
onto the sofa occupied by his wife and Melissa. His breath-

ing was a little rapid, and he complained, "I must be getting old—Jonathan wears me out."

Missy looked up briefly from examining April's pearls, which were adorning her small person at the moment.

"Nurse says Jonathan has rag manners," she announced coolly before returning her attention to her bedizened self.

"I do *not* have rag manners!"

The earl's eyes smiled into his wife's. "Someone sounds rather prissy," he remarked, *sotto voce*.

Jonathan heard this, and his indignation changed to teasing. "Prissy Missy, Prissy Missy!" he chanted at his sister, whose lip trembled warningly.

Mrs. Jeffries intervened, silencing her son with a stern look before all-out battle flared. April hugged the insulted Missy, who suddenly remembered something.

"Do you have a little girl like me at your house yet, Auntie April?"

"No, not yet, Missy," she replied hastily, keeping her head down to conceal the hot color that spread over her cheekbones and praying that Adam's attention was elsewhere.

"But you *said* you wished you had a little girl," the child pointed out in her clear, carrying treble.

"Yes, I know, darling, but—"

"It takes time to find a little girl as nice as you, Missy," finished the earl, coming to his wife's rescue. Their eyes met over the child's golden head. For a time the other occupants of the room receded to a far distance as husband and wife looked measuringly at each other, then the arrival of the first dinner guests shattered the intimacy of the moment.

They sat down ten to dinner, and as usual the conversation around the Jeffrieses' table was of the same high order as the delectable food that issued from the kitchen, whose control Jane never wholly relinquished to the resident chef. If the talk was weighted on the side of political issues and governmental happenings, that was only to be expected from guests involved in the daily process of governing the country.

When the men joined the ladies in the saloon later, the atmosphere shifted to an emphasis on music. Their host and hostess enjoyed listening and performing, and drew other enthusiasts to their home. April applauded the Jeffrieses' sprightly duets and was enthralled by the beautiful violin rendition of a Bach cantata by an undistinguished-looking king's councilor, but she realized as Jane begged Adam for a song or two that this was the moment she had been waiting for since first learning that her husband sang. She repressed the little pang that racked her at the thought that she was probably the only person present who had never been privileged to hear him, and composed her features to a listening attitude. He complied good-naturedly with Jane's requests for a couple of rollicking old country songs. April experienced the thrill that comes from hearing a superb artist performing with the ease of total control. Adam's speaking voice was rather low-pitched, so the range he displayed in singing was a revelation to her. Her shining eyes followed his every movement as he directed the songs smilingly and impartially to his eager audience. His wife led the applause with unself-conscious pride when the last note sounded. Only a stern recollection of propriety kept her from leading the chorus of requests for another number, and a delighted smile beamed when Adam leaned over and whispered to Jane, who was accompanying him at the pianoforte.

As the first notes of the introduction rippled softly, April sat up straighter in her chair, and her eyes, which had been fixed on the pianist's hands, sought her husband's in astonished, half-fearful questioning. The intensity of Adam's stare affected her so strongly that she missed the opening bars of the beautiful *Per la gloria d'adoravi,* but never could she be mistaken in this loveliest of all love songs Hadn't her father sung it to her mother on every musical occasion that she could remember from earliest childhood. It had been their special song and, consequently, one much loved by their daughter as she grew up. Memories washed over her and glazed her eyes with unshed tears as Adam sang the well-remembered lyrics in a voice as breathtakingly tender as a caress. *Amando penerò, ma sempre v'amerò*— in loving I shall suffer, but I shall always love you. How could he know, *did* he know what this song meant to her, or was it simply another number in his repertoire? Did he even know the meaning of the lyrics, or had he merely learned the Italian syllables by rote as children learned their ditties? Questions, doubts, hopes spun about in her brain, the internal activity at total variance with her appearance, which was that of a slender statue. Not a muscle moved in her face or body during Adam's rendition; she sat as one mesmerized by the power of his dark eyes which never left her face and the beauty of the rich voice rolling out the final tones of Bononcini's lovely melody.

Loud applause brought her back to her immediate surroundings with a start. Adam acknowledged it with a small smiling bow and prepared to resume his seat, firmly declining to sing anything else when pressed.

"I didn't understand a single word," declared Mrs. Elvin, the plump middle-aged wife of a Member of Parliament, "but I just know I'd love to have it sung to me, whatever it says." She waited for the general laugh this brazen confession elicited to die down, then pursued her line of thought. "What does that *luci care* mean, Lord Glenville?"

"It is difficult to translate exactly, ma'am," Adam replied, "but 'sweet eyes' is a fairly close rendering. When I saw my wife's eyes on our wedding day, the phrase came into my head. It seemed to fit."

"No need to look so conscious, my dear," Mrs. Elvin told the blushing Lady Glenville. "You should be pleased as punch to wring a public declaration from your husband. The most romantic thing Mr. Elvin ever said to me was that I had a good seat on a horse."

"Well, Adam's never seen me on a horse," replied April, rallying, "but I should consider such a compliment highly romantic indeed and shall endeavor to deserve it."

At this point another lady was reminded of a blatantly un-romantic compliment that had been paid by a gentleman in all sincerity, and this led to a spate of amusing recollections which reduced the company to helpless laughter. April summoned an alert look to her face and laughed at the proper places, but her laughter held a note of excitement unrelated to the story being told at the moment. Adam *had* known the meaning of the Italian lyrics of Bononcini's song! He thought the part about the eyes was applicable to herself. She stole a look at him as he threw his head back and roared with laughter at an incident being recounted by Mr. Elvin. Did the rest of the lyric apply to himself? Was it possible that he loved her in secret and expected nothing but suffering to come from such a love? At the moment he looked like a man unacquainted with the meaning of the word "suffering." Never had she seen him more completely relaxed and seemingly in spirits. Her own excitement mounted as the hour grew later. Never had she been so eager to see a delightful evening come to a close. Perhaps Adam would say something in the carriage, refer to the song he had sung to her. How would she respond? Should she reveal her own knowledge of Italian?

In the event, April's hopes came crashing down upon her during the drive home. They chatted quietly about the evening they had just spent, and Adam replied with perfect amiability, but his high spirits had evaporated, and he appeared thoughtful, leaving the burden of conversation on April's shoulders. Those slim shoulders seemed to sag literally as the carriage drew ever nearer to Hanover Square. At last she had to acknowledge that Adam was not going to refer to his singing. Her fingers were gripping her fan so tightly that she bent the sticks out of shape as she assessed her courage and found it wanting. Surely she was not such a sapskull that she could not even toss off a casual remark for fear of being thought to tread where she was not wanted! Where was her hard-earned worldliness? Every instant was bringing them nearer to the point when they would part for the night, for Adam never came upstairs with her. It was his invariable custom to detour to his study for a glass of brandy before retiring.

The door was open and the earl was assisting her down from the carriage when she said in desperation, "I have never heard you sing before, Adam. Yours is a magnificent voice. I enjoyed listening to you more than I can say."

Had his fingers tightened around hers for an instant, or had she imagined it? He inclined his head in acknowledgment but made no reply.

They were ascending the shallow entrance steps and April had admitted herself defeated when her husband said quietly, "I have always enjoyed singing."

"I . . . I hope you will permit me to accompany you at home sometimes. Diana will be enchanted with your voice," she added lamely, and mentally kicked herself for dragging her sister in as a shield.

Again he inclined his head politely. They were in the hall walking side by side, not looking at each other. The stairway was dead ahead. In less than thirty seconds the enchanted evening would be over.

"Would you care to drink a glass of brandy with me in the study?" Adam asked hesitantly. "It's not so very late."

"Thank you, I'd like that," said April, who loathed the taste of brandy. She thought she sensed a tension in his bearing as he stood back for her to precede him into the room. This was the first time she had entered it since that terrible night, but perhaps it was time to lay that particular ghost.

Neither spoke while the earl busied himself at the table holding bottle and glasses. Watching that strong back and bowed head and loving him fiercely, April was suddenly filled with resolution. What did her pride matter? If he wanted her, and she suspected he did, she was his, and somehow she'd find a way to tell him so.

As she accepted the glass from his hand, she met his eyes squarely. "That song by Bononcini is one of my favorites," she ventured. "My father used to sing it to my mother."

There was a flicker in the steel-gray eyes. "Do you know what the words mean . . . in English?"

Their eyes remained locked. A muscle twitched in Adam's lean scarred cheek as he awaited her answer. When it came it was scarcely more than a whisper.

"What do they mean, Adam . . . in English?"

"They mean that until I met you I had no idea of what love meant or what suffering meant."

"And now you do?" she prompted softly.

He gazed down into huge smoky eyes made even more luminous by a film of unshed tears, and his own softened, as did the straight line of his mouth.

"Oh, yes, although until this moment the emphasis has been on suffering. I never wished to put my heart into any woman's keeping. I thought I was in love once a long time ago, but when she turned me down I soon found consolation elsewhere. Loving you means there can be no consolation for me any longer." His mouth twisted wryly. "If you cannot bring yourself to love me, it will have to be more suffering. I won't rush you . . . I promise."

"Adam," April broke in with desperate earnestness, "please, *please* rush me!"

Through a mist she saw the light that entered those dark eyes as he closed the gap between them, then the impatient little frown as he registered the presence of two untouched brandy glasses in their hands. Time stood still as he disposed of them on the table and gathered her into his arms with deliberation. His eyes searched her face with a peculiar intensity that she knew, in a sudden flash of loving protectiveness, reflected a lingering concern that she might struggle in his embrace as she had on that other occasion. Her ardent response to his first kiss served to dispel any fears on that head, and his arms tightened convulsively about her as his mouth claimed hers in mounting passion.

"April! You *have* forgiven me!"

She heard his broken murmur over the accelerated clamor of her pulses as he released his lips for an instant, but she was beyond articulation by then. Adam had to accept the assurance conveyed by a warm slender body pressed urgently to his.

He had always sensed that her overactive conscience at having coerced the marriage would impel her to submit to him had he invoked his rights as her husband in the ordinary way. Now the wisdom of waiting and suffering was bearing abundant fruit. Tonight she clung to him with all the surprising strength with which she had resisted on that other occasion. He could scarcely credit that here was the silvery cool creature he had once assumed to be passionless. Lips, arms, body, all flamed into response at his touch. When he recalled his resolve to proceed slowly and woo her with gentle patience, he nearly laughed aloud with exultation. She was fire and ice, and the fire burned for him!

After a third consuming kiss, both were sorely in need of a respite to replenish their oxygen supply and take stock of their surroundings.

"Come on, darling," Adam said thickly. "The way I feel about you can best be expressed upstairs!"

Sudden mischief danced in April's eyes, and she lowered her lashes, then raised them in a provocative glance. "The last time, you carried me—no, Adam, please! I was only funning! Please put me down, I'm too heavy for you," she pleaded.

A quick hard kiss silenced her as he pushed open the door with his shoulder. "You asked for it, madam," he said on a note of reckless laughter. "You know you weigh a feather, and I'm in much better shape now."

His composure was sorely tested by the unexpected sight of Jacob in the hall as they emerged from the study. The footman was young but by no means lacking in wit. One swift glance from his mistress's crimson cheeks to the devilish gleam in his master's eye reassured him as to the state of health of the countess, and he wished them goodnight in the expressionless voice of the well-trained servant without even breaking his stride.

They were nearly at the top of the stairs before April mastered her embarrassment enough to meet her husband's gleaming eyes. "It will be all over the servants' hall by tomorrow, you know," she said with commendable command of her voice.

"Do you mind?"

"No."

His eyes were serious again as he paused outside her door and gazed hungrily down at the silver fair head resting confidingly against his shoulder.

"I promised once that I would not enter this room without an invitation. May I assume that I am welcome?"

April's face was irradiated with the love she bore this strong, sometimes difficult, and formerly lonely man.

"Now and forever," she replied with a throbbing note in her low, musical voice. "That is *my* promise."

About the Author

Dorothy Mack is a native New Englander, born in Rhode Island and educated at Brown and Harvard universities. While living in Massachusetts with her husband and four young sons, she began to combine a long-time interest in English history with her desire to write and emerged as an author of Regency Romances. The family now resides in northern Virginia, where Dorothy continues to pursue both interests.

More Regency Romances from SIGNET

(0451)

- [ ] **AN INTIMATE DECEPTION by Catherine Coulter.** (122364—$2.25)*
- [ ] **LORD HARRY'S FOLLY by Catherine Coulter.** (115341—$2.25)
- [ ] **LORD DEVERILL'S HEIR by Catherine Coulter.** (113985—$2.25)
- [ ] **THE REBEL BRIDE by Catherine Coulter.** (117190—$2.25)
- [ ] **THE AUTUMN COUNTESS by Catherine Coulter.** (114450—$2.25)
- [ ] **THE GENEROUS EARL by Catherine Coulter.** (114817—$2.25)
- [ ] **AN HONORABLE OFFER by Catherine Coulter.** (112091—$2.25)*
- [ ] **A SURFEIT OF SUITORS by Barbara Hazard.** (121317—$2.25)*
- [ ] **THE DISOBEDIENT DAUGHTER by Barbara Hazard.** (115570—$2.25)*

*Prices slightly higher in Canada